DEEP DARK

LAURA GRIFFIN

Pocket Books

New York   London   Toronto   Sydney   New Delhi

Pocket Books
An Imprint of Simon & Schuster, Inc.
1230 Avenue of the Americas
New York, NY 10020

This book is a work of fiction. Any references to historical events, real people, or real places are used fictitiously. Other names, characters, places, and events are products of the author's imagination, and any resemblance to actual events or places or persons, living or dead, is entirely coincidental.

First Pocket Books paperback edition June 2016

POCKET and colophon are registered trademarks of Simon & Schuster, Inc.

For information about special discounts for bulk purchases, please contact Simon & Schuster Special Sales at 1-866-506-1949 or business@simonandschuster.com.

The Simon & Schuster Speakers Bureau can bring authors to your live event. For more information or to book an event, contact the Simon & Schuster Speakers Bureau at 1-866-248-3049 or visit our website at www.simonspeakers.com.

Manufactured in the United States of America

10 9 8 7 6 5 4 3 2

ISBN 978-1-4767-7926-3
ISBN 978-1-4767-7928-7 (ebook)

New York Times and *USA Today* bestselling author

LAURA GRIFFIN

"DELIVERS THE GOODS." —*Publishers Weekly*

SHADOW FALL

"An expert at creating mystery and suspense that hook readers from the first page, Griffin's detailed description, well-crafted, intriguing plot and clear-cut characters are the highlights of her latest."

—*RT Book Reviews*

"Great lead characters and a spooky atmosphere make this a spine-tingling, stand-out novel of romantic suspense."

—*BookPage*

BEYOND LIMITS

"*Beyond Limits* is a page-turning, nail-biting thriller from the very first scene to the very last page."

—*Fresh Fiction*

"*Beyond Limits* has daring escapades, honest emotions, and heart-stopping danger."

—*Single Titles*

FAR GONE

"Perfectly gritty. . . . Griffin sprinkles on just enough jargon to give the reader the feel of being in the middle of an investigation, easily merging high-stakes action and spicy romance with rhythmic pacing and smartly economic prose."

—*Publishers Weekly* (starred review)

"Crisp storytelling, multifaceted characters, and excellent pacing. . . . A highly entertaining read."

—*RT Book Reviews* (4 stars)

"A first-rate addition to the Laura Griffin canon."

—*The Romance Dish* (5 stars)

"Be prepared for heart palpitations and a racing pulse as you read this fantastic novel. Fans of Lisa Gardner, Lisa Jackson, Nelson DeMille, and Michael Connelly will love [Griffin's] work."

—*The Reading Frenzy*

"*Far Gone* is riveting with never-ending action."

—*Single Titles*

"A tense, exciting romantic thriller that's not to be missed."

—*New York Times* bestselling author Karen Robards

"Griffin has cooked up a delicious read that will thrill her devoted fans and earn her legions more."

—*New York Times* bestselling author Lisa Unger

EXPOSED

"Laura Griffin at her finest! If you are not a Tracer-a-holic yet . . . you will be after this."

—*A Tasty Read*

"Explosive chemistry."

—*Coffee Time Romance & More*

"Explodes with action. . . . Laura Griffin escalates the tension with each page, each scene, and intersperses the action with spine-tingling romance in a perfect blend."

—*The Romance Reviews*

SCORCHED

Winner of the RITA Award for Best Romantic Suspense

"A sizzling novel of suspense . . . the perfect addition to the Tracers series."

—*Joyfully Reviewed*

"Has it all: dynamite characters, a taut plot, and plenty of sizzle to balance the suspense without overwhelming it."

—*RT Book Reviews* (4½ stars)

"Starts with a bang and never loses its momentum . . . intense and mesmerizing."

—*Night Owl Reviews* (Top Pick)

ALSO BY LAURA GRIFFIN

For Abby

DEEP
DARK

CHAPTER 0

Laney Knox blinked into the darkness and listened. Something . . . no.

She closed her eyes and slid deeper into the warm sheets, dismissing the sound. Probably her neighbor's cat on the patio again.

Her eyes flew open. It wasn't the sound but the light—or *lack* of light—that had her attention now. She looked at the bedroom window, but the familiar band of white wasn't seeping through the gap between the shade and the wall.

She stared into the void, trying to shake off her grogginess. The outdoor lightbulb was new—her landlord had changed it yesterday. Had he botched the job? She should have done it herself, but her shoestring budget didn't cover LED lights. It barely covered ramen and Red Bull.

How many software developers does it take to change a lightbulb? None, it's a hardware problem.

Laney looked around the pitch-black room. She wasn't afraid of the dark, never had been. Roaches terrified her. And block parties. But darkness had always been no big deal.

Except this darkness was all wrong.

She strained her ears and listened for whatever sound had awakened her, but she heard nothing. She saw nothing. All her senses could discern was a slight chill against her skin and the lingering scent of the kung pao chicken she'd had for dinner. But something was off, she knew it. As the seconds ticked by, a feeling of dread settled over her.

Creak.

She bolted upright. The noise was soft but unmistakable. Someone was *inside* her house.

Her heart skittered. She lived in an old bungalow, more dilapidated than charming, and her bedroom was at the back, a virtual dead end. She glanced at her windows. She'd reinforced the original latches with screw locks to deter burglars—which had seemed like a good idea at the time. But now she felt trapped. She reached over and groped around on the nightstand for her phone.

Crap.

Crap crap crap. It was charging in the kitchen.

Her blood turned icy as the stark reality sank in. She had no phone, no weapon, no exit route. And someone was *inside*.

Should she hide in the closet? Or try to slip past him somehow, maybe if he stepped into her room? It would never work, but—

Creak.

A burst of panic made the decision for her, and she was across the room in a flash. She scurried behind the door and flattened herself against the wall. Her breath came in shallow gasps. Her heart pounded wildly as she *felt* more than heard him creeping closer.

That's what he was doing. Creeping. He was easing down the hallway with quiet, deliberate steps while she cowered behind the door, quivering and naked except for her oversized Florence and the Machine T-shirt. Sweat sprang up on the back of her neck, and her chest tightened.

Who the hell was he? What did he want? She had no cash, no jewelry, just a few thousand dollars' worth of hardware sitting on her desk. Maybe she could slip out while he stole it.

Yeah, right. Her ancient hatchback in the driveway was a neon sign announcing that whoever lived here was not only dead broke but obviously home. This intruder was no burglar—he had come for *her*.

Laney's hands formed useless little fists at her sides, and she was overwhelmed with the absurd notion that she should have followed through on that kickboxing class.

She forced a breath into her lungs and tried to think.

She had to think her way out of this, because she was five-three, one hundred ten pounds, and weaponless. She didn't stand much chance against even an average-size man, and if he was armed, forget it.

The air moved. Laney's throat went dry. She stayed perfectly still and felt a faint shifting of molecules on the other side of the door. Then a soft sound, barely a whisper, as the door drifted open.

She held her breath. Her heart hammered. Everything was black, but gradually there was a hole in the blackness—a tall, man-shaped hole—and she stood paralyzed with disbelief as the shape eased into her bedroom and crept toward her bed. She watched it, rooted in place, waiting . . . waiting . . . waiting.

She bolted.

Her feet slapped against the wood floor as she raced down the hallway. Air *swooshed* behind her. A scream tore from her throat, then became a shrill yelp as he grabbed her hair and slammed her against the wall.

A stunning blow knocked her to the floor. Stars burst behind her eyes as her cheek hit wood. She scrambled to her feet in a frantic dash and tripped over the coffee table, sending glasses and dishes flying as she crashed to her knees.

He flipped her onto her back, and then he was on her, pinning her with his massive weight as something sharp cut into her shoulder blade.

She clawed at his face, his eyes. He wore a ski mask, and all she could see were three round holes and a sinister flash of teeth amid the blackness. She shrieked, but an elbow against her throat cut off all sound, all breath, as she fought and bucked beneath him.

He was strong, immovable. And terrifyingly calm as he pinned her arms one by one under his knees and reached for something in the pocket of his jacket. She expected a weapon—a knife or a gun—and she tried to heave him off. Panic seized her as his shadow shifted in the dimness. Above her frantic grunts, she heard the tear of duct tape. And suddenly the idea of being silenced that way was more horrifying than even a blade.

With a fresh burst of adrenaline she wriggled her arm out from under his knee and flailed for any kind of weapon. She groped around the floor until her fingers closed around something smooth and slender—a pen, a chopstick, she didn't know. She gripped it in her hand

and jabbed at his face with all her might. He reared back with a howl.

Laney bucked hard and rolled out from under him as he clutched his face.

A scream erupted from deep inside her. She tripped to her feet and rocketed for the door.

CHAPTER 1

This case was going to throw him. Reed Novak knew it the instant he saw the volleyball court.

Taut net, sugary white sand. Beside the court was a swimming pool that sparkled like a sapphire under the blazing August sun.

"Hell, if I had a pool like that, I'd use it."

Reed looked at his partner in the passenger seat. Jay Wallace had his window rolled down and his hefty arm resting on the door.

"Otherwise, what's the point?"

Reed didn't answer. The point was probably to slap a photo on a website to justify the astronomical rent Bellaterra charged for one- and two-bedroom units five minutes from downtown.

Reed pulled in beside the white ME's van and climbed out, glancing around. Even with a few emergency vehicles, the parking lot was quiet. Bellaterra's young and athletically inclined tenants were either at jobs or in classes, or maybe home with their parents for the summer, letting their luxury apartments sit empty.

Reed stood for a moment, getting a feel for the place. Heat radiated up from the blacktop, and the drone of cicadas drowned out the traffic noise on Lake Austin Boulevard. He glanced across the parking lot to the ground-floor unit where a female patrol officer stood guard.

"First responder, Lena Gutierrez," Reed said, looking at Jay. "You know her?"

"Think she's new."

They crossed the lot and exchanged introductions. Gutierrez looked nervous in her wilted uniform. Her gaze darted to the detective shield clipped to Reed's belt.

"I secured the perimeter, sir."

"Good. Tell us what you got."

She cleared her throat. "Apartment's rented to April Abrams, twenty-five. Didn't show up for work today, didn't answer her phone. One of her coworkers dropped by. The door was reportedly unlocked, so she went inside to check . . ."

Her voice trailed off as though they should fill in the blank.

Reed stepped around her and examined the door, which stood ajar. No visible scratches on the locking mechanism. No gouges on the doorframe.

Jay was already swapping his shiny black wing tips for paper booties. Reed did the same. Austin was casual, but they always wore business attire—suit pants and button-down shirts—because of days like today. Reed never wanted to do a death knock dressed like he was on his way to a keg party.

He stepped into the cool foyer and let his eyes adjust. To his right was a living area. White sectional sofa, bleached-wood coffee table, white shag rug over beige carpet. The pristine room was a contrast to the hallway, where yellow evidence markers littered the tile floor. A picture on the wall had been knocked askew, and a pair of ME's assistants bent over a body.

A bare foot jutted out from the huddle. Pale skin, polished red toenails.

Reed walked into the hall, sidestepping numbered pieces of plastic that flagged evidence he couldn't see. A slender guy with premature gray hair glanced up, and his expression was even grimmer than usual.

April Abrams was young.

Reed knelt down for a closer look. She lay on her side, her head resting in a pool of coagulated blood. Long auburn hair partially obscured her face, and her arm was bent behind her at an impossible angle. A strip of silver duct tape covered her mouth.

"Jesus," Jay muttered behind him.

Her bare legs were scissored out to the side. A pink T-shirt was bunched up under her armpits, and Reed noted extensive scratches on both breasts.

"What do you have?" Reed asked.

"Twelve to eighteen hours, ballpark," the ME's assistant said. "The pathologist should be able to pin that down better."

Reed studied her face again. No visible abrasions. No ligature marks on her neck. The left side of her skull was smashed in, and her hair was matted with dried blood.

"Murder weapon?" Reed asked.

"Not that we've seen. You might ask the photog, though. She's in the kitchen."

Reed stood up, looking again at the tape covering the victim's mouth. A lock of her hair was stuck under it, which for some reason pissed him off.

He moved into the kitchen and paused beside a sliding glass door that opened onto a fenced patio. Outside on the concrete sat a pair of plastic bowls, both empty.

"I haven't seen a weapon," the crime-scene photographer said over her shoulder. "You'll be the first to know."

Reed glanced around her to see what had her attention. On the granite countertop was an ID badge attached to one of those plastic clips with a retractable cord. The badge showed April's mug shot with her name above the words *ChatWare Solutions*. April had light blue eyes, pale skin. Her hair was pulled back in a ponytail, and she smiled tentatively for the camera.

The photographer finished with the badge and shifted to get a shot of the door.

"Come across a phone?" Reed asked, looking around. No dirty dishes on the counters. Empty sink.

"Not so far." She glanced up from her camera as Jay stepped into the kitchen and silently handed Reed a pair of latex gloves. "I haven't done the bedroom yet, though, so don't you guys move anything."

Reed pulled on the gloves and opened the fridge. It took him a moment to identify the unfamiliar contents: spinach, beets, bean sprouts. Something green and frilly that might or might not be kale. The dietary train wreck continued in the pantry, where he found three boxes of Kashi, six bottles of vitamins, and a bag of flaxseed.

Opening the cabinet under the sink, Reed found cat food and a plastic trash can. The can was empty, not even a plastic bag inside it despite the box of them right there in the cabinet. He'd check out Bellaterra's Dumpsters. Reed opened several drawers and found the usual assortment of utensils.

"That's an eight-hundred-dollar juicer." Jay nodded at the silver appliance near the sink.

"That thing?"

"At least. Maybe a thousand. My sister got one last Christmas."

Gutierrez was standing in the foyer now, watching them with interest.

"Did you come across a phone?" Reed asked her. "A purse? A wallet?"

"No on all three, sir. I did a full walk-through, didn't see anything."

Reed exchanged a look with Jay before moving back into the hallway. The ME's people were now taping paper bags over the victim's hands.

Reed stepped into the bedroom. A ceiling fan moved on low speed, stirring the air. The queen-size bed was heaped with plump white pillows like in a fancy hotel. The pillows were piled to the side and the bedspread was thrown back, suggesting April had gone to bed and then gotten up.

"Think she heard him?" Jay asked.

"Maybe."

The bedside lamp was off, and the only light in the room came from sunlight streaming through vertical blinds. Reed ducked into the bathroom. Makeup was scattered across the counter. A gold watch with a diamond bezel sat beside the sink. Reed opened the medicine cabinet.

"Sleeping pills, nasal spray, laxatives, OxyContin," he said.

"No shit, Oxies? Those are getting hard to come by."

Reed checked the doctor's name on the label.

"What about the sleeping pills?" Jay asked.

"Over-the-counter."

Reed examined the latch on the window above the toilet. Then he moved into the bedroom. Peering under the bed, he found a pair of white sandals and a folded shopping bag. On the nightstand was a stack of magazines: *Entertainment Weekly*, *People*, *Wired*. He opened the nightstand drawer and stared down.

"Huh."

Jay glanced over. "Vibrator?"

"Chocolate." Four bars of Godiva, seventy-two percent cocoa. One of the bars had the wrapper partially removed and a hunk bitten off.

Reed was more or less numb to going through people's stuff, but the chocolate bar struck him as both sad and infinitely personal. He closed the drawer.

"We ID'd her vehicle," Gutierrez said, stepping into the room, "in case you guys want to have a look."

Reed and Jay followed her back through the apartment, catching annoyed looks from the ME's people as they squeezed past again.

"What are you thinking?" Jay asked as they exited the home and got back into real shoes.

"I want that phone. I want her friends, her boyfriend, secret admirers at work, whatever." He glanced at Gutierrez. "What's the name of that witness? The coworker?"

"Mindy Stephens. She's in the leasing office with a patrol officer right now. She kind of lost it after she called it in, got sick all over the floor."

"I'll talk to her," Jay said.

Wallace was good with female witnesses. He had been a defensive tackle in college, where he'd been known as "The Wall" because of his size. But he'd stopped pumping iron and now had a teddy-bear thing that seemed to put women at ease.

Reed, not so much. He was tall and lean, and his skeptical eyes made people uncomfortable. At least that's what his ex-wife said. When they'd been married, she'd often accused him of interrogating her like a suspect, and maybe she was right. He'd gotten to where he expected people to lie to him right out of the gate, whether they needed to or not. Reed was thirty-nine and had been a cop for seventeen years. All that time on the job had made him jaded, but it had also made him good. It was a trade-off.

"Strange place to park," Jay observed as Gutierrez led them across the lot to a powder-blue BMW. Reed had been thinking the same. It would have been natural for April Abrams to park in front of her unit.

Police barricades had been set up around the victim's car, and a CSI was already crouched beside the driver's-side door. Reed recognized her—Veronica Greene. She was known to be abrasive, but Reed didn't mind, because she was crazy good at what she did. He'd once seen her lift a usable print off a charred envelope.

She glanced up as he neared the car. "You touch anything, you die."

"Print all of it, especially the passenger side," Reed said.

She lifted an eyebrow in a way that told him what he could do with his advice.

"Any sign of a phone?" he asked.

She leaned into the car and plucked something from the floorboard with a pair of tweezers, then dropped it into an evidence bag. "No, but I found a charger. Looks iPhone-compatible, which should help you track down the carrier, at least. There's a laptop computer in the trunk. And"—she reached in and lifted something from the cup holder—"a receipt. Dated yesterday, looks like a coffee shop."

Someone had scrawled a local phone number across the bottom of the receipt. Reed pulled out his phone to photograph it. It might be the best lead they had so far.

Or it might be nothing.

He glanced across the lot to where the ME's people were unloading a gurney from the van. The parking lot was filling in now, and Bellaterra residents were beginning to stop and gawk. In a few moments they'd realize what was happening, and then the phones would come out and pictures would end up on Facebook and Twitter.

"I need to notify the family," Reed told Jay. "And it's going to suck. I'm betting they're close."

"As in friendly or nearby?"

"Both."

"Why?"

"Call it a hunch." He glanced at the car. "Someone was giving her juicers and BMWs."

"Maybe she was good at her job."

"She was practically a kid."

Jay shrugged. "So was Mark Zuckerberg when he made his first billion."

Reed looked at him.

"Anyway, I need to move on that witness," Jay said. "What's our game plan?"

Reed watched the gurney being rolled inside. Twenty minutes into the case, and already they needed a game plan. That was how it worked now, and Reed didn't waste his energy cursing social media.

He thought of April's ID picture. He thought of her anxious smile as she'd stood before the camera, probably her first day on the job. She'd probably been feeling a heady mix of hope and anticipation as she embarked on something new.

He pictured the slash of duct tape over her mouth now. It would stay there until she reached the autopsy table.

"Reed?"

"No forced entry. No purse, no phone. But he left jewelry, pain meds, and a Bose stereo."

Jay nodded because he knew what Reed was thinking. At this point, everything pointed to someone she knew.

Jay glanced across the lot. "Shit."

Reed turned to see an SUV easing through the gate, tailgated by a white news van. Just in time for the money shot of the body coming out. In a matter of minutes the image would be ping-ponging between satellites.

"Dirtbags," Jay muttered.

"Right on time."

• • •

Laney rolled her chair back and let her system think. And think. It was sluggish tonight.

"Laney."

She tipped back and rested her Converse high-tops on the edge of the desk. She checked the script.

"Laney."

It was good. Better than good, it was perfect.

"Oh, La-ney? Hello?"

A row of numbers appeared, then another and another.

"*Yes.*" Her feet hit the floor. "I got you, you sick son of a bitch."

"*Laney.*"

She snapped her head up to see Tarek peering over the wall of her cubicle. "What's up?" She rolled forward and started creating a backup file.

"Are you coming with us or not?" he asked.

"Coming where?"

"The *Door*, Laney. God."

"What's at the Door?"

Silence.

She lifted her gaze. He looked annoyed now, maybe even a little hurt, and she stopped typing.

Tarek was one of the smartest programmers at the Delphi Center. He was tall and lanky and favored slogan T-shirts. Today's said, "I'm here because you broke something." Which tended to be true. Tarek was their fix-it man.

"You don't remember a word, do you?" he asked.

"No."

"The Cedar Door, ten o'clock, with me and George. Alex is meeting us for darts."

"Sorry, I'm out." She resumed typing. "Someone's waiting on this."

"But you said you'd come."

She very much doubted it.

Or maybe she had. She'd say almost anything to get people to leave her alone when she was working.

"Laney, we need four people."

She studied her list, her pulse pounding now because it was more than she'd expected. Way more. She grabbed her cell phone and texted her contact: *Execution complete.*

"Laney, come on."

"Man, show some respect." Ben Lawson's disembodied voice floated over from the neighboring cube. "Can't you see she's in the zone?"

"Hey, I wasn't talking to you." Tarek sounded ticked now, and she glanced up to see him glaring at Ben. "Whatever fed Laney's working for isn't waiting for a file *tonight*. I guarantee you he's off getting tanked or boffing his girlfriend."

"What're you working on, anyway?" Ben looked over their shared wall, which was lined with *South Park* bobbleheads. He glanced at her screen, and his mouth fell open. "Holy shit, you cracked it?"

"Yep."

"How?"

"*Wo ein Will eist, ist auch ein Weg.*" Where there's a will, there's a way. Ben, like Laney, had double-majored in German and computer science.

"I thought they had the firewall from hell," he said.

"I followed the money." A tried-and-true strategy. "They take credit-card payments, so I sent a trojan in through the payment company, then established a back door and went from there." She made it sound easy, but it had taken three days. The trojan alone had been a bitch to create. Criminals tended to be strangely paranoid about people poking around their networks.

"What about their AV?" Ben got out of his chair and came over, keenly interested now.

"The antivirus was okay, but I used a good wrapper, so . . ."

A text landed on Laney's phone, and she picked it up. *RU kidding??*

Encrypting now, she responded. *Look for a list of IPs, ETA 10 min.*

Laney skimmed the file for anything wonky, but it looked clean. Three days of work, pretty much around the clock. In moments the file would be on its way to Special Agent Maya Murray in Washington, D.C. In minutes Maya would be writing up a warrant. And a short time after that—possibly within forty-eight hours—a team of agents would swoop down on a crew that had hacked its way into an American electronics company that made webcams, nanny cams, and other Internet-enabled devices. After stealing usernames and passcodes, they'd set up an underground website called RealityKidPr0n and started streaming live footage of children's bedrooms to perverts across the globe.

Laney spent a few minutes double-checking everything. When she was finally satisfied, she hit send. Then she leaned back in her chair and heaved a sigh.

She glanced around. As always, she felt like she'd been in a time warp. She craned her neck to see over the sea of cubicles. Everyone but Ben and Dmitry had cleared out. They sat at Dmitry's computer now, probably deep into a game of *Settlers of Catan* while they waited on a scan.

Laney logged out and stretched her arms over her head. She stood up and slung her messenger bag over her shoulder, then navigated the minefield of crap that had accumulated on the floor of the lab over the past three weeks: pizza boxes, Nerf balls, several sleeping bags. The Delphi Center's cybercrime unit had recently landed a big fish client, and the past three weeks had

been a marathon of round-the-clock hacking runs as
Laney's colleagues channeled their collective brain-
power into ferreting out security holes in the systems
of various government agencies. Laney wasn't assigned
to the project, but she could appreciate the challenge.

Her phone beeped with a text, and she dug it from
the pocket of her hoodie.

W00t! U rule! Maya had texted, adding a Wonder
Woman emoji.

Laney smiled. She felt sore and tired but energized
now. Maybe she'd stop by the Door after all and whip
Tarek's butt at darts. Or maybe she'd spend a quiet
evening at home. Again. She could order takeout and
catch up on TV shows. Or she could curl up in front of
a movie and remind herself how relieved she was that
she didn't have a life outside work.

She wandered over to Dmitry's computer to check
out the game. When they weren't busy penetrating
highly secure systems, her coworkers were locked in
an intense competition with the computer science department at UT.

Ben cursed and jumped up from his chair. Dmitry
made a strangled sound and clamped a hand over his
mouth.

Laney glanced over. They weren't playing *Settlers* at
all—they were on Facebook.

"Who died?" she quipped.

Ben turned around, and Laney instantly regretted
the words. The look on his face stopped her in her
tracks.

CHAPTER 2

Reed hated gatekeepers almost as much as he hated hands-free phones.

"I need to talk to Greg Sloan," Reed said, flashing his ID.

The receptionist stared up at him from behind the counter, evidently flustered. He had brown eyes and freckles and wore a thin black tie that made him look at least twenty.

"Um, I'm sorry, but he's in a meeting."

"I'm going to need you to get him out of his meeting." Reed rested his elbow on the counter. "This is important."

"Uh . . ." The kid's Adam's apple bobbed, and Reed could tell he'd heard about the murder and guessed why Reed was here. "I'm afraid that's not possible at the moment. Mr. Sloan's in California."

Of course he was. Reed consulted his notepad and rattled off several more names.

"They're not here, either. Everyone's out right now."

"When will they be back?"

"I'm not at liberty to say."

Reed gave him a hard look.

"Tomorrow. They're on the nerd bird, San Jose to Austin, four fifteen arrival. Excuse me." The kid held up a finger. "ChatWare Solutions. How may I help you?"

Reed stepped over to the lobby's floor-to-ceiling window to call Jay. Glancing up, he noticed the golf-ball-size security camera staring down at him from the ceiling.

"How was the autopsy?" Jay asked right away.

"Frustrating."

"Why?"

Reed looked at the security cam again. "I'll fill you in later. What's the word on that phone dump?"

"Just got it," Jay reported. "Looks like she made eight calls on Tuesday. Two to her friend Mindy, like we expected, and six to an Ian Phelps."

"Who's that?"

"Don't know, but I happened to find out from the phone company that his phone number is under the same umbrella plan as April's. So I'm guessing it's someone at her office."

"I'll look into it. What are the times of the calls?" Reed gazed out the big window. ChatWare Solutions occupied a converted loft in the trendy business district just north of the lake. It was a sunny day, and the street below was busy with lunchtime traffic.

"Let's see . . . the six calls to Phelps happened between five fifteen and eight forty P.M."

"No kidding."

"All lasted about a minute, except the last one. That was three minutes."

Reed wrapped up with Jay and returned his attention to the receptionist, who was off the phone now but still had the microphone positioned in front of his mouth.

Reed walked over to him. "One more question. I'm looking for Ian Phelps."

Recognition flared, and Reed waited for him to say that Phelps was in California, too. "You just missed him," the receptionist said cheerfully. "He went to lunch."

"Any idea where?"

"Try Francesca's downstairs. If not, maybe the sushi shop across the street?"

Reed trekked down a free-floating glass staircase and stepped from pleasantly chilled air into sweltering heat. He paused on the sidewalk and texted Jay to run a wants-and-warrants check on Phelps.

Francesca's was on the corner, a cluster of dark red umbrella tables offering relief from the sun. The parking meters nearby were occupied by Fiats, Audis, and BMWs, and Reed remembered when the same corner had been staked out by drug addicts and homeless people who frequented the soup kitchen next door. Now the place was a yoga studio.

Nearing the restaurant, Reed spotted a guy at a shaded table talking on an iPhone, and the ChatWare badge clipped to his waist proved he'd hit pay dirt. He squeezed past a jogging stroller and stood over the table until the guy looked up.

"Ian Phelps?" He showed his ID. "Detective Novak, Austin PD."

Phelps hesitated a moment and then ended his call.

"You got a minute?" Reed pulled out a chair and sat down. Phelps glanced around before meeting Reed's gaze.

"You heard about April," Reed stated.

A slight nod.

"You don't look surprised to see me."

"I'm not." Phelps glanced around again, then leaned forward slightly. He wore black pants and a light purple dress shirt that looked custom-tailored. "April called me that night, so I figured you'd want to talk to me," he said.

"What night?"

"Tuesday." His eyebrows tipped up. "That's the night she died, right?"

Reed looked Phelps over. He had one of those carefully cultivated two-day beards, and he smelled like cologne, despite eating lunch out here in the ninety-degree heat.

Most people weren't so casual when it came to the details of a murder investigation. They tended to be distraught and tongue-tied.

Especially if they knew the victim well enough for six phone conversations in one night.

"What makes you think that?" Reed asked.

"It was in the news."

Reed watched him for a moment and decided to change course. "I understand you and April had several conversations Tuesday evening. What'd you talk about?"

"Well, first of all, she called me." Phelps nudged away a plate that held the remnants of a sandwich on ciabatta bread. "And I wouldn't exactly call them 'conversations,' because I couldn't talk and I told her I had to go."

"Six times?"

"What?"

"All six times she called, you told her you had to go?"

"Yeah, like I said, I couldn't talk. I've been slammed all week on a new project, barely time to breathe."

Reed glanced at the plate in front of him.

"Seriously." He sounded defensive now. "I couldn't

talk, and I told her I'd call her later, when stuff died down."

"Did you and April usually talk after work?"

He hesitated. "Not really."

"So what was she calling about?"

"She didn't say."

Reed leaned back in his chair and watched him for a long moment, and again the conversation felt off. This guy didn't seem nearly uncomfortable enough for someone discussing a woman's final hours. "What was your relationship with April like?" he asked.

"We were friends."

Reed lifted his eyebrows. "That's all?"

"Yes. I'm engaged to someone, all right? April and I were friends, no big deal. We worked a few accounts together."

"Accounts?"

"We're on the sales side. You know, software sales?"

According to the website, the company was a leading-edge provider of mobile messaging solutions. According to the *Austin Business Journal*, they were having a shit year.

Reed's phone *dinged* with an incoming text. He ignored it for now as he studied Phelps's body language. April's parents had said their daughter didn't have a boyfriend. Her coworker had said the same, but that didn't necessarily mean anything.

"Was April having any issues with anyone that you were aware of?" Reed asked.

"No."

"Anyone at work bothering her?"

"No. But I mean, why ask me? You should ask Mindy Stephens or someone who knew her better."

He shifted in his chair, finally getting uncomfortable. "Look, I know what you're driving at." He leaned closer and lowered his voice. "But you're wasting your time. I was here way late Tuesday, didn't leave till, like, two A.M. You can check the security tapes." He nodded down the street, and Reed knew he was indicating the security camera perched above ChatWare's front entrance.

Reed stared at him a moment, then pulled out a business card. He had a feeling he'd be talking with Ian Phelps again, and he wanted to keep things friendly. He jotted down his cell number and handed over the card. "Thanks for your time today. Call me if you think of anything helpful."

Phelps quickly got to his feet. "Yeah, sure."

Reed watched him walk away, already back on his phone and looking right at home among the neighborhood regulars. Reed glanced around the café. He was out of his element. The place served five-dollar coffee, and the average patron was probably twenty-eight.

Reed's phone *dinged* again and he checked the text.

OPEN ME. The words were followed by a link. Reed didn't recognize the number, but the area code was local. He debated a moment before taking the bait.

A photo appeared of a beautiful young woman with a cascade of auburn hair and a sultry smile. Reed frowned down at the picture. He checked the sender's number, but still it didn't ring a bell. Beneath the photo was a description, and Reed's frown deepened as he read the words.

He studied the picture, trying to reconcile the sexy red smile with the bloodless lips he'd seen during this morning's autopsy.

He couldn't. But the woman in the photograph was definitely April Abrams.

• • •

The volleyball court was empty, but Bellaterra's parking lot was almost full as Reed used his police emergency code to open the gate. He pulled up to April's unit and got out.

The victim's vehicle had been hauled to the crime lab, where it would remain until it could be cleared for release to the family. Reed glanced around as he approached April's door. He sliced through the scene tape and stepped inside, then donned a pair of booties and entered his name in the scene log. The CSIs had wrapped up last night, but the DA wanted to keep everything sealed for a while until the case took shape. Only one day in, and the man was already chomping at the bit to prosecute someone.

Reed stood in the foyer a moment, letting the air settle around him. A mix of smells lingered, the most notable being the Superglue that Veronica had used to fume the doorknobs. The familiar scent kicked his brain into gear as he stepped deeper into the apartment.

Walking a crime scene was something Reed did early and often. Things jumped out at him on a second or third pass, things he'd missed the first time, because death scenes had a way of being messy and chaotic, especially outdoor ones. But this scene was indoors. And uninhabited. It was a rare combination of circumstances that Reed intended to use to his advantage.

He walked through the kitchen again and looked

out at the patio. Still no cat. He pulled on a pair of gloves and went through the cabinets again. Then he tried the drawers, paying special attention to any slips of paper lying around. As he made his way into the bedroom, he called Jay.

"Sorry, I had a deposition at two," Jay said when he picked up. "I just got out."

"I'm at the apartment looking for passwords. Where are we on the laptop?"

"The techs tell me it's front of the line, but they haven't gotten to it yet. Passwords might help, though."

"I'll let you know," Reed said. "Hey, did you send me April's profile on this dating site?"

Pause. "She's on a dating site?"

Well, that answered that. Reed stepped into the bedroom and went straight to the dresser. He opened the small top drawers, where people tended to stash clutter.

"What, you mean like Match.com?" Jay asked.

"This one's called Mix. Looks like a smaller shop, and they're headquartered here in Austin."

"Interesting."

"I know. Maybe not a coincidence."

"You mean someone sent you her profile through department email?"

"Came in on my phone. I don't recognize the number, and it traces back to Chief Aguilar, only he didn't send it."

Jay snorted. "Someone's fucking with you, bro."

Reed stepped into the closet and flipped on the light. Besides the basic office clothes, April's wardrobe included sheer blouses, halter tops, and microskirts, along with a collection of designer shoes that would have made Reed's ex-wife green with envy. Not what Reed would have expected for a computer geek, which just reinforced the first thing he'd learned as a rookie detective: stereotypes amounted to shit. Criminals and victims were as quirky as everyone else, and relying on assumptions was straight-up laziness that could lead to problems down the road.

"Any idea who?" Jay asked.

"I'm running it down." He opened a shoe box to find a pair of rhinestone-encrusted stilettos. "Anyway, call me if you find anything."

Reed stepped out of the closet and stared at the bed. The sheets had been stripped and sent to the lab, but Reed could still picture April propped in the middle of all the pillows, maybe surfing around on her laptop or tablet before going to sleep. He walked over and opened the nightstand drawer. Beneath the chocolate bars he found a pink envelope he hadn't noticed yesterday. It contained scraps of paper showing words and email addresses.

"Gotcha," Reed muttered, thumbing through the notes. He took an evidence envelope from his pocket and wrote out a label, then sent Jay a text telling him he'd found the passwords and reminding him to run a check on Phelps. After a last quick walk-through, he let himself out.

The heat blasted him like a hair dryer. The parking lot was congested with people returning home from work and class. A trio of women in cutoff shorts crossed the patio beside the volleyball net and exited through the wrought-iron gate, which they held open for a man coming into the complex. Reed watched them with resignation. The killer could have gained access much the same way. Gates and fences and pass-codes were no match for the primal urge to flirt.

A young woman in workout clothes strode down the sidewalk. She had a yoga mat tucked under her arm, and Reed recognized her from yesterday's canvass.

"Excuse me, ma'am?"

She halted.

"My partner talked to you yesterday." Reed took out his ID, and she cast a wary glance over his shoulder at April's apartment. "Mind if I ask a few follow-up questions?"

Panicked eyes. "I don't really—"

"It won't take long." He ushered her into the shade of an oak tree. "I noticed you pull in a few minutes ago. You always get home around five thirty?"

She gazed up at him. "I . . . yeah, I guess. Most days."

She'd already been through all this with Jay and reported that she hadn't seen April Abrams or even her car all week.

"I'm wondering if you noticed any unusual vehicles here Tuesday evening," Reed said. "Maybe a moving van?"

"A moving van?"

"Or maybe a UPS truck? Something blocking the front-row spaces in front of your building."

"No moving van." She looked at the building. "But there was a truck here Tuesday. Furniture, I think? I saw some guys unloading a sofa."

Reed pulled out his notepad. "What time was this, exactly?"

"I don't know. Six? Maybe six ten?" She brushed her bangs from her eyes with the back of her hand. "I got stuck in traffic, so I was a little late getting home. I don't think I saw the name on the truck, but they took the sofa to that unit two doors down. The one on the corner there."

"Thanks." Reed would follow up, see if the delivery crew had witnessed anything. Or maybe they'd noticed April. The neighbor was watching him now with an anxious look, and Reed tucked his notebook away.

"So can you tell me . . ." She cast a glance at the crime-scene tape. "Did he break *in* or . . . ?"

"That's not something I can discuss," Reed said, feeling like an ass. "But you should take common-sense precautions. Lock your doors, etcetera, even during the day."

She nodded.

He pulled out a business card. "And don't hesitate to call us if you see anything unusual."

Another nod, and he knew he wasn't helping. She'd probably already started looking for a new place to live.

"Thanks, officer." She smiled awkwardly and started to leave.

"One more thing. You happened to see April's cat around?"

"Cat?"

"She had an outdoor cat."

She shaded her face with her hand and squinted at the building. "I don't know if it was hers, really. But there's a stray calico that hangs around here sometimes. Maybe she was feeding it?"

The woman tucked the business card into her purse and walked to her car as Reed's phone *dinged* with a text message.

A strange feeling settled in his stomach, and he

glanced around as he pulled out his cell. It was the Mix link again. This time the sender's number was all zeros.

WHO IS THIS? he queried.

FORGET IAN UR WASTING TIME.

Reed stared down at the words. A few seconds later a text bubble appeared showing the link again.

Reed gritted his teeth. How did the sender know about Ian Phelps? Someone was definitely screwing with him. He poised his thumb to respond.

The message vanished.

• • •

Laney drove down the row of condos, noting the familiar cars and the welcoming glow of porch lights. She'd picked this street specifically for its quiet feel, but her usual sense of relief at coming home was lacking tonight. Instead she felt stressed and irritable. Not to mention bone-tired. And she needed to snap out of it because she still had some code sprints ahead of her.

She reached her condo but on impulse kept on going. Throughout her drive home a vague feeling of unease had prompted her to check her mirrors over and over. Now she hooked a right at the stoplight. She circled the block twice before finding a parking space. She grabbed her messenger bag and got out, looping the strap over her head as she glanced around.

Urban Grounds was busy tonight but not nearly as bad as Saturdays, when they featured half-price microbrews and live music. She mounted the steps to the front porch where people lounged on mismatched armchairs under slow-churning ceiling fans. Inside, the place smelled like incense and coffee beans. Laney

made her way to the counter and ordered her usual
from a barista with blond dreadlocks and a lip ring.

"You seen Scream around?" she asked him, tucking
a bill into the tip jar.

"Not tonight."

"Tell him I'm looking for him, would you?"

"You got it."

She joined the cluster of people waiting for drinks
at the counter and eyed the cookies behind the glass.
Her stomach growled. She thought of her refrigerator,
which was suffering from severe neglect because of
the hours she'd been working. One of these days she'd
probably settle into a nine-to-five routine, but for now
she preferred to push herself. Predators didn't keep
business hours, so why should she?

"Night Owl, double jolt."

She grabbed her coffee and turned around, smack-
ing right into a broad chest.

A man gazed down at her with flinty blue eyes, and
her heart lurched.

"Delaney Knox."

CHAPTER 3

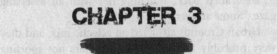

Laney stood frozen, her fingers burning against the cardboard cup.

Reed Novak's gaze didn't waver. "You got a minute?"

How had he found her? No way he'd spotted her tailing him yesterday. But he knew her name. Did he know where she lived, too? The thought unnerved her.

Then it pissed her off.

The detective eased closer, towering over her, attempting to intimidate her with his size. "We can do this here or at the station. Your call."

Laney stared up at him, debating how to respond. She avoided cops whenever possible. They were all about authority, rigidity, law and order. She wanted to tell him to get lost, and yet . . . she was curious. And impressed that he'd somehow tracked her down.

She stepped away from the counter and claimed an empty table. "Five minutes," she said.

The corner of his mouth lifted, and she felt a flutter of nerves. He took the metal chair across from her, turning sideways to make room for his long legs.

Up close she saw that his eyes were light blue, almost gray. He had thick salt-and-pepper hair and tanned skin and looked as though he spent time outdoors. Cop or not, he was definitely attractive. She'd have to be dead not to notice.

"What is it you want?" she asked.

He leaned back, watching her with an assessing gaze. "Some answers."

Urban Grounds attracted an eclectic mix, and they were probably the only two customers not sporting body art. But Laney still fit in. If the detective was bothered by the glances he was getting, he didn't show it.

Laney's heart was still thumping from the shock of seeing him here. She didn't like being caught off guard.

She looked at her watch again. "Four minutes."

He smiled. "You have somewhere to be tonight?"

"Yes."

The smiled faded and he held her gaze. "You hacked into my phone," he said evenly.

She didn't respond.

"You spoofed the unlisted number of the chief of police to pass information relevant to a homicide investigation."

He watched her and waited. Did he think she was going to explain? She didn't discuss her methodology. Her skills were her meal ticket, and she wasn't about to put herself out of a job.

"Well?" His eyebrows tipped up.

"No one's really unlisted."

He leaned farther back in the chair and looked her over, taking his time about it.

Laney's skin warmed under his gaze.

"How is it you know April Abrams?"

She sipped her coffee because her throat was suddenly dry. "Why would you assume I do?"

"I saw your Ford Focus parked near ChatWare Solutions yesterday."

Laney didn't say anything. He must have collected the security tapes and run her plate.

"I noticed it again near April's apartment," he said. "You seem interested in her murder."

"I'm interested in a lot of things."

He stared at her silently, but she refused to squirm. "Work? School?" he persisted. "A mutual friend?"

"That's not really relevant."

He leaned forward on his elbows, all trace of amusement gone now. "I'm the lead detective in her murder case. Far as I'm concerned, everything's relevant."

The words sent a chill down her spine. *Her murder case.* April had been reduced to a case number, a bar code.

The cold queasiness was back again. Laney had been trying to get rid of it, but she couldn't.

"I've got all night." His eyes settled on her, cool and determined. She felt as if she were sitting in an interview room with one of those two-way mirrors and furniture that was bolted to the floor.

She darted a glance at the door. She wanted to leave. She shouldn't have gotten involved in the first place. But the police had been wasting time, and she hadn't been able to sit idly by. Evidence was ephemeral, especially the digital kind. She knew that better than anyone.

"Delaney? How do you know April?"

A lump clogged in her throat, but she swallowed it down. She looked into his eyes. "She was my friend."

• • •

Her answer didn't surprise him. But the emotion in her voice did.

He watched her, trying to get a read. Her body language was guarded. She didn't like that he'd found her here in her own backyard, which was pretty ironic considering she'd hacked into his phone and didn't even bother denying it.

She sat there, staring at him defiantly with those brown-black eyes. Her dark hair was cut short in the back and angled sharply to her chin, with a hunk of bright pink on one side. She wore black Converse shoes, black jeans, and a thin black tank top that clung to her small, high breasts. Reed was making a valiant effort to keep his focus on her face, but God help him, he was only human.

"You and April were friends," he stated. "That how you knew she was on this dating site?"

"More or less."

"What's that mean?"

She looked impatient. "Yes, I knew she was on Mix."

So did that imply that she was on Mix, too? Somehow he couldn't picture this woman posting a dating profile for men to gawk at.

"Did she ever mention anyone she met there?" Reed asked.

"No."

"She ever mention anyone she was seeing at all?"

"No."

"You sure?"

"Yes."

"Where'd you two meet, anyway?"

She looked at him for a moment, maybe resigning herself to the fact that he wasn't going to leave her alone until he got some answers.

"At work," she said.

"ChatWare Solutions?" Her name wasn't on the current list of employees. Reed had checked.

"It was a long time ago," she said vaguely.

In her world, that meant what, six months? A year?

Delaney Knox was twenty-four, even younger than April Abrams, which made it all the more interesting that she had the balls to stonewall him.

Or it could be an act. After her little stunt yesterday, she might be worried that he intended to charge her with a crime.

She watched him, her hands clutched around a twenty-ounce double-shot coffee that would keep her up all night. He wondered what she planned to do later. And who she planned to do it with. His gaze dropped to her mouth. Her lips were full. Tempting. She had the kind of mouth that sparked fantasies. Reed dragged his attention back to her eyes, and the look in them told him she knew where his thoughts had strayed.

"So you knew April was on Mix," he said. "And you think this had something to do with her murder?"

"They've got security holes," she said. "Ones that can easily be exploited by any moron with a keyboard."

"How do you know?"

"Because I do."

"You ever work there?"

"No," she said, and something in her tone made him think it was a lie. But hell, why would she lie about something he could easily check out?

He was intrigued now, and not just by her nonanswers and screw-you attitude.

She glanced at her watch and stood. "Time's up."

This woman was a piece of work, no doubt about it.

Reed knew he'd be seeing her again, and he felt a buzz of excitement as he got to his feet.

"Don't follow me," she said, picking up her coffee.

"Wouldn't dream of it."

● ● ●

The security system beeped as Laney stepped through her front door and dropped her bag onto a chair. She silenced the noise with a few quick taps while her cat looked on in silent reproach.

Laney made a beeline for the fridge, where she found an expired yogurt and a carton of curry shrimp. She gave the carton a sniff and put it back.

"There's nothing to eat, Baggins."

She opened the pantry, but the options there were equally uninspiring. Baggins did figure eights around her ankles as Laney stared at the shelves that hadn't managed to replenish themselves while she'd been gone. She was famished, but even hunger wasn't enough to prompt her to pick up the phone. Sometimes she got like this. *I can tell you're in one of your hermit moods,* her mom would say on her voice mail. *Call me when you get this.*

Laney was definitely in one of those moods. She didn't want to face a single living person right now, not even the pizza guy. She poured cat food into a bowl and then returned to her messenger bag and dug out a half-eaten pack of Twizzlers.

She kicked off her shoes and sank onto her futon. She stared at her laptop for a few long minutes, gnawing on candy. Finally, she turned on her computer and watched her inbox fill. She had several messages about April, all from former coworkers at ChatWare.

That job seemed ages ago. It had been her first job out of college, and so much had changed since then. Over the past two years, she'd lost touch with the "normal" people she used to know, people who didn't live and breathe code.

But she'd gained some things, too, such as an unbelievably high security clearance. And what had once been a thrilling and subversive hobby had become a full-time job. Laney hacked for a living now, and she loved every minute of it.

What she didn't love was the fallout, because that was where people came in. And people could be incredibly shitty, in her experience. Not all people but plenty.

She thought of Reed Novak. She thought of his cool blue eyes and his relentless questions. Was he a good guy or bad? Hard to tell, and she'd been wrong in the past.

She'd expected him to take the lead that she'd generously sent him and run with it, without getting all hung up on where it came from. But the detective was thorough, apparently. She remembered the flare of attraction in his gaze, and the warm tingle was back again. There was something about him.

The men in Laney's world fell into two main groups. There were the smooth, overly manicured guys, who tended to be in software sales. And then there were the programmers, who tended to be smart and witty but awkward in social situations that didn't involve games.

Reed Novak was different. Maybe it was his broad

shoulders and the confident way he carried himself. Or maybe it was his ruggedly handsome face or the lines around his eyes that told her he'd seen a few things and had some life experience under his belt.

Maybe it was that he didn't mind making her uncomfortable. He probably made a lot of people uncomfortable in his line of work, and she liked that about him.

She thought of his low, easygoing voice, which had been at odds with his steely gaze. He hadn't been intimidated, and Laney was glad. April needed someone like that on her case, someone hard and persistent who would leave no stone unturned.

Baggins hopped onto the sofa and burrowed against her side. As he settled in for a nap, Laney surfed around for a few minutes before landing on Mix. She'd duplicated the answers to April's questionnaire and created a fake profile for herself to see what sort of response she'd get. So far it had been less than impressive. Most guys were idiots. They'd say something friendly or maybe ask to meet up, and when she declined they'd quickly devolve into insults. She read a few messages telling her she was a stuck-up bitch and then logged in under a different name and navigated over to April's profile.

Laney stared at the picture. Three full days, and no one had taken it down, not the system admin, not the family. Laney's cold and queasy feeling was back again.

She knew how it felt to be violated in the very place you called home. She knew the shock, the panic. Three years later, it was still seared into Laney's mind. She couldn't get away from it. Her life was forever divided into Before and After.

Before her attack, Laney had been aware of personal security but not vigilant. The danger had felt abstract, something she knew she should worry about—like cancer or air pollution—but in actuality, she didn't.

Now her fear was very real. She was fully attuned to noises in the night and hang-up calls and strangers watching her on the street. She habitually locked her car and set her burglar alarm. She no longer jogged at night or early in the morning. Her life was different now. Yes, she was safer, absolutely. But she also felt confined. Limited. As though her wings had been clipped when she'd only just learned to fly.

She stared at April's photo and wondered again what she'd felt in those final moments. Had she been paralyzed with terror, or had she managed to fight? Had she been aware of every agonizing second? Or had the stunning shock somehow blocked out the pain?

Looking at April's picture now, Laney felt a surge of anger. It shouldn't still be here, and yet it was. Three full days, and men were still shopping her. They were still leering, still critiquing, still imagining.

Even in death she wasn't out of their reach.

CHAPTER 4

"So what was wrong at the autopsy?" Jay asked as he stepped into the conference room. He plunked a giant Frappuccino on the table, and Reed immediately regretted not stopping for caffeine.

Reed handed him a copy of the pathologist's report, which he'd just pulled off the printer.

"ME spent a lot of time looking for things he didn't find," Reed said.

"Semen?" Veronica asked, getting straight to the point.

"Negative."

"Wait, back up." Lieutenant Hall pulled out his reading glasses.

The fact that the lieutenant wanted to sit in on this Saturday-morning meeting underscored the importance being placed on the case by the top brass.

"What's the cause of death?" Hall glanced at Reed.

"Blunt-force trauma."

"Weapon?"

"None recovered."

"He took it with him," Veronica added. "You can tell from the spatter pattern." She pulled a crime-scene photo from a file and slid it toward the lieutenant. "See how the droplets are comet shaped? The tail of the comet points toward the door, which is consistent with an object dripping blood as the perpetrator leaves the scene." She slid several photos to Reed and then Jay.

Reed studied the pictures. The tiny blood drops were denoted by evidence markers. Magnification revealed a clear pattern.

Hall glanced up from the photo in front of him. "What do we know about the weapon?"

"A hammer-like instrument, based on the skull fracture," Reed said.

"Hammer-*like*?" Hall's gaze narrowed.

"ME doesn't think it's a regular hammer but some sort of specialty tool. She was killed by a blow to the left parietal bone." Reed flipped through the pages to the diagram. As he studied the picture, something niggled at his subconscious, but he couldn't pinpoint it.

"What about the bruises?" Jay asked.

"She had bruising on her legs and torso," Reed said. "Plus a broken arm. By the looks of it, she was alive for most of the attack, resisting him, and then he killed her at the end."

The door opened, and Reed turned around to see Jordan Lowe stepping into the room.

"Sorry I'm late," she said, grabbing a chair next to him. She wore street clothes and a badge that dangled from a lanyard around her neck. Jordan was a homicide detective, but lately she'd been doing undercover work for vice.

What'd I miss? she mouthed, and Reed slid the autopsy report in front of her.

"Okay, what else?" the lieutenant asked. "I assume we searched the surrounding area for this hammer?"

"We covered everything," Jay said. "But you know,

chances are he ditched it. Town Lake is just across the street."

Reed wasn't convinced he'd ditched the weapon, but he kept his theory to himself for now.

"Also missing," Reed continued, "saliva, bite marks, hair, or skin cells belonging to the assailant, despite obvious signs of rape."

"So he wore a condom," Jay said.

"Tested positive for lubricant. Still working on a brand."

"I'm not surprised by the condom," Veronica said. "This guy's a real neat freak."

"Why do you say that?" Jay asked.

"No un-ID'd prints in the apartment. No outside hairs that we were able to find. Only one partial footprint, and that in itself looks weird."

"How come?" Reed asked.

"Shoe pattern's obscured." She passed him another photograph, this one showing a faint oblong shadow on the victim's Saltillo tile floor.

"You're sure this is a shoe print?" Reed asked.

"Positive. There's actually a trace of blood there at the bottom—the victim's blood—and it's clinging to a white fiber consistent with the synthetic material manufactured by Tyvek."

"You're saying he wore *shoe covers*?" Reed didn't bother to hide his disbelief.

"Looks that way."

Jay whistled. "Man, that's what I call premeditated."

Reed sat back in his chair, even more disturbed than he'd been during the autopsy.

"You're sure *we* didn't leave that print?" the lieutenant asked.

Veronica bristled. "Absolutely. The footprint was one of the first things the photographer captured when she arrived at the scene. Only person who'd been in there beforehand was Gutierrez, and she'd neglected to put booties on for her initial walk-through, so it wasn't her."

Reed flipped through the file, still digesting the implications of everything. No semen, no hair, no fingerprints. The victim's fingernail clippings had come back negative for skin cells, even though there were clear signs that she'd put up a fight. Reed had first thought the killer had gotten lucky, but now he thought maybe he'd worn long sleeves. And he might have worn some sort of head covering, too—maybe panty hose—to keep from leaving other trace evidence. Hell, maybe he'd even shaved his head.

"I did find some hair around the back door," Veronica continued, "all belonging to a cat, probably a calico, based on the coloring."

"No cat recovered, either," Jay said, trying to lighten the mood.

"What about method of entry?" Jordan asked.

"Unknown at this point," Reed said. "No sign of forced entry, but her sister said she was very conscientious about security, so it's unlikely she left her doors unlocked at night."

"You're thinking she let him in?" Hall asked.

"I wouldn't jump to that conclusion yet," Veronica said.

Reed looked at her. "You come up with something on the door?"

"No, but I'm working on it."

Hall turned to Reed. "What's this I hear about the

victim being on a dating site?" It was an abrupt change
of subject. Maybe they were getting around to the real
reason Hall had wanted in on this meeting.

"She has a profile on a site called Mix," Reed told
him. "They're headquartered here in Austin, coinci-
dentally. In terms of suspects, we're checking out guys
from this site, but there are a lot."

"How many?" Hall asked.

"Thirty-six thousand and twelve, to be exact," Jay
said. "And almost eight hundred who live locally. From
the messages, it looks like she only maybe went out
with two of them. This was back in October, and both
have alibis for the night of the murder."

Reed looked at Jay. His partner had interviewed the
men personally, and he had good instincts about people. The alibis had checked out, but Reed still wasn't
ready to let it go.

Delaney Knox seemed to think Mix was a good
lead. Reed had no idea why that should carry any
weight, but it did. The girl might be prickly, but she
was smart. Plus, she knew the victim, which gave her a
perspective he didn't have. He thought of the way she'd
looked at him last night. She'd been guarded, but there
was something else there, too—an expectation she
seemed to have of him.

"She might have contacted some other people from
this site off-line," Reed said. "So we're still checking her
phone and email records."

"This dating-site thing, that sounds like a huge time
sink," Hall said. "Unless we turn up a specific suspect,
let's wrap up that avenue as fast as we can. We definitely
don't want that angle leaking to the media, not with the
local connection."

Reed didn't respond. He disliked the media as much as anyone, but why should he worry about bad PR for some company, local or not? Reed despised this kind of politics. This case was bad enough already, with a young woman murdered inside her own home and not a single decent suspect four days in.

Hall looked at Jay. "What about people she knew at work?"

"We're checking into it."

"We're also investigating a phone number," Reed said. "It was scrawled on a receipt found in the victim's car."

"The receipt is dated the day of her murder," Veronica added, looking at Reed. "What'd you get on that?"

"Number comes back to a wellness studio on Barton Springs Road."

"Wellness studio?" Hall asked.

"Yoga, Pilates, meditation. They've got a health-food restaurant on-site." Reed's phone *dinged* with an incoming message. "I'll go by there later today."

"Who's going to the funeral?" Hall asked.

Silence.

"It's at noon, Sacred Heart Church," the lieutenant added.

"I'll go," Reed said.

Jordan looked at him. "No, you covered the last one. I'll take this one."

"I'll go with you," Jay offered, much to Reed's surprise. Jay hated funerals. Reed did, too, but they were part of the job. They offered a good chance to observe people close to the victim and sometimes a chance to pick up on any unusual family dynamics.

"Fine, Novak can cover the wellness studio, and

you two are on the funeral," Hall said, "but keep it low-profile. The press is going to be all over this one." He checked his watch and pushed back his chair as Reed read his text message.

SBUX ACROSS THE ST 5 MIN. Once again, the number belonged to the chief of police. Reed muttered a curse.

"Novak?"

He glanced up. "Sir?"

"Send me an update later today, and I want progress." Hall glanced around the room. "The minute that funeral ends, the media's going to be ringing my phone off the hook."

• • •

Delaney Knox wasn't hard to spot. She was the only one outside the coffee shop who wasn't drinking or staring at a phone, and she turned to face him as he approached her.

She wore faded jeans ripped at the knees, chunky black biker boots, and another tight-fitting black T-shirt. Her streak of pink hair was braided and tucked behind her ear today.

Reed stopped in front of her, and she gazed up at him with those brown-black eyes.

"Detective."

"Delaney."

"It's Laney." She looked away. "Let's go over there. This shouldn't take long."

He followed her to a circular fountain surrounded by stone benches. Reed glanced around, checking people's faces and body language, looking for suspicious behavior, but everyone seemed mellow on this sunny Saturday morning.

Reed took a bench in the shade. Laney remained standing and tucked her hands into her back pockets.

"You didn't tell me you worked at the Delphi Center," he said.

"Would it have made a difference?"

"Yes."

She watched him for a moment, then sat down on the bench, leaving plenty of space between them. "You've been checking up on me," she said.

"I have."

"That mean you've been checking up on my lead, too?"

"We're looking into it."

She stared out at the fountain, and he had a chance to study her profile. The hostility from yesterday was gone, but still she seemed tense. She appeared to be gathering her thoughts, and he took the time to look her over, fascinated by her smooth, bare arms. They were toned but pale, and he figured she spent most of her time indoors. His gaze drifted to her breasts again in that tight T-shirt.

Twenty-freaking-four, he reminded himself, looking away.

"Not to be rude, but—" He checked his watch.

"There's something you should know. Last night you were asking about Mix. About why I thought April was targeted through a dating site." She tucked her feet under the bench and glanced at the fountain, and he could tell she was uncomfortable with this conversation.

He waited.

"That's where he found her." She looked at him. "I can't prove it, but I believe he found her through that damn website."

"What makes you so sure?"

She sighed. "You know what I do, right?"

"You're a hacker."

"A white hat, the good kind. As opposed to black hat."

"Okay."

"So Mix was one of our clients. They hired us to check out their systems, run pen tests—penetration testing," she explained. "Looking for security holes, back doors, that sort of thing. Anyplace they'd be vulnerable to attack. I was tapped to be on the red team, the team that tries to sneak in."

He settled back against the bench to listen. He was intrigued by the fire he saw in her eyes. She seemed to like this topic. "When was this?"

"About ten months ago. They were concerned about operational security."

He smiled.

"What?"

"You make it sound like they were conducting nuclear tests," he said. "We're talking about a dating site."

"Do you have any idea how much money the on-line-dating industry is worth?"

"No, but I have a feeling you do."

"More than two billion a year. And it's a growing business."

He tried to look contrite.

"More important, it involves the private information of millions of people."

"Names, credit-card info?"

"And personal stuff," she said. "Location, physical description, sexual preferences. Some of the compatibility surveys get very personal. It's a predator's wet dream."

"Okay, so . . . I take it you found gaps in their security."

She scowled. "It was a joke. The system was wide open. They didn't need the Delphi Center—any script kiddie could have hacked them. And they did. Within a few months of Mix opening up shop, people started figuring out how to bypass the registration process but still use the site."

"To avoid paying fees?"

"Right, that was probably the goal. But they also ended up bypassing the background check. Mix's system is set up to run names through a criminal background check and also check them against sex-offender registries. A lot of dating sites don't bother with all that, so it's a feature that sets Mix apart. They added it to appeal to female users, hoping to gain market share. But this security gap, it's a major flaw, and the system admin didn't even know about it until a year ago, supposedly."

"Supposedly?"

"I think they suspected a problem before that but didn't have the resources or the motivation to really fix the bugs in the system. But once the problem started to become widespread, it was a PR liability. Competition for users is fierce, and Mix makes these promises about screening people and criminal background checks and keeping your personal information private. But that's all bullshit if they don't have the security in place to back it up."

"I assume you pointed out these problems?"

"Yes, immediately." She swiped her hair out of her eyes and looked at him. "Well, no. That's not true. First I warned April. I'd run across her name in their database. Then I pointed out all the problems in a formal report."

"What did they do about it?"

"Asked us to overhaul their security procedures, which we did. And I gave them a patch to address the specific holes I found. One of the problems was a secret back door that offered universal access. You could get anything—names, credit-card info, physical addresses—"

He frowned. "They keep physical addresses?"

"They keep home telephone numbers, which is the same thing. Takes about five seconds to trace."

"And you think April's killer found her on this site, through this back door."

"Or a different back door. And yes, I do. I think he found her and stalked her, maybe without her even knowing about it." She looked at him, her dark eyes somber. "And then I think he went to her home and killed her."

CHAPTER 5

Laney's heart was thudding now. She wasn't sure why. Maybe because she knew he was really listening.

He leaned back against the bench, watching her with that cop look designed to make people squirm. He probably used it on suspects all the time.

"You look skeptical," she said.

"I was born skeptical."

"You don't believe me."

"I didn't say that."

"Look, I investigate cybercrime. I'm an expert. And women get targeted online all the time, way more than anyone wants to believe."

"I'm sure you're right, but that doesn't prove that's what happened here."

She rolled her eyes. "Okay, how about you tell *me* something. How much time did your CSI spend examining the door at the crime scene? Or whatever his point of entry was?"

Reed didn't respond.

"How much?" She leaned closer.

"I don't know."

"Take a guess."

"Probably a lot."

"Right. Probably a lot. Because the point of entry is important to the case." She put her hand on his knee to make sure she had his attention, and his gaze darted down.

"Think of April's computer as another point of entry into her life," she said. "Maybe the most important one. I'm telling you, you should examine that, too."

· · ·

Reed watched her car pull away as he walked back to the building. Delaney Knox was full of contradictions. She lived in a pricey condo but drove a piece-of-shit hatchback. She was guarded about her privacy but didn't mind invading his. Her words were tough, but something in her eyes was achingly vulnerable.

The contradictions drew him in, like a puzzle he needed to solve. Who was she, exactly?

Reed stepped into the lobby and spied Jay. He immediately knew he was about to get grilled.

"Hey, you got a sec?" Jay stopped in front of him. "I didn't want to mention it in front of Hall, but I've got some thoughts on the autopsy report."

"What about it?"

Jay glanced at the elevator, then back at Reed. "Remember that young teacher who went missing two summers ago?"

"The one down in Clarke County, yeah."

"Olivia Hollis. You know she was bludgeoned, right? They never found out who killed her."

"Different MO," Reed pointed out. "She went missing, and her remains were found in the woods three months later."

"Four. I looked up the news story. Anyway, cause of death jumped out at me," Jay said. "And her age. And like I said, they never arrested anyone. So, you know, just a thought."

Reed watched him, considering it. "I know the sheriff down there. I can call him up."

"Wouldn't hurt." Jay looked at the window. "So who was that girl you were talking to?"

Here it came.

"Delaney Knox," Reed said.

"The one from the Delphi Center?"

"The hacker I told you about, yeah."

"She's hot." Jay glanced at the window again. "You asked her out yet?"

"She's twenty-four."

Jay lifted an eyebrow.

"I'll let you know what I hear from the sheriff." Reed walked away. "Don't be late to that funeral."

• • •

This time, the sand volleyball court was full, and Veronica admired the array of shirtless, sun-browned men as Jay pulled into a parking space.

"I'll keep this quick," Veronica said, shoving open the door.

"Ten minutes tops," he said. "I can't be late to this thing."

"I know, I know."

She grabbed her evidence kit and walked briskly up the sidewalk, ignoring the wary glances from the volleyball players. It was hard to forget about the homicide scene next door when the cops kept showing up.

"You remember the key?" Veronica dropped her kit beside the door and pulled out some shoe covers.

Jay silently produced a copy of the victim's key and unlocked the door. After tugging on his booties, he followed Veronica inside.

The apartment was dark and humid, and the scent of Superglue still hung in the air.

"Damn, you fume everything?" Jay made a face as he walked over to the scene log and entered their names.

"Just the interior doorknobs," she said. "The cabinet pulls I dusted."

Despite all the time she'd spent, she hadn't managed to lift a single print that didn't belong to the victim, her family, or one of her girlfriends.

"What exactly are we looking for?" Jay asked.

"Not sure. I'll let you know when I find it." She side-stepped the bloodstains in the hallway as she made her way to the bedroom. "I just keep thinking I missed something."

She started with the windows, checking the locking mechanisms for the umpteenth time. Then she moved to the bathroom. No sign of anyone tampering with the locks, and she doubted anyone had. Even if the perp had managed to get a window open, it would have been risky, because the bedroom windows faced a busy street.

Jay stood in the doorway watching her. "You're hung up on point of entry."

"Yep."

He moved aside so she could squeeze past him. He was a large man, tall and brawny, which was a big check mark in her plus column. Too bad she had a rule against cops.

"I thought we concluded she let him in," Jay said.

"No, you concluded that." She walked into the kitchen and crouched down beside the sliding glass door. "I'm still not convinced."

Veronica hated sliders. In terms of boneheaded ideas, they ranked right up there with hide-a-keys. But despite how easy it would have been for the perpetrator to pop the latch on the sliding door, she couldn't find the slightest bit of evidence that he'd done so. She pulled the magnifying glass from her pocket and examined the frame for scratches. Finding none, she stepped outside and looked around. She examined the top of the fence boards for torn fabric or blood or even a wisp of lint—anything that might indicate he'd come over the fence.

"You checked all that the first time," Jay said patiently. "I saw you with my own eyes."

She shot him a look. "Well, he didn't walk through the wall."

"Agreed."

"So how'd he get inside?"

"Gee, I don't know. Maybe she let him in?"

She huffed out a breath and pushed past him into the kitchen. "Put some food in that cat bowl, would you?"

He sighed. "Where's the cat?"

"I don't know, but I'm sure he's hungry."

Jay gave her a glare before bending down to get some food out from under the sink. Technically, she shouldn't change anything at a crime scene. But this one had already been processed, and she didn't see what it could hurt.

She returned to the front door.

This was his point of entry. She had a feeling about it.

But she couldn't swallow the idea that the victim had let him in. From the look of things, April Abrams had gone to bed alone on the night of her attack. So either someone she knew had come to the door and she'd unlocked it—possible but not likely, in Veronica's mind—or the killer had slipped in. April had heard him from the bedroom, gotten up, and confronted him in the hallway.

The second scenario felt right to Veronica. She could visualize it. It matched other elements at the scene—everything except the damn door lock.

She opened the front door once again and crouched down to study it. No marks or gouges on the wood anywhere.

Jay came up beside her, and she caught a faint whiff of his aftershave. She thought of her no-cops rule. Not that she could afford to be really picky. Her midthirties didn't offer nearly as many options as her midtwenties had. She worked hard to stay in shape, and she still looked good. But she had lines around her eyes now. And it was more effort than it used to be to keep the gray in her roots from showing.

Part of it was just life, but there was more to it, she knew. She'd spent the last decade lifting prints at crack houses and collecting blood samples from floors and swabbing semen off of children's sheets. She chose to do this job—every day and with her whole heart—but she knew her work had aged her much more than time.

She glanced up at Jay. "I know you have to go," she said, taking out her magnifying glass again. She examined the lock face but saw no signs of a lockpick.

He stepped over the threshold and started to remove his shoe covers. "Five minutes, Ronnie. I can't show up late to a funeral."

"I know, I know."

She took a flashlight from her kit and shined it in the keyway. She glanced at Jay, and he was staring down at something on his shoe covers.

"What's that?" She held her hand out. "What is that dust there?"

"Beats me." He passed the bootie to her. "Looks like glitter?"

Her heart jumped. "Damn it, I knew it!" She popped open her evidence kit and grabbed some tape.

"Knew what?"

Slowly, carefully, she used a strip of tape to lift the tiny metal shavings from the shoe cover. There were more bits of material on the ground, just beneath the lip of the threshold. She collected the material there, too, and placed everything in an evidence envelope. Then she turned her attention to the door lock. It was a typical pin-and-tumbler system, maybe a step above standard apartment-unit hardware. She tore off a new strip of tape and sealed it over the keyway, and her fingers trembled slightly from excitement.

"What's that for?" Jay asked.

"Transport to the lab. We don't want to lose anything."

"Don't tell me you want the whole lock."

"I want the whole door." She smiled up at him. "And it's a good thing you're here, because I'm going to need a hand."

• • •

The basement of the Clarke County Sheriff's Office smelled like pot, and Reed had no trouble identifying the source as he neared the evidence room.

"Don't you guys ever incinerate anything?" Reed asked the deputy leading him down the hall.

"'Bout twice a year." The man shook out a key from his big ring. "That load we got now is headed to trial."

After Reed's stop at the wellness studio failed to generate any leads, he'd driven down to Clarke County to take a look at the Olivia Hollis case. The sheriff was out, but he'd assigned Reed a deputy. Henry Krueller was short and bald and had a beer gut that hung over his utility belt, but he didn't seem to mind getting up from his desk to show Reed around.

Now they stepped up to the evidence room, which was actually a steel cage roughly forty by forty feet and ten feet tall. It had a lid on it, too, presumably to keep people from scaling the walls and helping themselves.

Evidence theft was a widespread problem that departments didn't like to talk about. Just last year, a police storage room in east Texas had been pilfered following a drug bust. Thieves had made off with sixteen kilos of coke by puncturing the plastic-wrapped bricks and emptying out the product inside, then filling the cavities with baking soda. The swap wasn't discovered until the case went to trial.

"That load there, we seized that down on I-35 back in March." Krueller nodded at a table with a pile of marijuana bricks stacked two feet high. "Got it off an eighteen-wheeler. Made it right past the border check."

"Fake cargo area?" Reed asked.

"Nah, hidden in the spare tires. Trial's in September, so until then we got it here under lock and key." Krueller motioned with his head for Reed to follow him. "Come on back. It's around the corner."

Reed followed him down a narrow passageway between metal shelves packed tightly with banker's boxes, each labeled with a case number. Some of the cases dated back to the '70s.

They rounded a corner to find more shelves. Oversized evidence that didn't fit in the boxes lined the cinder-block wall to Reed's right. He saw hunting rifles, pool cues, a mangled bicycle, all labeled with evidence tags. In the corner was a heavy-duty gun safe. It looked like someone had tried to get into it with an ax.

"We're switching our files to digital," Krueller said. "Haven't gotten very far back yet." He stopped in front of a box and stooped to read the label. "Here we go. Olivia Hollis."

"Two boxes?"

"Four."

Reed nudged the top off a box and found it filled with manila folders. The second box contained more of the same. "Looks like this may take a while."

"Don't be messing things up, now." Krueller gave him a stern look. "The deputy on this one, he's very particular with the files."

"I understand."

"Anything you look at, put it back where you found it."

"Will do."

Krueller stood for a moment, watching him. He seemed reluctant to go.

"Thanks for your help," Reed said. "Thank the sheriff for me, too, when you see him."

"There's a worktable up front. You can set up there." Krueller gave a stiff nod and lumbered off.

Reed read the labels again and moved all four boxes to the worktable. He parked himself in a chair and rolled up his sleeves.

The first carton contained personal items. He found a phone and a set of car keys and also a brown leather wallet-purse thing that was big enough to hold a cell phone. Fingerprint powder clung to some of the items, and they'd been zipped into plastic freezer bags. Reed shook his head. Everything should have been put in paper evidence envelopes where any biological material would be less likely to degrade over time. But maybe Clarke County wasn't up to date on evidence procedures. Reed thumbed through the bags, looking at everything through the plastic. Olivia's driver's license and credit cards had been collected in a clear sandwich bag with the case number scrawled across the front in black Sharpie. Reed studied the driver's license photo. Olivia had pale skin and soft brown eyes. Her tentative smile reminded Reed of April Abrams.

He moved on to the file box, searching for a case summary, which he located in a black three-ring binder that included key documents. He settled back in his chair. Amid the stale marijuana scent, he started to read.

Twenty-five-year-old Olivia Jane Hollis had been a teacher at Clarkesville Elementary School. Police were called to her apartment the second week in June after a friend stopped by to visit and discovered Olivia's back door ajar and blood smears on the floor.

Olivia's car was parked in the carport behind her unit. Her purse was on the kitchen counter, along with her keys and her cell phone.

Local police immediately shifted into high gear. But because the police department included a grand total of three full-time officers, the sheriff's department was quickly called in to assist. They combed the town and the surrounding area on foot and horseback. They brought in canine teams. Olivia's family mobilized hundreds of people to help search and blanketed the area with flyers. They held a press conference that attracted statewide media and even set up a tip line. But the tips went nowhere, and searchers turned up nothing for months. Finally, in October, a young couple hiking in northern Clarke County came across some bones in a ravine.

Reed flipped through the binder until he found the autopsy report. Given the advanced state of decomp, the county coroner had turned everything over to a forensic anthropologist. Reed checked the signature on the report: Dr. Kelsey Quinn at the Delphi Center Crime Lab. The private forensics lab sat in the middle of a body-decomposition research center, better known as a body farm. Reed had heard of Dr. Quinn but had never met her in person.

He flipped through the pages, skimming over the diagrams. Manner of death: homicide. Cause of death: blunt-force trauma. The victim had sustained two skull fractures. The likely instrument was listed as a *hammer, circular face, 1.5-inch diameter*.

Reed paused. It was the hammer. *That* was the detail that had been lurking at the back of his mind since he'd talked to Jay. He must have heard it somewhere, maybe from a cop or a crime-scene tech. A detail like that wouldn't have been in the news, but Reed had known it somehow.

Both Olivia Hollis and April Abrams had been killed with a hammer. Both had been twenty-five. Both had been attacked at home.

I think he found her and stalked her, maybe without her even knowing about it.

Laney's words came back to him, along with the imploring look she'd had in her eyes. She was convinced of her theory, convinced enough to elbow her way into his investigation. She simply wouldn't let it go, and Reed knew how that felt because he'd been there.

He reached into the banker's box and pulled out another binder. This one was packed with interview notes, all neatly typed by someone with a fondness for all caps. He flipped through the pages, skimming names and dates. The sheriff's guys had interviewed quite a few friends of the victim, most of them male. Reed counted eight different names, some interviewed multiple times. They had addresses in Clarkesville, San Marcos, Austin. Reed skimmed the pages but didn't see any mention of Mix or any other dating site. He didn't see anything computer-related mentioned anywhere at all, in fact. The closest thing was a phone dump, which showed a long list of cell-phone calls during the sixty days preceding Olivia's disappearance. Someone had marked up the report, highlighting numbers and scrawling notes in the margin: *mom, sister, fmr. roommate.*

Reed heard shuffling in the hallway. The vending machine groaned, and a soda can *clunked* down. Reed leaned his head out of the cage as Krueller hiked up the stairs.

"Hey, you guys have any chargers around here?"

Krueller stopped and turned around. "What's that?"

"Phone chargers? You have any plugged in up there? I'm looking for an iPhone charger, older model, probably a four."

Krueller stared at him.

"It's probably white. Maybe plugged into the wall or someone's power bar?"

"I'll look around," he said.

Reed set the phone aside and continued with the binder. It was packed with interview notes. For a small department, they'd covered a lot of ground, and he knew they'd been under intense pressure. Not unlike the pressure his department was under, which was mounting by the day.

Damn it, he owed his lieutenant a phone call.

His cell buzzed in his pocket. He set the binder aside and checked the number. Jay.

"How'd the funeral go?" Reed asked.

"How you'd expect."

"Anything interesting?"

A heavy sigh on the other end. "No. Good turnout, though. Lot of people from her work were there. Ian Phelps, Greg Sloan. Mindy What's-her-name."

"Stephens."

"Right. And your friend was there, too. Delaney Knox."

Reed stopped what he was doing.

"I tried to approach her, but she lit out right after the service ended," Jay said. "So how'd it go at the yoga place?"

"They never heard of April Abrams. Looks like maybe she was just calling to inquire about class schedules or something."

"Where are you now?"

"Clarke County."

Reed went back to the autopsy report and flipped to the diagram drawn by the forensic anthropologist.

It was one of those fill-in-the-blank pictures, only instead of a human body, as Reed had seen in April's case, the diagram showed a skeleton with various injuries marked.

"And?" Jay sounded eager. "You turn up anything?"

"Still working on it, and I've got another stop to make. I'll let you know when I'm back."

"Shit, you found something, didn't you?"

Reed studied the drawing and read Dr. Quinn's notes in the margin: *Depressed fracture, left parietal.*

"Reed?"

"I don't know yet. Maybe."

The Delphi Center was on the outskirts of a college town between Clarkesville and Austin. It was on Reed's way home.

He checked his watch. It was almost six o'clock on a Saturday, which meant lots of cops stopping by the crime lab to drop off evidence from weekend incidents. Reed figured he had a fifty-fifty chance of catching her.

"Well, what's the other stop?" Jay asked.

"I need to swing by the Delphi Center."

CHAPTER 6

The sun was getting low by the time Laney logged off her computer and packed it in for the day.

Alex Deveraux breezed into the lab. She had a cup of coffee in hand and looked ready for action.

"Graveyard shift?" Laney asked.

"I'm on the Homeland Security project with Tarek. He here yet?"

Laney stood up and grabbed her bag. "Haven't seen him."

"We're running a DDoS attack against ICE tonight."

They typically did simulated attacks at night or on weekends, when it would be less disruptive to normal operations.

Alex set her coffee beside her keyboard. "By the way, there's a cop downstairs asking about you."

Laney froze. "What, now?"

"He was at the reception desk when I came in."

"What's he want?"

"Don't know. I didn't talk to him."

"How do you know he's a cop?"

Alex shot her a "get real" look as she pulled out her chair. Alex was married to a cop, so she could probably spot them a mile away.

Laney's desk phone buzzed, and Alex nodded at it. "See?"

She picked it up. "Knox."

"Hey, it's Reed."

She didn't say anything.

"Reed Novak."

"What are you doing here?"

"Looking for someone."

"Who?"

"Doesn't matter, I missed her."

Laney slung her bag over her shoulder and waited. She could feel Alex's eyes on her.

"I saw your car out front," he said. "I need to talk to you about something. You have time to meet up?"

Laney felt a rush of warmth. It wasn't just the invitation but the low timbre of his voice.

"I'll buy you a cup of coffee," he added.

Laney glanced at Alex, who was watching her with blatant curiosity now.

"Laney?"

"There's a place in town called the Cedar Door. You know it?"

"No."

"Corner of Main and River Road," she said. "I'll meet you over there."

She got off the phone, and Alex was smiling at her. "Hot date?" she asked.

"I wish."

• • •

The Cedar Door was a hangout for college students as well as tourists who'd spent the day tubing on the river and drinking copious amounts of beer. On Saturdays especially, the place was a meat market, which was exactly why Laney picked it.

She pulled into the gravel parking lot and created a space for her car at the end of a row of pickups. She tossed her hoodie into the backseat and looked around. The outdoor deck overlooking the river was already filled to capacity.

She spotted Reed waiting by the door. He still wore his usual detective attire, but his sleeves were rolled up and his hair was mussed as though he'd raked his hand through it a few too many times. His blue eyes pinned her as she walked over, and she got a warm tingle in the pit of her stomach. For a moment, she just gazed up at him.

"Any trouble finding it?" she asked.

"No."

He pulled open the heavy wooden door, and she stepped inside. The place was filled with sunburned men and lots of women in cutoff shorts and halter tops.

Perfect.

Maybe it was the funeral getting to her. Or maybe the fact that Reed had caught her off guard last night. Or maybe she just had a mean streak. Whatever the reason, she was determined to screw with his head tonight.

She turned around to see him skimming his gaze over the crowd. He glanced down at her. "What do you want to drink?"

"Shiner Bock."

He started toward the bar, but she caught his arm.

"No, I'll go—it'll be faster. What would you like?"

"Shiner's good," he said.

She wove her way through the crowd. At the bar, she leaned forward and waited to be noticed by one of the bartenders. A few minutes later, she rejoined Reed with the drinks.

"There's a spot," she said, moving toward some empty stools beside a life-size cardboard cutout of a bikini-clad woman holding a tray of tequila shooters. But Reed took her elbow and steered her toward a corner table instead, and just the touch of his fingers gave her a warm shiver.

Laney sat down, glancing around to see if she knew anyone.

"Looks like you come here a lot," Reed said, taking a seat.

"Sometimes after work. It's a popular hangout." She sipped her beer, watching him. He seemed uneasy. Mission accomplished.

Laney was good at reading people, and she could tell Reed thought she was young. Much too young to be taken seriously as an investigator. And definitely too young for whatever thoughts put that smoldering look in his eyes.

She placed her bottle beside his. "So what did you want to talk about?"

He didn't answer. He turned his Shiner on the table, and his attention veered to the trio of blondes who'd stepped up to the dartboard. They barely looked old enough to drink.

He looked at her. "You always work Saturdays?"

"Sometimes. A lot of the tests we do go better on nights and weekends. We usually don't want to crash our clients' systems during peak hours." She tipped her head to the side. "What about you? You work a lot of weekends?"

"Sometimes."

He held her gaze, and she waited.

"You like working at Delphi?" he asked.

"It's interesting. Pays really well."

"I'd imagine it does. Especially for someone, what, two years out of college?"

"Three."

He lifted an eyebrow. "You shotgunned it."

"I was in a hurry to finish."

"How come?"

She debated how much to tell him. She didn't usually talk about her family. "When I was twelve, my dad took off with my college fund," she said. "He and his girlfriend needed it for a nest egg."

"You're serious?"

"Yeah."

"That's—wow." He shook his head. "That must have sucked."

"I don't know." She shrugged. "It wasn't all bad. It forced me to motivate. I mean, nobody's entitled to go to college, right?"

"He betrayed you and your mom. That must've hurt."

It did. Still. Her mom's whole life had imploded— both of theirs had. Laney didn't like to dwell on it, and she wasn't sure why she was talking about it now.

"No wonder you're a workaholic," Reed said.

"How would you know?"

"It's Saturday evening, and you're just starting your weekend."

"So are you."

He swilled his beer and smiled. "Fair point."

"Is that why you're divorced?"

The smile disappeared. "What makes you think I'm divorced?"

"Because," she said, glad to shift the focus. "You're obviously straight. Outwardly likable—"

"'Outwardly'?"

"You seem like someone who'd get married. But I'm guessing your hours weren't conducive to domestic bliss, right?"

He watched her warily, and she got the feeling she'd hit on the truth. "That's more or less accurate," he said, and she could see he wanted to change the subject. He took another sip of beer and watched her. "So what's interesting about working at the Delphi Center?"

"A lot of things. I used to be a software developer. This is much better. For one thing, there's a point."

"You're saying software's pointless?"

"Well, I started out with ChatWare Solutions, which is a messaging platform. So it has a function, but I'm talking about a *point* point. Something meaningful."

He looked genuinely interested. "What's meaningful at Delphi?"

"I don't know. Lot of things."

"Such as."

"Such as . . . we have one of the best cybercrime units in the country. We go after thieves and pimps and pedophiles."

He had to know all about their unit. They'd even teamed up with Austin PD a few times. "You're an idealist."

She scoffed. "Right."

"No, it's good."

She watched him silently. She wasn't sure why the label made her uncomfortable, but it did. She never thought of herself as an idealist. It seemed to imply she was naive, and she wasn't.

"One of your coworkers over there at Delphi," he said. "Dmitry Burkov?"

"What about him?"

"I remember his arrest four years ago at the University of Texas."

She didn't respond.

"You remember that?"

"No," she lied.

"He wormed his way into the school computer and was selling grade adjustments on the black market."

She didn't comment.

"Too bad they didn't get the charges to stick." He watched her steadily. "Could have been ten years for hacking and online theft."

"Dmitry's smart. He doesn't leave footprints."

"Yeah, I don't know how smart it was risking his freedom—not to mention his student visa—over a few bucks." He gave her a long, cool look, and she wondered if he was trying to intimidate her again, maybe with the threat of charges. Where was he going with this?

She turned her beer on the table. "Most people don't do it for the money."

"Do what?"

"Hack."

"Why do they do it?"

"I don't know. Boredom. Entertainment." She shrugged. "Because they can. Nothing's unhackable—the challenge is to figure out how."

"Why do you do it?"

"Better than a life of suits and office plants."

His gaze settled on her, dark and serious. It was his cop look again. "I want you to tell me more about Mix."

"There's nothing more to tell."

"I doubt it."

"You're the investigator. Why don't you investigate instead of asking me?"

He leaned forward on his elbows, and she had to make an effort to keep from squirming in her chair. "You hacked your way into my case, Delaney. What'd you think, that you could just drop a lead into my lap and disappear?"

She didn't answer.

"That's not how it works."

"Yeah, well, that's how it works for me," she said. "I've got my job to think about. I've signed nondisclosure agreements. Every one of my clients has an NDA with the Delphi Center."

"Fuck your NDA. A woman is dead."

The words were like a slap.

And regrets flooded her mind again. April was dead. And Laney should have followed up. She'd warned April about the security breach, but then she'd basically checked it off her list and forgotten about it.

She should have done more. If she'd pressed the issue, April might have taken more steps to protect herself and she might be alive right now.

Reed's stare was hard and unyielding. He'd laid a conversational trap, and she'd walked right into it. Now she felt petty for worrying about her job.

And then she felt angry at herself.

Since when did she give a damn about a bunch of dot-com executives? Since when was she a corporate lackey?

"Fine." She tore her eyes away from his and looked down at her beer. "What is it you want to know?"

• • •

Everything shifted, and he knew he had her. She was going to talk to him. For now. But who knew how long it would last? This girl was evasive.

He waited for her to lift her gaze.

"You told me you were on the red team investigating Mix last fall," he said.

"What about it?"

"Why do you think they hired the Delphi Center?"

"They wanted to beef up their security," she said.

"Yes, but why?"

Something flickered in her eyes. Hesitation? "They said they thought they were losing revenue. Some users had found a way to bypass the payment procedures."

Reed didn't respond for a moment. He just watched her. "Is that the real reason? The Delphi Center is a world-renowned institution. And expensive. Seems like there are cheaper ways to check out credit-card fraud."

"That's what they *said*." She traced her thumb over her beer label. "I always thought . . ."

"You always thought what?"

"There were rumors they were trying to go public. And they weren't just rumors. I heard that from one of the top executives. They're hoping for an IPO this year. I think they hired Delphi to help get all their ducks in a row, you know, security-wise, before it was time to open everything up to public scrutiny."

Reed leaned back in his chair, thinking about it. It

was a plausible reason, one he hadn't considered. But it wasn't the reason he'd expected.

"You have some new lead about Mix, don't you?" she asked.

He didn't answer.

"Don't you?" She eased closer.

"I can't share details about an ongoing investigation."

Her jaw dropped. "Are you freaking kidding me? You just pressured me into revealing confidential client information. You just—"

"I'm gathering facts."

Her eyes simmered. He'd offended her, but there wasn't much he could do about it. Investigations weren't a two-way street, and she needed to wise up to that fact.

She shook her head and looked away.

"That's the way it is, Laney."

"I get it."

"It's nothing personal."

She watched him coolly and seemed to be waiting for his next move. It was a conversational chess game. He was a skilled interrogator, so skilled it felt almost unfair now. She acted so guarded, and she didn't realize what she'd already told him. In the time it took her to finish one beer, he'd learned that she had a daddy complex that probably made her insecure in relationships. He'd bet she was fiercely loyal to her mother, too. And slow to get close to people, especially men.

And then he felt bad psychoanalyzing her as she sat there watching him with that frustrated look in her eyes. She shook her head and glanced away. Every time she started to open up to him, he did something to piss her off.

"Laney?"

"What?"

"It's my job to ask questions. To push."

She looked at him again, and her expression softened. "No, you're right." She glanced down at her bottle and picked at the label. "I'm glad she has you."

"Who has me?"

"April. You seem . . ." She paused, like she was searching for the right word. "Committed."

He didn't answer. It wasn't really a question, but the way she looked at him gave him the feeling she wanted a response.

She drained her beer and plunked down the bottle. "I should get home." She stood up.

Reed stood, too. He left a tip on the table and followed her through the throng of people. The bar was packed, and the music had gotten louder since they'd first walked in.

They stepped into the warm, muggy air. It was dusk now, and a neon Lone Star Light sign cast a blue-and-red glow over the sidewalk. As they walked in silence, he thought of what she'd said about her job being meaningful. It was refreshing. Maybe he'd been a cop too long, but he didn't know anyone who talked about things being *meaningful* anymore. If they thought about work in those terms, they kept it to themselves.

Maybe he was jaded.

No, he definitely was jaded. But it had more to do with his failed marriage than anything he'd seen on the job. Laney had gotten in a little psychoanalyzing of her own on that one.

Reed spotted her white car and felt a twinge of regret. He'd enjoyed talking to her, enjoyed being near her. And he couldn't remember the last time that had happened with a woman. Having a beer with Laney had been the highlight of his crap week. Hell, of his month.

She looked around. "Where are you parked?"

"Around back."

She gazed up at him. He couldn't read her expression. "Thanks for the drink," she said.

"You bought it."

He couldn't read her tone, either. The thrum of music seeped through the thin walls of the bar as they stood there in the light of the beer sign.

She stepped closer, and a jolt of heat went through him. She looked up at him with those bottomless brown eyes, and he knew he was in trouble. It was a bad idea to involve this girl. Whatever useful info she might have was outweighed by the fact that she was young and edgy, and he wanted her. And she must have seen something in his face, because her eyes sparked.

She went up on tiptoes and kissed him, pulling his face down to hers and nibbling his lower lip. Reed flinched, but he didn't pull away. Her tongue found his, and it was soft, sweet. He pulled her against him, gripping the back of her T-shirt in his hand and feeling the warmth of her body. Her fingers slid up around his neck, and he felt her nails sinking into his skin, and he was responding without even meaning to, kissing her back and pulling her in tight.

God, she was hot. Her mouth, her body. Lust surged through him, and he lingered a moment before he managed to pull away.

"What was that for?" He was still gripping her shirt, and his voice sounded husky.

She smiled. "Nothing."

He gazed down at her and felt a spurt of panic. What the fuck was he doing?

He let her go, and she stepped back, still smiling.

"Good night, detective."

CHAPTER 7

Laney swung into her driveway and glanced around. Everything was quiet, and her street seemed normal.

With the notable exception of the man sitting on her doorstep.

She grabbed her messenger bag and got out. She walked up her sidewalk, looking Ben over in the glow of the porch light. Disheveled hair, rumpled suit. His arms rested on his knees, and he had a tall-boy beer parked at his feet.

"Nice disappearing act," he said, slurring the words slightly. "You took off."

"I had to go in."

He got to his feet. "We missed you at the wake."

"I hate those things."

"Everybody hates those things. That's why they get drunk."

She stepped around him to unlock her door. She walked inside and silenced her burglar alarm as Baggins greeted her with an extra dose of feline disdain.

"What're you working on?" Ben asked, sauntering into her living room.

She set her bag and keys on the kitchen counter. "The task-force thing."

She'd spent her afternoon helping San Antonio investigators trace the email account of a fifty-two-year-old man who'd been posing as a high school kid and luring teen girls into sending him nude photos. It was a depressingly common scenario, but this perp had an uncommon talent for covering his tracks using anonymizers.

Ben wasn't listening. He was standing at the window now, looking at the Buddha statue on her back patio. Laney dumped some cat food into a bowl and filled another with water.

Ben turned around. "You got anything to eat?"

"No."

"Drink?"

She opened the fridge and grabbed a pair of Shiners. As she popped the tops off, she thought of Reed. His jaw had been scratchy when she'd kissed him, and he'd smelled faintly of weed, which had surprised her.

And he was a good kisser, which hadn't surprised her at all.

Ben collapsed onto her futon and leaned his head back. Laney walked over and handed him a beer.

"You look like shit," she said.

"Thanks."

She sank down beside him. He propped his long legs on her coffee table and crossed his ankles. Then he closed his eyes and heaved a sigh.

"I told the police about Mix," she said.

He opened one eye and peered at her. "What about 'em?"

"The red team."

He frowned at her. "You think that's relevant?"

"Don't you?"

He didn't answer, and Laney sipped her beer. It tasted bitter, and she didn't really want it. She set it on the table beside Ben's shiny black shoes. She'd never seen him dressed up before today. His suit was solid black, same as his tie. He looked like a missionary on a bender.

He closed his eyes and sighed again. "I dunno."

"I think it is."

He took his feet off the table and leaned forward, resting his elbows on his knees. She looked at his wide shoulders in the ill-fitting jacket.

"I talked to Mindy," he said. "You know, the cops didn't find any forced entry." He turned to look at her, and she saw that his eyes were bloodshot. "Sounds like April knew him and let him in."

"That's a disturbing thought."

"Not hard to believe, though, right?" He combed his hand through his hair. "I mean, she's always had shitty judgment about guys. She dated me, didn't she?" He turned away and bowed his head. His shoulders slumped.

"Hey."

He didn't respond.

"*Hey.*"

He turned, and his gaze looked tortured now. "You know if she was seeing anyone?"

"I don't know." Laney searched his face, trying to gauge whether this was a real conversation or just drunken ramblings. "I hadn't talked to her in about six months. You?"

He nodded. "I talked to her a month ago."

She waited. It seemed like he had something to get off his chest.

"She called me up one night. In one of her moods. She wanted to go out. I got the feeling some guy had blown her off or something. She seemed pretty upset."

"Did you go?"

He sighed. "I went to her place. Slept with her. Left right afterward."

"Nice."

He rested his head in his hand. "I'm such a shithead."

Laney didn't say anything.

He turned to look at her, and the guilt on his face gave her a sharp pang.

She put her arm around him. He slumped against her and buried his face in her hair. "I'm a total shit, Laney."

"God, you smell like a distillery." She pushed him away.

He scooted away from her on the futon, and she gave him another shove. He tipped over and rested his head in her lap. His face crumpled, and she felt a flurry of nervousness because she really, really didn't want him to cry.

"Where was the wake?" she asked.

He slung his arm over her lap. "O'Toole's."

"Who was there?"

"Dmitry. Mindy. Ian. You shoulda gone," he mumbled.

"Was Scream there?" she asked.

"No. Why?"

"I've been trying to reach him."

"It was mainly ChatWare people. It was a good crowd."

She waited for more, but he seemed tapped out. His eyes were closed, and his face suddenly looked relaxed.

Baggins walked over and rubbed against her ankles. Laney sighed and looked around at her messy house. Empty Starbucks cups littered the counter. Unopened mail blanketed the breakfast table. The black heels she'd worn to the funeral sat in the middle of the rug.

This was not what she'd wanted to be doing tonight. She'd wanted a man here but not this one.

She gazed down at Ben. His hair was brown, with light streaks from all the hours he spent outside playing Ultimate Frisbee. Gently, she stroked her fingers through it. She wasn't the cuddle type, but he was too drunk to remember. In fact, he looked unconscious. She feathered his hair off his forehead. It was shaggy, but she'd always liked it.

He turned his head and kissed the top of her thigh. She ignored him, and he did it again. She started to push him off, and he caught her hand.

"Don't." He looked up at her with those sad eyes, and her heart ached for him. "Please, Laney? Don't kick me out."

• • •

A dull pounding noise pulled Laney from sleep. She sat up in bed and looked around. Sunlight streamed through her mini-blinds, casting yellow stripes over the cat curled at the foot of her bed.

More pounding.

She got up and glanced around the room. She grabbed a pair of boxers off her floor, pulled them on, and went to the front door to check the peephole.

"Crap," she muttered.

She deactivated her alarm and jerked open the door. Reed looked showered and freshly shaven and much too alert for a Sunday morning.

"Why don't you answer your phone?"

She sighed. "I didn't hear it."

"I need to talk to you."

She pulled the door back to let him in. He glanced down at Baggins stretching his paws in the middle of the foyer. Then he glanced at her futon, where from the corner of her eye she could see Ben stirring.

Reed looked at her. "Something's come up with the case."

"What?"

"Step outside, I'll tell you." His voice sounded normal, but the muscle in his jaw twitched as Ben got up and crossed the living room in only his boxer briefs, pants in hand.

Laney stepped onto her porch and pulled the door shut behind her. She glanced at her wrist, but she wasn't wearing her watch.

"Ten thirty," Reed informed her.

She brushed the hair from her eyes and tried not to look flustered. "So what's going on?"

"I got a call this morning from a sheriff's deputy in Clarke County. It's looking like you may be on to something with your theory."

"What theory?"

"The dating website."

Her brain clicked into gear as she gazed up at him.

"There's an unsolved homicide down there. Victim was twenty-five, female." He paused. "Looks like she might have been on Mix."

She stared up at him, processing the words. "They . . . told you she—"

"They didn't tell me anything. The app was on her cell phone. We found it when we charged the phone up."

"When was she murdered?"

"Two years ago. Same cause of death, too, blunt-force trauma." He watched her closely, maybe trying to gauge her reaction.

Laney felt numb. Disoriented. And it wasn't because two minutes ago she'd been sound asleep.

There was another case. A pattern. Until now it had only been a theory. A slimy, monstrous theory that had taken up residence in her mind and refused to go away.

She cleared her throat. "What's her name?"

He didn't answer.

"I'll find out anyway. You already told me the county."

"Olivia Hollis," he said.

Laney leaned back against the door. "God, I remember it. It was all over the news."

She recalled footage of the anguished parents at a press conference. She recalled the flyers and the search parties and all those yellow ribbons tied around trees.

"Does Mix know about this?" she asked. "If they did, they never said anything when they hired us."

"I'm not sure what they know," Reed said. "That's why I'm here. It could be they're clueless that this happened to one of their users. Or it could be this is the real reason they wanted Delphi to overhaul their security. The credit-card thing might have been a cover story."

"It probably was. But they've likely deleted her file by now. Deleted everything about her."

Reed gazed at her expectantly, and she realized what he wanted. And why he wanted *her* versus some police department flunky who probably didn't know his ass from his elbow.

"I'll need her hardware," she told him. "Computer, phone, tablet, whatever you have."

"I'm working on that, but we've got jurisdictional issues, for starters. And that's *if* the victim's computer is still around from two years ago. I know the cell phone is in evidence, but—"

The door creaked open, and Ben stepped outside in his rumpled suit, smelling like old beer. He gave Reed a once-over before turning to Laney.

"I'm taking off, Lane."

"Ben, this is Reed Novak with Austin PD. Reed, this is Ben Lawson."

They traded cool nods as Ben pulled the door shut. And then, in case things weren't awkward enough, he planted a kiss on her forehead—no doubt his way of thanking her for sticking him on the couch last night.

"Need a ride?" she asked tersely.

He smiled. "Nah, I'm good."

She watched him walk down the sidewalk, then crossed her arms and turned to Reed. "You were saying about the phone?" she asked.

"The phone's still in evidence. I'm working on the rest."

"What about April's phone?"

"We never found it. We've been through her laptop, though, and we didn't find any messages from people on the dating site. We know she had a profile over there, but looks like she only communicated through the site itself, and so far that hasn't produced any leads."

"Where is it now? April's laptop?"

"Our computer guys have it."

"I want to see it."

His brow furrowed. "Why?"

"Because I've got a hunch."

CHAPTER 8

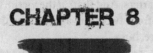

Laney had never actually been inside police head-
quarters. She'd pictured something loud and hectic,
with cops rushing around and phones ringing on
every desk. But Reed's workplace was eerily quiet as
they stepped off the elevator and she scanned the cubicles.

"Is anyone here?"

"At the moment, maybe not." He glanced at her.
"What do you think?"

"It's dead."

"This is the bullpen. Booking's a little more lively."

He led her through a maze of desks awash in paperwork. Framed photographs competed for space
with files and coffee cups. Cardigan sweaters were
draped over several desk chairs. It could have been an
accounting firm except for the mug shots pinned to
many of the walls.

Laney felt strange being here with him. She'd kissed
him last night to let him know she was interested, and
he'd definitely responded. But after seeing Ben at her
house, he was all business again, as though their kiss
had never happened. He was in detective mode, Mr.
Polite. She definitely sensed his reluctance to get involved with her sexually. But all that just made her
more determined to put herself in his way.

He led her into a break room. "Coffee?" he asked, grabbing a mug.

"I'm fine." She glanced around the room, doing a double take as she noticed the boxes on the counter. "I thought that was just a myth."

"What?" He replaced the coffee pitcher.

"You guys actually bring in doughnuts?"

"I think it was someone's birthday yesterday."

She stepped over to a bulletin board where the FBI's top ten fugitives were on display.

Reed walked over. "Recognize anyone?"

"No."

"Good. Come on."

He stopped at a cubicle and started culling through papers in a wire basket. Laney stepped into his work space, burning with curiosity. It was stacked with paperwork and files, but she zeroed in on the few personal items—an autographed baseball and a pair of framed photographs. One picture showed a large group of people standing in front of a barn. A tall, wide-shouldered man who looked remarkably like Reed stood at the edge of the group manning a huge barbecue pit made from an oil drum. He wore an apron with the words "Pit Boss" printed across the chest.

"Your family?" She glanced over, and Reed was checking his email.

"Yeah."

"There are a lot of you."

"Czech Catholic. We tend to multiply."

She counted nineteen people ranging in age from maybe five to seventy-five. They looked relaxed together, which said a lot. So many families didn't.

The second picture showed Reed on a boat with his

arm hooked around the neck of a smiling man who was holding a speckled fish.

"This your brother?"

"My nephew. He's at UT." Reed glanced at her. "He's about your age, too. You guys would get along."

She ignored the comment and turned her attention to a pile of police photos on the corner of his desk. The top one showed a patch of dirt that had been staked out with orange twine. Laney picked up the photo and read the date stamp. She realized it was a picture of the recovery site of Olivia Hollis's bones.

Reed was tapping out an email using a rapid-fire hunt-and-peck method.

"What exactly are the connections?" she asked.

"What's that?" He stopped to see what she was looking at.

"Between the cases. April and Olivia. I mean, the crimes seem different. Are there any other links besides Mix?"

"Age of the victims. MO." He resumed typing. "The lightbulbs, the cause of death."

"Lightbulbs?" She replaced the photo.

"He unscrews a lightbulb beforehand to conceal his entry."

Laney went still. "He . . ." She swallowed. "You mean the outside lightbulb or—"

"The porch light, yeah." Reed closed out of his email and glanced up. "In both cases they'd been unscrewed. So we think he does it beforehand, then comes back and enters the home under cover of darkness."

Laney stared at him, suddenly cold all over.

"What's wrong?" he asked.

"Nothing."

He led her from the cube, and they wound back through the labyrinth. Laney's heart was pounding. Her palms felt sweaty. She trailed behind him, and her thoughts were sprinting in a dozen different directions.

"Is that a common technique?" she asked his back.

"What?"

"Unscrewing a lightbulb."

"You see it from time to time. Sometimes they leave fingerprints, which is always helpful." He glanced over his shoulder. "Not in this case, unfortunately. But with April we got lucky, because a neighbor remembers the bulb being out the day before the murder, and she called maintenance—which tells us he was there at least a day in advance, scoping things out. The DA's going to like that, because it proves premeditation."

"But how do you know she didn't just forget to turn on her porch light?"

"Outdoor security lights are on a timer over there. So they automatically go on at night, unless they're burned out or tampered with." He stopped in front of a door. "Here we are."

She followed him into a large, windowless space with an abundance of putty-colored workstations and fluorescent lighting.

"Paul Doher's our computer analyst," Reed said. "Paul, this is Delaney Knox."

She wiped her palms on her jeans as the man got to his feet. She tried to get her nerves under control. She couldn't focus on lightbulbs right now—she had a job to do.

"Nice to meet you, Delaney."

"It's Laney."

The police techie was stout and balding and wore

a short-sleeve button-down that reminded Laney of her high school chem teacher. He even had the armpit stains to match.

"Reed here tells me you'd like a look at one of our notebook computers."

"The April Abrams case," Reed said, glancing around. "I got your message that you finished with it?"

Paul stepped over to a table where clear plastic evidence bags sat in a long row. Inside each bag was a laptop. Beside each was a smaller plastic bag containing a power cord.

"Let's see." Paul consulted a clipboard, then walked over and picked up a thin silver laptop. "Here we go." He handed it to Reed, who looked at Laney.

"You want to work in here or—"

"Wherever," she said, glancing around at all the empty chairs and tabletops. "Here is fine."

She took a chair and pulled the computer from the bag, noting the gray smudges on it.

"No interesting prints," Reed said.

She opened the laptop and took a deep breath. "Password?" She glanced at Paul.

"You'll never guess."

"One-two-three-four-five."

He smiled. "Close. It's numbers and letters."

"April-one-two-three-four-five."

"You got it."

"You're kidding," Reed said.

"It happens all the time," Paul told him. "First rule of informational security, have a decent password. Second rule, make it different across platforms."

Laney swiftly got into the system. April's desktop background showed an amateur photograph of a beach at sunset. The pair of feet in the foreground had rainbow-painted toenails.

"We went through all her email and browsing activity," Paul said. "Her last available visit to Mix was last November."

"Exactly when was the last visit?" Reed asked.

"I believe the twelfth."

Laney's stomach knotted. That was the week before she had warned April about the security breach. So she *had* listened.

Sort of.

Laney had advised her to pull her profile down, but she'd evidently ignored that.

Laney perused the desktop. As she clicked open a file folder, she felt the men behind her leaning closer. She hated shoulder surfing.

"Do you mind?" She glanced up at them.

"Reed?"

Everyone turned around at the voice. A slender, thirtyish woman with bottle-blond hair and huge boobs stood in the doorway.

"I need you to take a look at something," she said.

Reed glanced at Laney. "You good here?"

"Sure."

"I'll be back in a few minutes."

Laney turned back to the screen and made an effort to ignore the remaining spectator. She didn't like working with an audience.

Paul was a computer analyst, which was a catchall title that in Laney's experience could include everything from forensic computer analysis to troubleshooting software problems, depending on the budget of the police department. Laney was pretty sure this department had enough money for a designated investigator, but she didn't want to make assumptions.

"So the Delphi Center," he said, and she got a waft of coffee breath. "I bet that's a nice place to work."

She glanced up at him. He was fairly tan for a computer geek, and she pictured him in wraparound sunglasses on top of a bike. Austin had an abundance of techies who fancied themselves cyclists.

"How long have you been there?" he asked.

"A while," she said vaguely.

Laney tapped open a folder. It seemed to contain a mixture of business and personal files, pretty routine. She opened April's email and had a quick look around, although she didn't expect to find anything. The person she was looking for wouldn't be careless enough to leave tracks there.

"I assume they pay pretty well?"

She glanced up.

"Just asking. I hear it's good money. Better than DPS, at least. And DPS pays better than Austin PD does, so . . ." In response to her stony look, he gave her a sheepish smile. "Sorry—I should let you get to work."

She returned her attention to the screen, and he wandered back to his chair. When she felt sure he was distracted, she clicked out of April's email.

She darted a glance over her shoulder, opened up a directory, and got down to business.

· · ·

Veronica had the victim's front door mounted on sawhorses in the evidence lab. It looked big and out of place, like an elephant in a petting zoo. For a moment, Reed just stared at it.

"Take a look at what she found," Jay said, pulling his attention to the microscope on the far side of the room.

Reed stepped over and peered into the viewfinder. He hated this game, because he never knew what he was looking at.

"What am I seeing here?"

"Brass shavings," Veronica said. "Ten-times magnification. They're from the lock on the victim's front door."

"You're telling me someone picked her lock?"

"Appears so."

"I thought we ruled that out."

"This was no ham-handed job with a screwdriver," Veronica said. She walked up to a computer on the counter and started pecking around. "This involved some skill. It's taken me hours just to analyze the evidence and piece together what happened."

Reed traded looks with Jay. Jay had mentioned that he'd been at the lab last night, but Reed had figured it was personal, not work-related. Veronica was pretty and single, and Jay had been talking about her for months.

"What did you find out?" Reed asked her.

"Are you familiar with how pin-and-tumbler locks work?" she asked.

"More or less."

"Basically, inside the lock you have several pins of different lengths that keep the lock from opening without a key." She pulled up a diagram on her computer. "When the correct key is used, the gap between the top pins and the bottom pins is aligned with the edge of the plug, which means the plug is able to rotate and—*presto*—the lock opens. In this case, I found evidence that someone used a pick gun."

Reed glanced up as Hall stepped into the room.

"That from the April Abrams crime scene?" the lieutenant asked, looking at the door.

Veronica looked surprised to see Hall here, but she quickly recovered. "That's right."

"You said something about a pick gun?"

"Yes, an electronic pick gun. It vibrates rapidly to separate the pairs of pins, and then the plug is able to rotate without a key. It's fast, usually. And battery operated. It creates tiny marks on the metal, though, and leaves behind brass particles, which we found on the inside of the lock itself and scattered near the front door."

Hall glanced around at all the equipment, as if he was seeing it for the first time. Maybe he was. The lieutenant wasn't known for being hands-on and tended to stay upstairs.

"How much does a tool like that run?" Jay asked Veronica.

"Anywhere from a hundred to five hundred dollars, depending how fancy you want it. Some are loud, like dental drills. The nicer ones are quieter and don't leave as much evidence behind."

"And this one?" Reed asked.

"I'd say medium. It left behind some brass shavings but not a lot. And it was probably quiet but not silent."

Jay looked at Reed. "Seems like a risk."

"You mean a risk that she'd hear him?"

"Yeah. I mean, she probably did, right? She confronted him in the hallway."

"You're overlooking something," Veronica said, and

by the look on her face, Reed could tell what she was thinking about.

"He might have done it earlier," Reed said.

"Exactly." She nodded at the door. "This tool didn't leave a lot of damage. Even looking for it, we nearly missed it. So maybe the victim missed it, too."

Jay frowned. "You're saying he was *inside* her apartment when she came home from work that day?"

"He could have been hiding," she said. "He could have been there for hours, waiting for her to go to sleep. Which, basically, is any woman's worst nightmare."

Jay looked at Reed. "The more I know about this guy, the more I hate him."

"We need to talk to those furniture movers," Reed said. "Maybe they saw something."

"Furniture movers?" Hall asked.

"There was a furniture delivery in front of April's unit on the day of the murder."

Hall nodded. "And what about the boyfriend? Ian Phelps. How's it coming with him?"

"His alibi checked out, so we've bumped him down the list for now. We're working some other leads."

"Speaking of which . . ." Reed glanced at his watch. Laney had been at it twenty minutes. "I'll see about that laptop."

He left Jay to handle Hall and went to check on Laney. As he took the elevator up, he got a sour feeling in his stomach.

Veronica's lie-in-wait theory bothered him. This case had been bad from the beginning, but with every new bit of evidence it got worse. They weren't looking for some punk kid here. This was someone experienced. And smart. And deliberate.

Reed crossed the bullpen and found Paul alone in the computer lab.

"Where the hell did she go?" Reed asked.

"Who, Laney? She left."

"When?"

"Oh, I'd say . . ." He looked at the clock. "About five minutes ago? She had to check something at work, something important. Said to tell you she'd call you."

CHAPTER 9

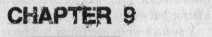

The sun was setting as Reed pulled up the winding road to the Delphi Center.

"Damn," Jay said as the building came into view.

"Ever been here before?"

"No." He craned his neck to get a view through the gnarled oak trees. "Looks expensive."

"Private money. Some oil heiress donated her millions after her daughter was killed by a convicted sex offender. They specialize in DNA here."

A buzzard swooped over the road and landed in a thicket of junipers.

"I thought it was mainly a body farm." Jay looked at him.

"That, too. They study human decomp, but the real money's in DNA. All the private testing they do subsidizes the pro bono work, which is mostly running rape kits and cold-case evidence."

They swung into the parking lot, which was fuller than he would have expected for a Sunday evening. Reed noticed the battered white Focus in the front row.

So Laney had spent her whole day working, just as he had. Evidently, they were both workaholics, and she'd been right last night when she guessed the reason for his divorce. Reed's job was a marriage wrecker.

At least that's what Erika thought—that his job had

killed their marriage. Reed wasn't completely sold on that view of it. Yeah, his long hours had definitely been a factor, but so was infidelity.

Way back when everything had been going downhill, she'd accused him of wanting her to have an affair, of practically pushing her into it with all his late nights and weekends, just so he'd have an excuse to get out.

Right. Like he'd wanted the humiliation of finding out his wife was cheating on him. Like he'd wanted those visions stuck in his head for months and months, which was how long it had taken him to face up to the fact that things were damaged beyond repair and go through with the divorce. He'd been ashamed on so many levels—for giving up on his marriage, for failing to keep his wife happy, for failing to see that she was screwing around when the evidence was right under his nose. All in all, he'd been burned. And the experience had made him even more cynical than he already was.

But the crazy thing was, he still cared about her. Even after all the crap and the lies and the accusations, he still wanted her to be happy.

Reed glanced at Laney's car again as he hiked up the steps to the entrance. She'd been dodging his calls all afternoon, and he wanted to know why. He also wanted to know why she'd left APD in such a hurry.

He and Jay checked in with the weekend security guard and were met in the lobby by Dr. Kelsey Quinn. She wore a lab coat and jeans, and her auburn hair was piled up on her head and secured with a pencil. She'd sounded distracted over the phone this morning, but she didn't really seem annoyed to have her Sunday interrupted. Maybe she was used to it.

"Right this way," she said, leading them down a sloping hallway. "You ever been to our Bones Unit?"

"No, ma'am," Jay said.

"Once," Reed told her, looking at his partner. Jay broke out the "ma'am" when he felt nervous, and Reed wondered what the deal was. It wasn't like they were going to an autopsy.

"I have to warn you, it's cold," the doctor said, using her badge to swipe her way through a door. "Helps with the smells. So I took a look at the remains to freshen my memory."

"You mean X-rays, right?" Jay asked. "I thought they had a burial after the body was found."

"They did." Another swipe of her badge, and she led them into an office with several workstations crammed into it. She crossed to a desk and picked up a folder. "Before the remains were released to the family, I decided to make a plaster cast of the skull."

She skimmed her file as Reed tried to imagine just what that entailed. The scent of formaldehyde wafted into the room. Reed glanced at Jay, who was looking a little green around the gills as he gazed through the door into the adjoining laboratory.

The doctor looked at Jay. "You okay, detective?"

"Yes, ma'am."

Her attention shifted to Reed. "Given the unusual nature of the case, I thought it would be prudent to keep something readily available, in addition to X-rays, in case this case came under scrutiny at a later date. We like to avoid exhumation whenever possible. It's very hard on the family."

No doubt it was. Reed imagined that having your child murdered was about the only thing worse than having to exhume your child's remains to bring the killer to justice. Reed didn't know this doctor very well, but he liked that she seemed to think long-term, like an investigator.

"What do you mean, 'unusual'?" he asked.

"You'll see." She stepped around Jay and into the laboratory. She led them past a row of stainless-steel tables, all empty, to a tall slate counter. On it was a flat cardboard box containing a human skull.

Or at least a damn good replica.

The doctor reached up and switched on an adjustable overhead lamp.

"Here we have the cranium," she stated, picking it up. "Which means the skull, minus the mandible. As you can see here"—she rotated it under the light—"the victim sustained two blows to the left parietal bone near the coronal suture. Both resulted in a depressed fracture. It is this fracture here"—she pointed at the shallower fracture—"where we're able to discern the most detail. Microscopic examination reveals a unique shape to this wound, corresponding to the murder weapon."

"Your report said it was a hammer with a one-point-five-inch face. You're saying that's unusual?"

"That's right. A regular garden-variety hammer has a smaller face but a heavy head, which makes it a much clumsier instrument. In an attack like this—a violent struggle—we would expect to see a regular hammer leave a deeper wound. This wound is wide and shallow, and the edges are refined, almost delicate."

"How can you be sure there was a violent struggle?" Reed asked.

"It's an inference from some of her other injuries.

She sustained a spiral fracture to her humerus, which can result when someone grabs a person from behind and wrenches their arm around."

Reed was all too familiar with the injury, common in child-abuse cases.

"She also sustained a broken wrist, likely from fighting with her attacker."

"So . . . we're looking for a delicate hammer?" Jay sounded skeptical.

"A specialty hammer," she said. "I had our tool-marks examiner take a look at this back when we first got the case. Actually, he looked at the skull itself, not this replica. He's of the opinion that this wound was inflicted by a body hammer."

Reed's gaze narrowed. "Like from an auto shop?"

"Precisely. The tools they use to hammer out dings on cars are very specialized in shape, texture, and weight. Our expert believes that's what we're looking at here."

"I'm surprised this wasn't in your report."

"Well, it wasn't my finding, so I couldn't sign off on it," she said. "But the Clarke County investigator knew about my colleague's opinion. Why he chose not to include it in the file, I couldn't say."

Reed studied Kelsey's face, and he knew that she *could* say. If the detective documented in the files that the victim's wounds were made by a body hammer, then he'd have a problem on his hands if they found a suspect with some other kind of hammer sitting around his garage.

Reed looked at Jay and saw that he'd also picked up on the doc's unspoken implication.

"Like I mentioned on the phone," Reed said, "we're

investigating a second case with similar circumstances, and the ME's telling us the murder weapon was some sort of specialty hammer. You think your tool-marks guy would be able to make a match?"

Kelsey tipped her head to the side. "We don't use the word *match* very often. Defense attorneys jump all over it. He could tell you if the instrument used on your victim was *consistent* with the one used on Olivia Hollis."

Reed's pulse picked up. It was a solid lead, and it was based on physical evidence—his favorite kind. Eyewitness accounts carried less and less weight these days, and the CSI effect was very real. Juries, especially in homicide cases, expected to see forensic evidence and often had a hard time convicting without it.

"I can tell you something else." Kelsey folded her arms over her chest. "If you want my two cents, that is."

"I want it."

"My team and I spent three full days in Clarke County excavating this crime scene." She nodded at the skull. "We used alternative light sources, cadaver dogs, metal detectors, everything we could get our hands on to recover every last shred of physical evidence from that ravine. Besides the victim herself, we found nothing, not even a scrap of clothing. I think that's no accident."

"You think he dumped her there naked so nature would cover his tracks?" Reed asked.

"That's exactly what I think. As for why he needed them covered? I'll leave that question to you. Maybe he bled on her during the struggle, or maybe he raped her and the condom broke or something else happened that wasn't part of his plan, and he needed to get rid of the biological evidence. But whatever happened, he was very thorough, very deliberate, and very skillful in concealing the evidence. Which leads me to conclude what you two have probably already figured out."

Reed waited for her to say it.

"Olivia Hollis wasn't his first victim," she said. "And I very much doubt she was his last."

• • •

Laney knew who it was when she heard the knock on her door. She padded across the house in her bare feet and peered through the peephole. In those brief seconds of privacy, she took the opportunity to *look* at him, the way she'd wanted to since they'd first met. She liked his tall, athletic build. She liked the confident way he carried himself. She even liked the bulge in his jacket, because it reminded her that he was armed and dangerous.

He gazed directly at the peephole, and she felt a jolt of heat. She unlocked the door.

"Hi," she said, silencing her beeping alarm as he stepped into the house. He watched her actions without comment. If he had a burglar alarm, she doubted he set it at nine P.M.

She led him into the kitchen, where she'd been busy contemplating her empty fridge.

"Drink?"

"No." He leaned back against the counter, planting a hand on either side of his lean hips. "You keep disappearing."

"Yeah, well. I had some stuff to check out."

"And?"

"And I have some info for you." She settled back

against the sink and watched him. She liked having him in her kitchen. She'd never admit it to him, but his presence had a way of making her feel safe.

Safer. She hadn't felt truly safe in years. Maybe she never would again.

"I confirmed the link," she said.

"You mean Mix?"

"Olivia definitely had a profile there. It was taken down after her disappearance. Three weeks after, to be exact. It was removed by the site admin."

His brow furrowed. "If it was removed, how—"

"I was on the red team, remember? I know their setup. It was a soft delete. The public-facing profile was removed, but there's still evidence of it in their system, provided you know where to look."

He watched her silently. Something was wrong. Maybe he'd been expecting her to call throughout the day with updates, but that wasn't how she worked.

"That's not all I found," she said. "April's laptop contains some important evidence."

"Paul told me it seemed like you discovered something, but you wouldn't share."

"April's webcam has been compromised."

He cocked an eyebrow. "Compromised?"

"*Hijacked* might be a better term. It was accessed remotely and turned on without her knowledge. Someone's been watching her."

"Since when?"

"I can't say for sure when the monitoring started, but what I *do* know is that the malware found its way onto her computer back in October. The week after she first signed on to Mix."

He stared at her. "You're saying the killer's been spying on her—"

"For months, yes. And he got to her via the dating site. I'm willing to bet he was spying on Olivia, too, but I'll need her hardware to check it out. Her laptop, her tablet, her phone, whatever you can get me."

She watched him closely. He looked calm but tense. And she couldn't shake the feeling that something was off. She stepped closer, watching his reaction, but he didn't move. She looked at the shadow of stubble along his jaw and reminded herself that he'd had a long day, even longer than hers, because he'd been up early this morning while she'd been sleeping off her drinking binge with Ben.

"So that's it. That's what I learned today," she said. "We have a definite link between both victims and this dating site, which suggests the killer found them online. And we know in at least one case, he used malware to spy on his victim."

Reed said nothing, just watched her. She was standing so close now she could feel his body heat. His gaze held hers, and she wondered if he'd learned something about her that she didn't want him to know.

She'd avoided telling him about her attack because it hadn't seemed relevant. Until today.

You see it from time to time.

But what did that mean, exactly? Laney didn't have any statistics on how often criminals scoped out the crime scene ahead of time and tampered with lightbulbs. She'd looked for that info but had come up short.

She'd looked for other information, too, but April's and Olivia's case files were off-limits to her, and investigators had made a concerted effort to keep details out of the news. They wanted to maintain as much confidentiality as possible so they could gauge the truthfulness of anyone who came forward with a tip or even a confession.

Laney stared at Reed now and felt the urge to tell him. But she didn't know for certain whether her attack was even related. What she *did* know for certain was that if he discovered she had a personal connection to this case, he'd yank her off it in a heartbeat. Of that she had no doubt. And being pulled from the case would be a problem, because she was the only person with the skills to pick up this UNSUB's trail in cyberspace. That wasn't her ego, it was a hard fact.

"What's that look?" She stepped closer and noticed his jaw tighten. "You're all quiet. What is it?"

He gazed down at her with those penetrating blue eyes, and her pulse started to thrum.

"There's something you're not telling me, Laney."

CHAPTER 10

Reed watched her reaction, and he knew he was right. She was holding out on him. He didn't know what or why, just that she wasn't telling him everything she knew.

There was something elusive about her, something he couldn't quite pinpoint, but he felt it every time he tried to get personal. He'd been interviewing suspects and witnesses for years, and he could spot evasiveness a mile away.

"Well?" he asked.

"Well, what?"

Reed tried to tamp down his frustration. He couldn't *make* her tell him. He couldn't make her do a damn thing, including stay out of his thoughts. She was standing so close now he could smell her hair, her skin. He couldn't stop thinking about her lithe body and her tight breasts. He wanted to kiss her, and he knew she could see it in his face, because her gaze heated.

She stepped closer, watching him with those dark brown eyes. She slid her hand over his chest and rested it on his sternum, where she could feel his heart thudding.

He took her wrist. "Laney—"

"You have a problem with me?"

He moved her hand away. "With you? No. With your age? Yeah, I do."

"What's the big deal?"

"I'm fifteen years older than you."

"So?"

She went up on tiptoes and kissed him, and this time it wasn't a shock at all. This time he'd been expecting it, and still he did nothing to stop her. There was something wrong with him. With this. But he kissed her anyway, sliding his hands around her waist and pulling her to him as he hungrily took her mouth.

She tasted good again, hot. And he couldn't stop, even as the cool, logical side of his brain told him this was a distraction. She didn't want him right now—not really. She just wanted him to stop asking questions, stop trying to pin her down. He shifted her hips, pinning her back against the counter, still kissing her and still frustrated with himself for falling for what he knew was a ploy. Her fingers tangled in his hair, and he kissed her harder, driven by a surge of lust. What the hell was it with her?

A phone buzzed, and she stopped. She stared up at him, wide-eyed and breathless, and he saw something in her look—something real, not fake. A genuine yearning that mirrored his own. Did she really want this?

His phone buzzed again. He stepped away and pulled it from his pocket, both grateful and disappointed at the interruption.

He cleared his throat. "Novak."

"Where are you?"

It was Jay. And by the tone of his voice Reed knew something was very wrong.

* * *

The blue-and-red whir of emergency lights signaled their destination well ahead of the outdated navigation system in Reed's pickup truck. He glanced at Laney in the passenger seat. She stared out the windshield and had a white-knuckled grip on the door handle.

"Ever been to a homicide scene before?" he asked.

"No."

He passed the row of haphazardly parked emergency vehicles and found a space beside Jay's black Tahoe. Jay had been at a baseball game in Round Rock when he'd gotten the call, so he must have sped all the way down here.

"No reason for you to enter the crime scene," Reed said. "It makes sense for you to wait in the car. That way you don't have to sign the scene log."

She nodded stiffly as an ME's assistant crossed the crowded parking lot with his evidence case in hand.

"Don't be nervous."

"I'm worried I know her." She glanced at him, and something in her eyes made his chest tighten.

"You ever been here?"

She shook her head.

"Given the neighborhood, odds are it's a drug thing," he said, but she didn't look convinced. He reached over and squeezed her hand. "Sit tight."

He got out and glanced around, getting the lay of the land. Jordan Lowe stood at the door talking to a uniform, and Reed caught her eye as he walked over.

"Caucasian female, midtwenties, still working on an ID," she said.

"You caught the case?"

"No, but I happened to be in the area. It's Montoya's."

Reed looked over the building. It was old and poorly

maintained, judging by the chipping paint and sagging second-story gutters. Just inside the door stood a cluster of uniformed officers.

"Jesus, what's with the crowd?"

Jordan glanced inside. "Slow night. Plus, it went out over the scanner." She looked at him. "The first responder's new."

Reed shook his head. It would have been much better if the responding officer had kept things over the phone, at least initially. It would have given investigators a jump on the media, who would no doubt be arriving soon.

"Where's Jay?" Reed asked.

"In the bedroom."

Jordan moved aside, and Reed stepped into a moldy-smelling living room. A faded blue sofa sat beside a plastic patio table. No lamps in the room, and the only light was provided by a dim ceiling fixture. He glanced at the kitchen, where a CSI was dusting the refrigerator door for prints.

Jay squeezed past the two uniforms milling in the hallway and walked over. "Montoya's about to kick everyone out so the gurney can get through."

"He's in the bedroom?"

Jay nodded. "Victim's in bed. Clothes torn off, duct tape, the whole thing."

"Blunt-force trauma?"

"That's right. And I talked to Montoya. He caught the case, but I think he'll toss it to us if we think it's related."

"It's related."

"That's my take, too. You seen the back door?"

"No." Reed glanced down the dark hallway as Montoya's voice echoed from the bedroom.

"Everyone out," he bellowed. "Unless you got a body bag or an evidence kit, I need you on the other side of the scene tape."

Reed looked at Jay. "Where are we?"

"ME's guys have been here a while. They're fixing to roll. Veronica's on the back steps now, examining the door."

"What about a computer? Or a tablet or even a cell phone?"

"No phone. Not that we've found yet, anyway." Jay glanced over Reed's shoulder, and his brow furrowed. "Damn, who invited the mayor's people?"

Reed turned around and spotted about the last person he wanted to see right now. His ex-wife stood in the doorway arguing with Jordan. She was tall and slim, with a cascade of thick dark hair that hung down her back. As always when she argued, she did it with a slight smile and a gleam in her eye.

Reed muttered a curse.

"You were asking about computers," Jay said. "There's a desk in the bedroom with a laptop on it—"

"Get it," Reed said. "Make sure the photog documents it, and then bring it out here. I have Laney with me."

"Laney?"

"Delaney Knox, from the Delphi Center."

Reed walked over to the doorway, where Jordan now had her arm physically barring the door. Reed's ex was a head taller, but Jordan didn't seem intimidated.

Erika's gaze landed on him. "Reed. Glad to see someone's in charge here."

Jordan shot him a look. "I was just explaining that

this is a *closed* crime scene." She dropped her arm as a parade of bulky officers squeezed past.

Erika stepped back and watched them. Sunday night, and she looked fully put together in a suit and heels, ready for any contingency—such as a briefing with reporters.

"We don't have a statement yet," Reed told her. "You'll be the first to know."

She smiled sweetly. "Could I have a moment, please? In private?"

Reed eased past Jordan and stepped onto the patch of weeds that constituted the building's landscaping.

"Why didn't you call me?" Erika asked in a low voice.

"It's not my case."

"Then why are you here?"

"Professional curiosity."

She gave him a baleful look. Then she glanced over his shoulder as another uniform exited the apartment. "Tell me this isn't related to the other one."

"I've been here ten minutes, Erika. I can't tell you jack shit."

"Do you guys at least have a suspect yet?"

"We're working on it. Obviously. When there's something more to tell you, we will."

"The mayor is getting concerned, as I'm sure you're aware."

"I am."

"Great. Then you're also aware that in three weeks about forty thousand students will be descending on this city. And their parents are not happy to know there's a murderer on the loose."

"Yo, Reed."

He turned around to see Jay motioning him inside.

"Stay here," he told Erika, stepping back into the apartment to find Laney standing at the bar that separated the kitchen from the living room. He wasn't sure how she'd slipped in, but she seemed to have a knack for getting in and out of places discreetly. She had a laptop computer open in front of her, and her latex-gloved hands flew over the keyboard.

"It's password protected," Jay said. "I don't know how she's going to get in."

Reed looked over Laney's shoulder. The screen was flat blue with lines of code scrolling up. "We still need a name?"

"Affirmative," Jay said. "The neighbors say this apartment's being sublet for the summer. We haven't tracked down the lease holder yet. We're running vehicle tags in the parking lot."

"Detective."

Erika was standing beside the uniform who was guarding the door now. The man was doing an admirable job of keeping her outside. It helped that he was built like a tank.

Reed walked over as she pulled her phone from her pocket and checked a message.

"You have to give me *something*," she said. "You know I can't call Bob with nothing."

"Tell him to call the chief."

"The chief doesn't know anything. That's why I'm here talking to you."

"I'm in."

He darted a look at Laney and returned to the bar to watch as a personalized desktop appeared on the computer screen. The desktop background was a candid photo of a smiling blonde with her arms around the neck of a golden retriever.

"How'd you crack that so fast?" Jay asked.

"It was a simple key walk."

"Key walk?"

"C-D-E-three-two-W-S-X." She shifted so Reed and Jay could view the keyboard. "See? It's one of the more common passwords."

Jay gave Reed a look that said *holy shit*, and Reed had to agree. She ran circles around the computer techs back at the station.

Reed touched her shoulder. "Nice work."

"You say you need a name?" She clicked into an email program and skimmed a few outgoing messages. "Looks like . . . Isabella Marshall. Bella for short. I can give you her email."

"Give us everything you can," Reed said, and Jay was already taking out a notepad.

"It's a dot edu." Her gaze met Reed's. "Looks like she's a student."

Reed leaned closer and read some of the subject lines. He picked up on a legal theme. Maybe she was at the law school. Shit.

Laney was in a blue screen again, and Reed watched lines of code scrolling at dizzying speed.

"What are you—"

"The webcam," she said. "Looks like . . . we've got an anomaly."

Jay leaned closer. "A what?"

"He's been spying," Reed said.

"Same thing I found on April's system. Where was this laptop recovered?" She looked up at Jay.

"The bedroom." Jay glanced at Reed, his look dark. "You think she was on that same dating thing?"

"We're about to find out," Laney said.

"Hey, found the phone."

Reed glanced across the kitchen where a crime-scene tech crouched beside the open refrigerator. He glanced at Reed. "We need the photographer over here."

"It's in the fridge?" Jay walked over to take a look. "Weird-ass place for a phone."

"Not really," Laney said.

Reed looked at her. She glanced up at him, then returned her attention to the computer screen.

Reed looked back at Erika. She was watching everything from the door, and Reed knew she wouldn't leave until he gave her something, so he walked over.

"We've got a tentative ID on the woman living here," he said. "I have no idea whether she's the victim. The ME should be able to tell us within twenty-four hours."

"Who's that?" Erika nodded at Laney.

"A cyber investigator."

"I don't recognize her."

"She's with the Delphi Center."

Erika studied his face for a moment, then shifted her attention back to Laney.

It was the shoulder pat, damn it.

"She's cute," Erika said. "In an alterna-teen kind of way. You seeing her?"

"She's twenty-four."

She lifted an eyebrow. "Nice."

Reed stepped back to let a CSI through the doorway.

"Really, I'm happy for you." Erika pulled out her

phone and checked a message. "Anything that gets your mind off work. *I* sure as hell never managed to do it."

• • •

It was after eleven when Laney finally left. Reed was still tied up, and one of his coworkers had offered her a ride home. The woman was polite but brisk, and Laney appreciated that she didn't try to talk Laney's ear off as she gave her a lift in her unmarked police vehicle.

Laney stared out the window. She couldn't get the crime scene out of her head. She'd been standing at the bar working on the computer when the medical examiner's people had removed the body.

Isabella. Bella to her friends. The sight of the body bag being wheeled out had stolen the air from Laney's lungs. She hadn't been able to breathe or even move.

Reed had noticed her noticing and asked some meaningless question to distract her. But it was too late. The image was etched into Laney's mind.

The ID hadn't been confirmed yet, but Laney felt certain it was Isabella Marshall, twenty-four, a second-year law student at the University of Texas. She'd been in summer school. Based on her email exchanges, she'd apparently spent the weekend with family in Dallas before returning to Austin to study for exams.

No one had said how she'd died, but Laney could guess. It hadn't been a gunshot. The CSIs had been talking about blood spatter and castoff patterns. And then Laney had seen a pair of detectives—including the big one, Jay—remove the back door from the apartment and load it into the crime-scene van.

The lock had been picked, evidently.

A cold ball formed in Laney's stomach. She glanced at the woman beside her, Jordan Lowe, a detective who worked with Reed. She was slender and brown haired—pretty in an understated way. She wore a linen blazer over jeans, and Laney noticed the bump at her hip.

"What kind of gun do you carry?"

Jordan glanced over. "Glock twenty-two."

"You keep it with you all the time?"

"Yep."

"This is your exit up here."

She sailed across three lanes without signaling. Traffic was light this time of night.

"Does it feel heavy?" Laney asked.

"Not really. Honestly, when I'm not carrying? That's when I feel weird. You get used to the weight of it." Jordan gave her a sidelong glance. "Why?"

"Just curious."

"You worried about something?"

Laney looked out the window. "Isn't everyone?"

She didn't comment right away, and Laney wished she hadn't brought it up.

"A Glock twenty-three is more compact." Jordan glanced at her. "You're petite, so that might be a better bet for you."

"You're turning left at the light here."

"A concealed-carry permit shouldn't be a problem. If you don't have a sheet, that is." She smiled slightly. "Which I assume you don't, if you're working for us."

Laney didn't answer the implied question.

"There're some reputable dealers in town. Reed could hook you up."

Laney didn't comment. She had no doubt Reed could hook her up. In a lot of ways.

But if she asked him for a favor, that would put him in some kind of power position over her. The idea made Laney uncomfortable. Intensely uncomfortable. She'd never owed a man for anything in her life, and she didn't want to start with Reed Novak.

Jordan rolled to a stop at the light and glanced at her. "What's up with you two?"

"Nothing."

Another faint smile. "He'll be disappointed to hear that. Reed likes you."

"How do you know?"

"The way he looks at you. And the way his ex looks at you."

"His ex?"

"Erika Cowan. The PR flack from the mayor's office. You didn't know?"

"No."

Laney had noticed the woman eyeing her but had thought she was just pissy over being barred from the crime scene. Laney couldn't picture her with Reed. She seemed too . . . artificial, with her designer suit and her dragon-lady fingernails. How had Reed ended up with her?

But it was obvious, really. How did men end up with anyone? She was built like a Victoria's Secret model.

"The other way I know?" Jordan looked at her. "Because—no offense—your house is way the hell out of my way. Not that I mind or anything. But normally Reed would have let a uniform drive you home. He asked me because he didn't want anyone hitting on you."

They finished the drive in silence. Jordan pulled up to the curb, and Laney pushed open the door.

"Thanks for the ride." She glanced at Jordan's gun again. "And for the tip about the Glock."

"No problem. And you know, for what it's worth, homicide scenes are always disturbing. It's a normal reaction."

Laney watched her drive away, feeling more unsettled than ever.

There was no way she'd be able to sleep. She was wired and hungry and more than a little unnerved. She should make herself a snack and then slide into her computer world where she could lose herself until her head cleared. She pictured that body bag again, and a shudder rippled through her from the top of her head to the soles of her feet.

She glanced up and down her block, trying to calm her thoughts. There was no moon tonight, and it was dark but peaceful. Her neighbors' familiar cars were parked along the street. A warm breeze wafted over her. She turned toward the bright glow of the convenience store on the corner. Still open.

She walked quickly, thinking about Reed again.

He'd said the crimes had a similar MO, but what did that mean, exactly? She knew the details of her own incident, but that was it. News articles about April and Olivia had included little information about the crimes themselves. In April's case, most of the news coverage focused on the fact that she was young and worked for a local tech company. Olivia's case was sensational for totally different reasons— the small-town teacher who had disappeared without a trace and the intensive search that failed to yield even a single clue until her skeleton was discovered by hikers.

Laney shuddered again. She picked up her pace and hurried into the squint-inducing brightness of the grocery store. She nodded at the clerk as she stepped inside. He had turquoise ear plugs and a ponytail down his back, and he always reminded Laney to buy a lottery ticket when the pot was big.

She bypassed the "fresh" food section, where brisket sandwiches languished under a heat lamp, opting instead for a frozen pizza and a Raspberry Snapple.

"Ticket tonight?" the clerk asked her.

"No, thanks."

"Six mil."

"Ten's my floor."

She left the store swigging her tea, buoyed by her purchases. She had dinner now, and probably breakfast, too, and she could work on her computer until her nerves settled.

What she definitely wouldn't do was stare at her phone all night hoping Reed would call. He wouldn't—he probably had hours of work ahead of him. And she wouldn't stare at her door, either, because she definitely did *not* want him to come over when he was finished.

She pulled her phone from her pocket and checked it. No messages.

The breeze kicked up again. Moths flitted around the streetlights. Her street was calm and empty, and she couldn't really account for the sudden queasiness in her stomach.

She glanced over her shoulder.

Nothing.

She scanned both sides of the sidewalk for threats.

No shadows between the cars. No dogs barking. No sign of anyone on the street right now, but—

Scrape.

She whirled around.

It had sounded close. Too close. But there was no one there.

She kept walking, focusing on her house, scanning her yard for anything out of place.

Snick.

Her heart did a flip. She glanced around. She quickened her stride and pulled out her phone.

She didn't have pepper spray or even a purse. She had nothing but a pepperoni pizza and a phone. And, yes, two years of kickboxing under her belt, for all the good that would do her. She wished she had a Glock on her hip. She rushed down the sidewalk, feeling ridiculously paranoid as she neared her house.

"Screw it," she muttered, breaking into a run. She clutched the pizza to her chest and glanced over her shoulder as she dashed for her door. Relief surged through her as she reached her sidewalk.

An arm snaked around her, grabbing her from behind.

CHAPTER 11

The Snapple bottle shattered as Laney shrieked and kicked.

"Fuck!"

It was a male voice, and she lunged away from him, turning on her heel to nail him with a side kick. She missed his leg and threw herself off balance, landing on her butt. Her motion-sensitive floodlight went on. She scrambled to her feet, punching at her attacker, who was on his hands and knees on her sidewalk now, spewing curses.

"Scream, is that you?"

"Shit, Laney!"

She rushed forward, crunching glass under her shoes. Her ankle burned, and she realized it was bleeding.

Scream was bleeding, too. He pushed himself to his feet, dripping blood from a gash in his hand. He wore a T-shirt, cargo shorts, and combat boots.

"What the fuck?" He glared at her.

"What are you *doing*?" She clutched her chest, where her heart felt like it would pound right through her skin. She looked him up and down and resisted the urge to kick him in the shins.

Which, she now noticed, were bleeding pretty badly.

"What the hell *was* that?" he asked, looking around at the chunks of glass scattered across the pavement.

"My drink. What the hell are you doing skulking around my house at night?"

"I was looking for you."

"You grabbed me!"

"I was kidding around." He stripped off his T-shirt and wrapped his hand.

She stepped over to him, feeling guilty now that she could breathe again. She eyed the rivulets of blood streaming down his shins.

"Here. Come inside." She picked up her pizza, which perched like a Frisbee on the hedge beside her door. She fumbled with her keys and managed to get the door unlocked, then tapped in her alarm code and dumped all her stuff on the kitchen counter.

Scream went directly to the sink and started rinsing his hand as Laney switched on a light.

"Damn it, Laney." He plucked a shard of glass from his palm and dropped it on the counter.

"Hey, not my fault. You freaking attacked me."

"I was joking. Christ. Good thing you're not packing heat."

A sour lump lodged in her throat. She swallowed it down. If she *had* been armed, she probably would have killed him.

Blood flowed from his hand as he held it under the faucet. She eased closer to watch. He smelled like cigarettes, and she took a closer look at him.

He'd put on weight since she'd seen him last. He was still thin, but his arms were more defined. The tattoo on his shoulder—a picture of Edvard Munch's *The Scream*—had been embellished since she'd last seen it. Now it was framed by a ring of barbed wire.

Laney dampened a dish towel and crouched down

to examine his injuries. The blood looked alarming, but when she wiped away the streaks, she saw that the cuts were pretty small.

"Ouch!" He scowled down at her.

"Fine, you do it."

He stepped back and propped his foot on the counter, and she watched as he pulled a sliver of glass from his shin.

Laney tended to her own cut, squeezing out a thin splinter.

"What did you want, anyway?" He looked at her. "You've been leaving messages everywhere."

She sighed. "You want a beer?"

"Hell, yeah. Something to numb the pain." He smiled slightly, and she felt relieved. Teasing meant he didn't need to go to the ER.

She switched on the oven and slid the pizza inside. Then she grabbed a beer and used the bloody dish towel to twist off the cap. Scream took his leg down and leaned back against the sink, and Laney had a sudden memory of Reed pinning her against that very spot. Had it really only been a few hours ago?

The two men couldn't look more different. Reed was tall and powerfully built, with thick dark hair that curled at the nape of his neck, and just the thought of touching it again made Laney's fingers twitch.

Scream was . . . odd-looking. Pale, thin, awkwardly long-limbed. At first glance, most people took him for a skinhead, but his body art didn't fit. His tattoos included literary references, Egyptian symbols, Chinese characters.

"What about you?" He swigged his beer, watching her.

"I'm not thirsty."

She eyed his cuts again and felt a tug of guilt. She dreaded asking for favors, and she wasn't good at chitchat, but she at least needed to try. She tossed the bloody towel into the sink.

"So how are you?" she asked.

"Fine. You?"

"Fine." This was why she hated small talk. She crossed her arms. "How's business?"

"Can't complain," he said. The smug tone of his voice told Laney he was making money hand over fist.

Scream's underfed homeless look was basically an avatar. In reality, he was a millionaire several times over.

Scream sold zeros for a living, which was one of the reasons Ben hated him. Ben believed he operated without code. Not computer code but ethics. As in, Scream had none, at least not according to Ben.

Once upon a time, Scream had been the best cyber-intrusion expert at the Delphi Center. During his years at the lab, he'd built a name for himself.

But then he'd gone rogue. He'd gone from helping companies test and fix their security vulnerabilities to selling those vulnerabilities on the black market as zeros. Fresh zeros, or zero-day exploits, were hugely valuable because they'd been known for zero days, which meant they could be exploited until someone had a chance to fix them. Individuals, companies, and even the U.S. government spent millions of dollars a year buying up zeros to gain unauthorized access to computer systems all over the world. Another lucrative part of the market was companies that purchased their own zeros to prevent rivals from snapping them up.

Once Scream's original business was running smoothly, he'd started buying up zeros found and created by *other* people, then selling them to the highest bidder. And when he sold a bug, he didn't care what his client's intent was. Scream didn't care if the buyer wanted it to hack, steal, or spy—he was all about the money. If the Net was a war zone and zeros were weapons, then Scream was an arms dealer.

"I need a favor," Laney said now. "I understand you've been doing some work in the social-media space."

He arched his eyebrows but didn't confirm.

"I need to know if you've sold any zeros lately that could be used to target a dating website."

"What's it called?"

"Mix."

"I've heard of it."

"What have you heard?"

He shrugged. "They're small. Local. They're trying to grow their customer base by appealing to the young demographic that comes to town every year for ACL Fest and SXSW. It's a good niche. Some people think they're headed for an IPO soon if their vulture capitalists don't pull the funding."

So he knew all about them, maybe more than she did. This was exactly why she'd wanted his help. Scream kept his ear to the ground. And as someone who dealt in information, he knew rumors had value, whether they were true or not.

He swigged his beer. "What are you investigating, a credit-card scam?"

"I can't say."

He rolled his eyes.

"It's a sensitive case," she added.

"Okay, what's your budget?"

"I don't have one."

"Yeah, right."

"Really, I don't. I'm doing this on the side, sort of pro bono."

He smiled slowly. "You're going to have to do better than that, Laney."

She hesitated to go into it. But if she wanted his help, he needed information.

"It's for a friend of mine," she said. "He's a detective, and his department's pretty cash-strapped."

He sipped his beer and watched her, and she could see his interest in doing this favor was quickly evaporating.

"What's this detective of yours investigating?"

"A murder."

He tipped his head back. "Shit, I should have known." He looked at her and shook his head. "Always the crusader. You should have been a cop, Laney."

She bristled. "Are you going to help me or not?"

"Not." He plunked his beer on the counter, and she felt a surge of desperation.

"But you have to. I don't know anyone else."

"Sure you do."

"Not for this."

He gave her a long, cool look, and she realized he was right. He *didn't* have to. He didn't owe her anything, and her guilt trips weren't going to work if he truly had no moral compass. And she really didn't know if he did. She didn't know much of anything about him, not even where he lived. Scream popped in and out of her life at odd intervals, mostly without cause or explanation. He was temperamental and mysterious, and he liked that image and worked hard to cultivate it.

So the question was, would he help her for free? Because she sure as hell wasn't going to sleep with him.

His gaze locked on hers, and she felt like he could read her thoughts.

Laney checked the pizza to stall for time. She needed a new strategy.

"Listen, I wouldn't have called you if this wasn't important," she said. "I need your help."

"And why do I get the feeling there's more to this favor than you're telling me?"

"There is. And you're the only one who can do it."

"Help me, Obi-Wan Kenobi. You're my only hope." He said it in a high-pitched Princess Leia voice.

"I'm being serious here."

"Then cut the crap," he said. "What is it you really want?"

"There's another zero I need. And there's no one else who can get it."

"You mean get it for free."

"Yes. I need a way into the FBI."

He stared at her.

"Specifically, I need access to their ViCAP system," she said. "That's the database where—"

"They store info about violent crimes, I know."

She could tell he was intrigued, and she felt a flicker of optimism. Scream hated the FBI, so maybe he'd help her defeat their security just for kicks.

"I want to see if there are any similar cases out there," she said. "The victims—"

"How many?"

"We don't know. At least three with a similar MO,

maybe more. The UNSUB goes to their homes and unscrews a lightbulb near his point of entry. Then he comes back to rape and bludgeon them."

Scream was listening closely, but she couldn't read his reaction.

Her phone chimed, and she rushed to answer it. It was Ben, so she took the call out on the patio, pulling the door shut behind her and giving Scream a chance to think. She had a feeling she'd hooked him.

"What's up?" she asked Ben.

"Did you see the news?"

"No. Why?"

"There's been another murder."

"I know."

Silence.

"So you're on the case?" Ben sounded confused, and she didn't blame him. She wasn't on anything yet. APD hadn't really hired the lab. She was essentially free-lancing, and that wasn't accurate, either, because Reed hadn't officially hired her. But she had a sense that was coming. Whether he liked it or not, he needed her help.

"More or less," Laney said. "We're still trying to establish a firm connection between the cases."

"What's the holdup?"

"I haven't seen all the evidence," she said.

"Well, what else is new? We never see all the evidence. Do they realize the trail's getting cold while they dick around?"

"I can't talk about this right now, Ben. I have to go."

"Call me in the morning."

"I will."

Laney stepped back inside and halted. The kitchen was empty now.

"Scream?"

She checked the bathroom and the bedroom, confirming what she already knew.

He'd left. She'd turned her back for one minute, and he'd taken off. She returned to the kitchen and glanced around. The pizza sat on the counter with a big wedge missing so it looked like Pac-Man. Beside it was a paper towel that had a message scrawled across it.

Mission accepted. But it's going to cost you.

CHAPTER 12

By Monday morning, Bella Marshall's murder was all over the news. By noon, Reed was in the chief's office, and by late afternoon, he was back at Delphi, this time to meet with one of the nation's top experts in cyber-profiling.

Reed wasn't much on profiling, but he tried to keep an open mind as he rode the elevator up to the Delphi's cybercrime unit alongside the guy who'd spent the night on Laney's couch.

"You ever met Mark?"

Reed glanced over. "No."

"We poached him from the Bureau a few years ago. He's the best in the world."

The doors *dinged* open, and Ben Lawson led him down a corridor lined with windows. To Reed's left was a view of rolling green hills bathed in sunlight. To his right was a dimly lit computer lab with rows of glowing workstations. Reed quickly spotted Laney seated at one of them. Several men watched over her shoulders as she pointed at something on her screen.

Reed scanned the lab. Cargo shorts and flip-flops seemed to be the uniform. It was a large work space, and busy, but Reed wondered how much crime fighting actually got done with so many dartboards and basketball hoops around.

"Always interesting to watch Smurfette work."

Reed looked at Ben. "What's that?"

"Smurfette." He smiled. "That's her nickname. She ever tell you about it?"

"No."

Ben propped his shoulder against the window and smiled. "Then I guess she never told you how she landed a job here."

Reed glanced at Laney again. She was a female island in a sea of men. And most of them looked half Reed's age.

"It goes back to this hack she did in college," Ben said, determined to tell his story. "Not sure how she got tipped off to this, but there was a teacher at one of the local high schools who frequented this kiddie-porn site." He glanced through the window. "So Laney hears about it, decides to check into it. She penetrates their system, has a look around. Turns out, it's a major operation based in Phoenix. And this isn't some jerkoff in his garage uploading photos, this is a sizable enterprise, one of the biggest in the country. At least it was back then. Anyway, Laney starts nosing around, getting pissed off, and decides to launch a DoS attack. You know what that is?"

"Denial of service."

"Exactly. Basically, it crashes the site. So she uses what we call a smurf attack, which means she sends a ping from the spoofed IP address of the target to the network's broadcast network. What happens is all the systems in the subnet respond to the spoof and flood the device."

Reed didn't really know what he'd just said, but he caught the gist of it. "So she took them down?"

"Man, she *owned* them. It was wizardly. Meanwhile,

she sent an anonymous tip to a detective over at Phoenix PD explaining what they were up to and providing all kinds of details they could use for a bust. Only problem was, the FBI was already on to this shop. They had a sting operation in the works, and she basically beat them to the punch. So, you know, they were pretty pissed. They couldn't figure out whether they wanted to arrest her or hire her."

Reed looked at Laney again. "I thought she started out at ChatWare?"

"She did." Ben nodded. "Worked there for almost a year, right after she graduated. That's how long it took the feds to catch up with her."

"A whole year?"

"Yeah, it was months before anyone could piece together exactly what she'd done." He looked through the window, and Reed followed his gaze.

Laney was by herself now, leaning back in her chair and resting her feet on the desk as she stared at her screen. Ripped jeans again, black tank top. The streak in her hair was purple today, and Reed couldn't explain why his heart was thrumming just from watching her at her computer.

"She's a master at covering her tracks. That's why the FBI wanted her." Ben smiled. "Too bad we snagged her first."

"How'd you do it?"

"Money," he said. "Although, to tell you the truth, that probably wasn't the real reason. Laney doesn't really care about money. But Delphi's got some other advantages. You can work flex hours, wear anything you want. And they pretty much turn a blind eye to hacktivism, so . . ."

"Hacktivism."

"Doing it for a cause." Ben looked at him. "You know, like that thing with that middle-school kid last year. The one who was getting bullied and tormented because he was gay, and so he hanged himself?"

"The boy in Houston?"

"Right. Some crackpot church was planning to picket his funeral with their 'God Hates Fags' signs. Laney and some other people launched a DDoS attack—that's like a regular DoS but bigger because you use a botnet, which is basically a fleet of zombie computers programmed to ping the site all at once. They crashed their systems and then doxed the congregation, using the church's own website to publish everyone's names and emails so they'd get inundated with spam. It was a sweet op. Signature Laney."

A man stepped out of an office down the hall. In contrast to everyone else on this floor, he looked over forty and wore a suit and tie instead of a *Warcraft* T-shirt. This would be Mark Wolfe, the former fed.

Ben stood silently by as Reed introduced himself.

"You coming to the meeting?" Mark asked Ben.

"I've got something else."

"We ready?" Laney asked, appearing in the doorway. She had a file under her arm and didn't make eye contact with Reed.

Laney's boss led the way into a conference room. Reed waited for Laney to sit and took the chair across from her, where he wouldn't be distracted by her closeness.

He looked at Mark Wolfe. "Thanks for meeting on short notice."

"Aguilar said it was urgent." He leaned back in his chair. "He sounded pretty rattled, actually."

Rattled wasn't a word Reed had ever heard used to describe the chief of police. But the media was all over him, and, as Erika had pointed out, classes were resuming soon at the state's largest university. Both Austin victims had lived near campus, and one had been a student. The last thing the chief wanted was a public panic.

"I went through the reports." Mark flipped open a file. "I've got some preliminary feedback, but you're not going to like it."

"Let's hear it."

"I have a basic profile, which you've probably already come up with on your own. The UNSUB is a white male, twenty-five to fifty, living in or near the Austin area, and probably working in a technical or computer-related field."

His rundown came as no surprise. Sexual predators tended to operate within their ethnic group, and the tech connection was obvious.

"That's a pretty big age range," Reed said. "I'd expected younger."

"I did, too, at first, especially with the online-targeting angle. But when you look at the murders themselves . . ." He shook his head. "His MO is revealing. He exercises tremendous patience and impulse control, which indicates we might be dealing with an older perpetrator. These crimes demonstrate a good deal of premeditation. To approach a door with a specialized tool and pick a lock without being seen—it's probable he scoped the place out ahead of time." Mark tapped his pencil on the table. "Another important factor is the webcams. In the April Abrams case, the report suggests he might have hijacked the webcam as early as last October."

"He did," Laney confirmed.

"That's a long time to watch and wait to select your moment. A long time to construct the fantasy."

"But that's part of the thrill, isn't it? I'm no psychologist," Reed said, "but seems to me he likes the buildup."

"That's correct," Mark said. "He's driven by deep-rooted fantasies about controlling women and causing pain. It's likely he was abused by a parent—no surprise there—and I also think he's probably been treated for depression at some point."

"That narrows it down."

"Look, I realize it's not a lot of specifics," Mark said, picking up on the sarcasm. "Most online predators I see have some of that in their background. Many of them also have difficulty fitting into normal social situations, so the Internet is something of a haven. But let's talk about what sets this guy apart." He leaned forward on his elbows and looked Reed in the eye. "Studies indicate that at any given time, there are as many as eight hundred thousand child sexual predators online. And that's only *child* predators. Add adults, and we're dealing with an enormous number. It's bad enough that these people are out there spying, surfing kid-porn sites, and harassing people. I'm not saying those aren't real crimes, because they absolutely are, and they cause harm and pain. But this UNSUB took it all a step further."

"He went after them in real life."

"Exactly." Mark nodded. "So you have to ask yourself, what kind of person would do that?"

"Someone who thinks he can get away with it," Laney said.

"That's right. He believes he's beyond the reach of law enforcement, immune to punishment. This is someone who has spent years online shrouded in a cloak of anonymity, frequenting the Internet's dark side, sometimes called the darknet."

"He likes the anonymity," Reed stated.

"Thrives on it," Mark said. "Many people online construct these alter egos. They feel free to say and do things they would never say and do in a face-to-face encounter, and they feel immune to consequences."

Reed watched him, digesting it all. He glanced at Laney, who was being unusually quiet.

"This UNSUB made a leap that many online predators do not," Mark continued. "He went from spying and stalking online to actually tracking down his victim in the real world, entering her private home, and carrying out a remarkably violent attack. All without leaving much of anything in the way of physical evidence. All this tells us he's adept at operating and concealing himself in two entirely different environments, not just one. And that definitely sets him apart."

"Did you see the note in the report about the shoe print?" Reed asked. "Our lab tested the fiber found with that print, and it looks like he wore shoe coverings."

"He's very meticulous. And he knows about police procedures, or else he's watched a lot of CSI shows. You shouldn't discount that possibility." Mark glanced at the file in front of him. "Another thing I notice, he's got a keen sense of his targets. He finds a victim he wants and hones in on her digital vulnerabilities."

"You mean portals into her life." Reed glanced at Laney.

"Right," Mark said. "Where has she left herself open to attack? Internet-enabled devices are so ubiquitous now, there are more and more places for predators to get in. Everything from your fitness tracker to your smart refrigerator can provide a doorway into your life. We let ourselves be tracked and monitored, then we have no control over how that info is later used. Laney here can tell you better than anyone. She's our top cyber-intrusion expert."

"Take the webcams," she said, finally chiming in. "Many devices come with built-in cameras. And a lot of people don't bother setting up passwords. They leave the default passwords that were set at the factory, which means if someone knows what they're doing, it's not that hard to remotely take over a device."

"The key word here is *remote*," Mark said. "So much of the planning, the fantasizing, the stalking can be done from a distance, and it adds to the UNSUB's sense that he's anonymous and out of the reach of law enforcement."

"It's part of his game," Laney said. "He's screwing with you."

"Me?"

"Investigators. Take the phone, for example." She looked at Mark. "The most recent victim's cell phone was found in her refrigerator."

Mark raised an eyebrow. "I hadn't read that."

"It wasn't in the preliminary report. You'll have to go through the crime-scene photos."

"Wait." Reed looked at Mark. "Explain the phone."

"It could be a reference to certain low-tech tactics

used to hamper surveillance by spy agencies," he said. "If you put your cell phone in the refrigerator, it's harder for the NSA or whoever to use it as a listening device."

Reed stared at him. "So you're saying—"

"He killed her and stashed her phone in the fridge for investigators to find," Laney said. "He's being sarcastic. It's a taunt."

"In other words, he knows that *we* know he's monitoring his victims," Mark added. "He's escalating the game."

The room went quiet as Reed digested that. "I take it you think he's not done," he said.

Mark shook his head. "All evidence points to the contrary. He's been doing this a while, and he's very patient. He has long-term commitments to these women, and he targets multiple people at once. What we're seeing now is a shrinking interval between murders. It's getting harder for him to control the urge, to make himself wait. Which might be good for us because he might slip up."

"Can you predict when the next one will happen?" Reed asked, not bothering to hide his skepticism.

"It's not an exact science," Mark said, refusing to be baited.

"I'm pulling together a list." Laney opened her file. "We've done research here at the lab, basically linking certain online behaviors to future violent attacks."

"We want to pinpoint which online behaviors pose a nuisance or are simply bizarre," Mark said, "and which can be correlated with future criminal acts in real life."

Laney's phone chimed, and she pulled it from her pocket to check the number. "Sorry." She looked at her boss. "I need to take this."

She stepped out, and Reed looked at Mark. He'd gotten more than he'd expected, but it still felt too theoretical. He still didn't have anything that actually put him on to a particular suspect.

"You look pensive, detective."

"It's pretty depressing," Reed said.

"What is?"

"This whole topic. Makes me glad I don't have kids."

"I know what you mean. Some people blame technology, like it somehow creates aberrant behavior. I happen to believe it's there naturally—a dark side to human nature—and the Internet provides an ideal environment for it to flourish. Degradation, abuse, violence—these things have been around forever. But now we have a whole new setting in which predators can find and victimize people."

Reed looked at the man, and he knew he must see a lot of ugliness on a day-to-day basis. Laney had to see it, too.

"Well, that about covers it," Mark said. "I should be able to flesh out the profile when I get more info, such as the autopsy report in the Bella Marshall case."

"I'll have that by tomorrow." Reed checked his watch and stood up.

"One more thing." The profiler stood, too. "You seem reluctant to involve Laney."

He'd picked up on that. Maybe there was something to this profiling thing after all.

"She's obviously young," Mark said, "but she's very talented, one of the best we have."

"I like to keep my team lean. For a lot of reasons."

"I understand. But if you're worried about leaks, don't be. Laney's very professional. She won't talk to the media."

"Good to know."

Reed stepped into the hallway as Laney slipped her phone into the pocket of her ripped jeans.

"You're leaving?" she asked.

"I have to drop something off at the DNA lab first. I hear it's on this floor."

"I'll show you." Laney led him down the corridor. "What'd you think of the profile?"

"It's interesting."

"Wow. Damned by faint praise."

"It could be useful. Or it could be a dead end. I'm always partial to physical evidence." He cut a glance at her.

"What?"

"This work you do, it can get bleak, especially the child stuff. And the Internet's full of these dirtbags." He paused. "I'd think you'd burn out. Why do you keep doing it?"

"Same reason you keep taking rapists and murderers off the street. It's my job. For better or for worse, it's what I chose."

"You could shift into something else. White-collar crime. There's plenty of identity theft to go around."

"I'm good at this." She shrugged. "Anyway, I know the ecosystem. I can navigate it easily, and not many people can, so I guess I feel obligated."

Would she always feel that way, that she had to devote the best years of her life to tracking down scum?

Reed looked at her. So young and idealistic. And so damn smart. Why couldn't she have chosen something easier, like designing apps or video games?

She stopped in front of a door labeled DNA AND SE-ROLOGY. Through a large glass window, Reed saw people in white lab coats hunched over microscopes.

"What do you have there?" She nodded at his evidence envelope.

"Duct tape."

Her eyebrows tipped up.

"From the autopsy this morning."

"He uses—"

"Twice before," Reed said. "I spoke with one of your DNA tracers on the phone, Mia Voss. She agreed to take a look at it, see if she could recover something."

Laney's mouth opened, but she didn't say anything. She looked pale suddenly.

"You all right?" he asked.

"Fine."

But he could tell she was lying.

CHAPTER 13

Reed lived in a '60s-style ranch house in north Austin, and his gray pickup was in the driveway when Laney pulled up. The flicker of the television in the window told her Reed was still awake. Whether he was alone or not, she had no idea.

Her stomach fluttered with nerves as she walked up to his door. The lawn was green but needed mowing. She wondered if he hired someone or if he did the work himself. She glanced at the garden hose coiled at the corner of the house.

Himself, she decided. He seemed like the type.

He answered the door, and Laney's breath caught. He'd shed his crisp white button-down and now wore a plain white T-shirt that clung to a very impressive chest. Same business slacks and shoes as before.

She cleared her throat. "Hi."

He looked her over with those flinty blue eyes. "Cops are unlisted. You know that, right?"

"Can I come in?"

He pulled the door back, and she stepped inside. Without a word, he led her into a kitchen that was dark except for a light glowing over the sink.

She glanced around, absorbing details about his house. It had the sparse look of a bachelor pad, right down to the black leather sofa and glass coffee table.

His kitchen wasn't fancy—Formica and linoleum with black appliances. His breakfast table was stacked with unopened mail, just like hers.

"I finished the online indicators," she said.

"Indicators?"

"A component of the profile Mark was telling you about. The online behaviors."

He leaned back against the counter, watching her. His eyes were cool, and he seemed guarded.

"This is based on studies we've done. Correlating various types of criminal behavior with other online activities." She cleared her throat. "I believe we're going to find that he has a number of online identities that he changes frequently. He uses code names and pseudonyms, and they likely have meaning to him."

"Do you know any of these pseudonyms?"

"No, but I will. I also believe he trolls people, particularly women, and has probably been banned from sites for harassment."

Reed seemed to be listening now, probably because she was getting out of the realm of conjecture and into the realm of actual criminal activities that investigators could track.

"It's also likely he has a history of impersonating others, stealing their identities, and communicating publicly. It would be something he does for the thrill of it. I think he's into gamesmanship."

He lifted an eyebrow. "You think he's a gamer?"

"Not necessarily. Although he could be," she said. "What I'm saying is he considers this a game. Outsmarting people. The voyeurism is part of that. He gets an intense thrill from entering a woman's living room or bedroom without her permission and watching her private moments. It helps him build the fantasy. A lot of online predators are into voyeurism. What makes this guy unique, like Mark said, is that he takes it into the physical world. His fantasy isn't complete until he's made that physical contact. Everything culminates with extreme violence."

He was watching her closely, but she couldn't read his expression.

"So those are the indicators I've come up with. They're based on studies of hundreds of predators. And they're useful, because they help us pick up his trail. I'm already following up on various pseudonyms. I hope to have a lead for you soon."

Reed didn't say anything.

"What's wrong?" she asked. "I thought you'd be happy."

"Happy?" He shook his head.

"Okay, encouraged. We're getting a picture of who we're looking for." She stepped closer, watching his re-action. "It's like a jigsaw puzzle, and we're filling in the pieces." She paused. "What's the problem?"

He folded his arms over his chest, creating a barrier between them. "I've been doing some research of my own, Laney."

"Yeah. So?"

"So you want to tell me about your record with Austin PD?"

CHAPTER 14

"I don't have a record."

"Okay, your history with us," he said. "The incident at your home several years ago."

Everything changed in her face. One second she was open and talkative, and the next her expression was shuttered. Her gaze darted to the door. She wanted to leave, but she wasn't going anywhere until he got some answers.

He eased closer. "Why didn't you tell me up front that you'd been the victim of a similar attack?"

The word *victim* made her flinch, but he didn't let up.

"Did you think I wouldn't find out?"

"No, I thought . . ." She looked flustered. "I thought it's none of your business."

He stared at her, gritting his teeth with frustration.

"It isn't something I talk about with people." She sounded defensive now. "And I didn't think it was relevant, not until recently."

He didn't respond.

"You don't believe me?"

"When you first texted me that link, did you or did you not know that April's case bears a striking resemblance to what happened to you three years ago?"

"I didn't know."

"Don't lie to me, Laney. I'll find out."

"I'm not lying! And where do you get off interrogating me like I'm some kind of criminal? Keeping something private is not the same as lying. Why the hell am I explaining myself to you?" She pushed off the counter and turned away, but he caught her arm.

"Wait—"

"Screw you. I don't need this." She yanked her arm, but he wouldn't let her go.

"Would you wait a minute?"

She glared up at him, then glanced down at his hand clenched around her arm.

He released his grip and stepped back. "Sorry." He raked his hand through his hair. "I'm being . . ."

"A dick?"

He looked at her.

And he knew she was right. *Interrogated.* It was the word Erika always used.

Frustration bubbled inside him. He was going about this conversation all wrong. Laney had been attacked in her own home in the middle of the night. He'd read her police report thoroughly. Twice. He'd memorized every detail, including the part about her being assaulted on her living-room floor before she'd managed to escape. Had she been raped, too? People didn't always give law enforcement the full story, and the investigating officer had been a rookie. He'd basically chalked her case up to a burglary gone wrong.

Laney was watching him with simmering eyes now. She'd calmed down some, but she was clearly still pissed.

This was his fault. He'd involved her in the investigation without checking her background. And now she might actually become a witness in the case, which would create all kinds of problems.

Shit.

Reed stepped over and reached for the cabinet behind her. She ducked out of the way, and he watched her as he took down a pair of glasses.

"You want a drink?" He opened the liquor cabinet and got out a bottle of Jack Daniel's.

"Sure."

"Ice?"

"No."

He poured two generous shots and handed her a glass. She eyed him over the rim as she took a sip. She wrinkled her nose at the taste, and Reed almost laughed.

This was so fucked up. He was in his kitchen drinking whiskey with a girl who would probably get carded if he took her to a real bar.

She was beautiful. She was smart and manipulative, and that mouth of hers set him on fire.

And he wanted her. Still. Even with all the complications.

"What's that look?" She stepped closer. "What are you thinking?"

"You don't want to know."

"You're thinking of pulling me off the case, aren't you? I can tell."

He didn't answer.

"I hate to break it to you, but women get assaulted all the time, Reed. It happens. And what happened to me might not be related to this. I'm extremely careful about my online security, and I've never used a dating site. And it's entirely possible that what happened to me *three years ago* has nothing to do with what's going on now."

She gazed up at him, and he wasn't sure if she was trying to convince him or herself. He hated the fear he saw in her eyes. God *damn* it, why hadn't she told him? He never would have let her get involved.

"I read the report filed by the responding officer." Reed watched her face carefully. "Did you tell him everything?"

"Yes."

"Were you sexually assaulted?"

"No."

He watched her eyes, trying to gauge whether she was telling the truth. He wanted to believe she'd tell him, that she trusted him enough. "You said you didn't see your attacker well. That he was wearing a ski mask."

She nodded. "Also, he'd taken out the back light, so it was pitch dark."

"But you got a feel for his size. You told the officer—"

"He was bigger than me. But that's about all I know. It's not enough for a forensic sketch or anything."

And no evidence had been collected. No blood or saliva or semen. The responding officer had treated it like a burglary, basically dusting the door for prints and that was it. It should have been handled differently because of the assault, but it hadn't been. And it was too late now. What was done was done.

Reed sighed heavily and rubbed the back of his neck. "I'm sorry." He looked up at her. "It should have been handled better at the time. We let you down."

"Forget it, it's over. And anyway, it's not your fault." She lifted her chin. "You still want to pull me?"

"Laney—"

"Don't." She got up in his face. "Don't you dare. *I'm* the one who managed to uncover evidence that these women were targeted online. That's the best lead you have, and I can help you follow it. You'd be stupid not to use me."

"That's tactful."

"It's true. I know their system inside out. Do you? Does Paul? That guy couldn't penetrate a Gmail account."

Reed stared down at her, his heart still pounding way too hard. He knew what he should do. He should tell her to stay the hell away from the case and from him. And he didn't want to do either of those things.

"Well?"

"I'm sorry, Laney. You're off."

Her breath *whooshed* out. "But you can't do that!"

"I'm the lead detective. It's my call."

"But—"

"It's for the best. It's for your own safety."

Her eyebrows shot up. "My safety?"

"Yes."

"What is that, some sexist crap, Reed? You can't work with a female investigator who's ever been assaulted before?"

"I'm not sexist. And I don't believe it was some random assault."

"How would you know?"

"Look at the circumstances! The method of entry, the duct tape, the lightbulb—it all adds up to a connection." He was yelling again, but he couldn't help it. "Do you realize you could be the only woman who's been targeted by this guy and lived to tell about it? You could end up being a witness."

"Reed—"

"I don't want you involved."

"But my work is in the background."

"Not even in the background! Off the case means *off*. Stay away from it."

Silence settled over the room. And he saw defiance in her eyes. It didn't matter what he said, she was going to do what she damn well pleased.

His phone buzzed across the room. He sidestepped her and grabbed the call.

"Hey, sorry to call so late," Jay said.

"What is it?"

"I'm down at the station. You need to come see this."

• • •

Reed stood at Veronica's microscope, and everything about his body language was tense. Maybe he'd had a crappy day. Or maybe he hadn't appreciated being called away from whatever he'd been doing at nine o'clock this evening.

Veronica was going with the second option. Reed Novak was known to be a workaholic, but he also struck her as a man who had plenty of female companionship.

"What am I looking at here?" he asked impatiently.

Jay edged closer. "You don't see it?"

"No."

Veronica nudged him aside and checked the view-finder. She adjusted the focus. The lightbulb she'd col-lected from Isabella Marshall's apartment was secured to the stage with a few dabs of putty.

"Upper right quadrant. You don't see that?" She moved aside so he could look again.

"I see dirt. Or maybe rust."

"It's blood," Veronica said.

Reed glanced at her. "You sure?"

She rolled her eyes. "Jeez. What is it with you guys? I've been doing this ten years. I think I know blood when I see it."

Reed shot a look at Jay. He'd been skeptical, too, when she first showed him, but now he was convinced, not only that she'd found blood but of what it could mean for the case.

"Walk me through it." Reed's gaze settled on her, and she couldn't help but feel intimidated. "Our UNSUB left no prints behind at her apartment, right?"

"Right. Not at Isabella's or April's."

"And no prints on either of the lightbulbs he un-screwed, either."

"Right," she said.

"But you're saying he left this smudge of blood here?"

"That's what I think." She nodded. "It fits with ev-erything we know. We know from the blood-spatter patterns that he takes his weapon away from the scene with him. The hammer or whatever."

"A body hammer," Reed said.

"Exactly. And we know he brings a lockpick, duct tape, condoms—everything he needs. He's obviously got a murder kit. Maybe he's got a favorite pair of gloves in there, too. Not disposable gloves but maybe work gloves or something. Let's assume he uses those same gloves when he scopes out the crime scene ahead of time, unscrewing lightbulbs and whatever."

Reed looked at her, seeming to consider it. "You're saying he left this blood on the lightbulb *before* he committed the murder, in which case it comes from one of his previous victims."

"Exactly. Or if we're really lucky, it could be his blood. Maybe he cut himself in a struggle with someone, got blood on the glove, but didn't notice it and ended up depositing it on the lightbulb."

"We won't get that lucky," Jay said.

"But even if we don't, it's someone's blood. And I think the killer left it there, so it's bound to tell us something useful."

"Now you just have to analyze it," Reed said. "Run the DNA."

"And that's the tricky part." Veronica sighed. "I can't do it here. The sample is much too small, and I don't want to use it all. I'd rather send it somewhere where they have better equipment." She glanced at Jay and caught him looking at her cleavage. "Somewhere like Quantico."

"You can forget it," Jay said. "Hall won't want the FBI anywhere near this thing."

"The Delphi Center could do it, and probably fast, too," she said. "Problem is, they're expensive."

Reed looked at her for a long moment, and she could see his wheels turning. It was a very tiny amount of material, hardly visible to the naked eye. But it could be a critical break in the case. He stepped up to the microscope again and took another look.

Veronica huffed out a sigh. "It's blood, all right?"

"You hope." He glanced up at her.

"Don't be so damn skeptical. I *know*."

CHAPTER 15

Laney pulled up to the curb and double-checked the address. It wasn't what she'd expected. She glanced up and down the block, noting the empty parking lots, the gang graffiti, the burglar bars on the windows across the street. She'd heard this part of town was making a comeback, but from the looks of things, it still had a long way to go.

Laney grabbed a tube of pepper spray from her console and tucked it into her pocket. Then she gathered up her stuff and got out, looking over her shoulder as she locked her car.

Scream lived in a vintage four-story walkup in the middle of the block. Laney couldn't afford to pay him, so instead she'd brought food.

She approached the building, shifting her bags to free her hands. The downstairs was dark, but lights glowed on the second and third levels. She stepped through the unlocked front door and found herself inside a musty hallway with a stairwell. Using her phone as a flashlight, she checked the row of mailboxes. Most of the names had been scratched out or taped over multiple times. Scream's real name, Edward Gantz, was nowhere to be found.

The whine of a table saw echoed down the stairwell. Laney followed the noise up and came to a dimly lit landing. Hammering sounded above her head, and dust rained down as she glanced at the ceiling. It seemed late for construction work, but maybe it was an off-the-books job.

She checked her text message again before knocking on the door labeled 2C. She waited. And waited. She knocked again.

The door swung open, and Scream stood there, shirtless and scowling.

"You're early," he said. "I'm not done yet."

"I brought dinner. I remembered you like Hut's."

He took the bag and retreated into the apartment.

"You're welcome," she said, stepping inside.

She followed him, gaping at everything. She'd expected a choppy turn-of-the-century floor plan, but it was a large open space with high ceilings. Lumber was stacked at the far end of the room beside a pair of sawhorses. The furniture consisted of an overturned milk crate and a lone metal folding chair near the window.

"You have the whole floor?" she asked.

"The whole building."

She looked at him. "You *own* it?"

"My latest project," he said, stepping into a half-finished kitchen. There was a row of cabinets without doors. Hookups for appliances but no appliances yet. He set the food down beside a stainless-steel sink and peeked into the bag.

"Bacon cheeseburger?" he asked.

"And onion rings." She glanced around. "How many square feet is this?"

"All four floors, about twelve thousand. The bottom two levels are for business. I plan to live upstairs."

"Then why the kitchen?"

"Break room." He chomped into an onion ring. "You want to see the rest?"

"Sure."

"My office is down here." He led her down a corridor with freshly installed drywall. "We'll have a couple of conference rooms, server storage, the whole deal."

They entered a spacious room where he'd set up a desk with three workstations. On the wall behind the computers hung a large black pirate flag, an allusion to his black-hat roots. The two windows in the room had been sealed off with butcher paper and masking tape. Laney noticed the cot in the corner with a sleeping bag bunched at the end.

"You're living here?"

"Haven't moved in yet, but I've been putting in some late nights getting our systems set up." He sank into a rolling leather chair. "I'm just finishing your download."

"What did you get?"

"Not a lot—"

The whine of a saw directly above them drowned out his words. Laney glanced at the ceiling. "How do you work with that?" she asked when it was quiet again.

"You get used to it." He popped a thumb drive into the middle computer. "I couldn't find any zeros in the marketplace that work against Mix's system. And they have surprisingly tight security. Whoever designed it knew what they were doing."

"Thanks."

"It's yours?"

"I overhauled everything after they had some security breaches. So you didn't find anything off the shelf?"

"No."

"What did you find on ViCAP?" she asked.

"Give me a sec."

"You got something?" Hope welled in her chest. He had to have found a back door, or he wouldn't have bothered calling her.

He glanced up at her with a sly grin. "You're going to like it." He ejected the thumb drive and handed it to her, then popped in a new one.

"What's on this?"

"I'll show you."

There was a knock at the front door, and he pushed back his chair. "That's my workmen. Don't touch anything." He went to the doorway, and she took the vacated chair. "I mean it, Laney. Paws off."

"All right, all right." She held up her hands.

When he disappeared, she returned her attention to his computer. Whatever file he was downloading was twenty percent finished. She shifted her attention to the neighboring computer and tapped the mouse. The screen came to life, showing a Facebook page for Bella Marshall.

A chill crept down Laney's spine as she studied the picture. Why had Scream been looking at this? Did he know Bella? She glanced at the door, then scooted her chair closer. Maybe he'd heard about her murder and made the connection to Laney's investigation.

Thud.

She glanced over her shoulder. The noise had come from the front room, and it sounded like someone falling to the floor. She strained to listen and heard a low-pitched sucking sound.

Laney's blood turned icy. Was that . . . a gunshot?

She jumped to her feet. A gun with a silencer. She'd

only heard the sound in movies, but it was unmistakable. She rushed for the door, then halted beside it, heart pounding as she tried to decide what to do. Had Scream been *shot*?

Voices. Low, monotone. She didn't know them. Did they know she was here? She glanced around frantically, but there was no place to hide.

The shrill noise of the saw was back, and she darted a look at the ceiling. She couldn't go into the hallway—they might see her. Her gaze landed on the window, and she dashed across the room to peel back the paper. It was two floors up, but there was a fire escape where she could hide. She ripped the paper away, praying the construction noise would cover the sound. She flipped the latch and pushed on the window frame.

Stuck.

The whine of the saw abruptly stopped. She heard a voice, closer now. She grabbed a pen from the desk and managed to wedge it under the window frame. It started to move, just barely, but she kept working the lever, darting glances at the door. Her heart was racing. Her hands shook.

Footsteps in the hallway. A distant door creaking open.

She managed to get her fingers under the window frame. She cast a look at the door and gave a mighty pull just as the wail of the saw started up again.

Laney stuck her head out the window. It was an old-fashioned fire escape, brown and rusty, and she wasn't sure it was attached securely to the building. But she scrambled onto it anyway, keeping an eye on the door to Scream's office as she rolled onto her side on the metal slats. She could see the alley below, dark and empty. There wasn't a ladder, not even one of those drop-down ones. Maybe there had been one at some point, but now it was gone.

The saw noise ceased. The butcher paper flapped in the wind, and she worried the sound would attract attention, but then the breeze died down. Panting from fear and exertion, she glanced up at the glowing windows of the third floor, where the workmen were. Hadn't they heard anything?

A gun. It had definitely been a gun.

Her heart thudded wildly as she crouched on the metal slats and tried to get her bearings. She had to stay hidden. Or get out of here before the person in the hallway noticed the open window. The construction noise had covered her escape, but—

A soft scraping sound. Laney's nerves skittered as she looked at the windowpane. It was sliding shut. She lunged to catch it, but she wasn't quick enough, and it crashed down with a bang.

CHAPTER 16

The noise reverberated through the alley—louder than a rifle shot, she thought, although it probably wasn't. Her terrified brain had probably amplified it. She sprang into action, scrambling up the metal stairs, desperate to get away from the man with the gun.

Footsteps in the office as Laney reached the next level. The third-story window was dark, but she pounded her fists against the glass. Could the workmen hear her? She eyed the light spilling from windows several rooms over and pounded again, but the whine of the saw drowned her out.

Noise below her. The fire escape shifted. Laney rolled back on the platform and bucked forward with a powerful kick. Glass shattered around her legs.

A soft sucking noise as something whizzed by her head.

He's shooting.

She pulled her hoodie over her face and dived through the broken window, landing with a graceless flop on the dusty floor, shocked and gasping.

Noise on the fire escape.

Laney rolled to her feet and looked around. Everything was dark. She could hear the workmen nearby, but they seemed to be separated from her by a thick wall. Her eyes adjusted, and she rushed through the

doorway, only to find herself in an even darker hallway. Was it a mirror of Scream's floor plan? She rushed
toward the door and smacked into something hard.
Reeling with pain, she stood stunned for a moment.
Then she groped her way along the wall until she found
a doorknob.

The sound of crunching glass in the darkness. Laney
fumbled with the door and yanked it open.

Hallway.

She raced down the stairs, toward the light. She
whipped around the landing, taking the steps two at
a time. She hit Scream's floor and kept going. He must
still be in there, either dead or injured.

Footsteps thundered above her. She rounded the
next landing, digging for her phone in her pocket as
she flew down the steps. Something clattered to the
floor—her pepper spray! She couldn't go back for it.
She yanked her phone out and pressed the emergency
button as the footsteps pounded closer and closer—

Wffftt.

Sheetrock exploded beside her head. She dropped
to her knees, then grabbed the handrail to haul herself
up and took the last four stairs in one leap. It wasn't
the same stairwell she'd used the first time. There were
two? She spotted a door at the end of the corridor and
made a sprint for it, still jabbing at the buttons on her
phone. She heard the operator's distant voice in her
hand: *Nine-one-one, please state your emergency.*

Wffftt.

She tripped and crashed to her knees. She couldn't
look back, couldn't do anything except stumble to
her feet and bolt for the door. She reached it, jerked it
open, and rushed into the muggy night air.

The alley behind the building was dark and narrow. Laney looked in both directions, then raced for the light. She ran and ran, spurred by the knowledge that someone was right behind her and he had a *gun*.

She reached the corner and ducked around the building. It wasn't the street she'd parked on, but this was better. It had cars and people.

Footsteps in the alley, coming closer.

Laney sprinted down the street waving her arms and yelling, hoping to flag down a cop or a cab, anything. She spotted a neon sign ahead. A liquor store. A quick look over her shoulder told her he wasn't there, but still she kept running, pushing and pushing until she thought her lungs would burst. Reaching the neon sign, she slid to a stop, yanked open the door, and raced inside.

CHAPTER 17

Laney sat in the police car with her feet firmly planted on the asphalt. The big detective, Jay, rested his arm on the top of the door and gazed down at her.

"Sure you don't want to get that cut looked at?" he asked.

"I'm sure."

He returned his attention to his phone, where he'd been checking messages for the past twenty minutes. Or maybe he was playing *Angry Birds*. She didn't know. Whatever he was doing, his real purpose was to guard her.

As if she might be planning to run away.

Laney rested her arms on her knees and stared at the ground. She felt dizzy. Nauseated. And she was shivering despite the ninety-degree heat. Blood had trickled from the gash on her ankle and made a sticky puddle under her heel. Laney stared at her shoe, wanting to take it off but not wanting to attract anyone's attention, least of all Reed's.

Her gaze settled on him. The liquor store parking lot had become a makeshift command center, and Reed was on the far side of it now, talking to some uniforms beside the crime-scene van. Twice he'd started to walk toward her, and twice he'd been waylaid by people in suits. There was a grand total of nine cops on the

scene now—five uniforms and four in street clothes—
and every last one of them was armed with something
better than pepper spray.

That was the good news.

The bad news was that they'd been arriving steadily
for the past hour and showed no signs of either wrapping things up or allowing Laney to leave.

She checked her watch. "How much longer is this
going to take?"

Reed's partner looked amused. "You got someplace
else to be?"

"Yes."

He sighed heavily and glanced at the crowd of officers, then looked at her. "Lemme check."

He left his post, and Laney returned her attention
to her feet. Little shards of glass clung to her shoelaces
from when she'd kicked through the third-floor window. She plucked them out one by one, making a shim-
mery mound on the asphalt beside her foot. Her hands
trembled as she did it, and she thought about Scream.

At the liquor store, she'd talked to the emergency
dispatcher while the manager locked and barricaded
the door, even though the gunman seemed to have
fled. The police had shown up quickly and found
Scream on the floor of his apartment bleeding from
two gunshot wounds. He'd barely had a pulse when the
EMTs loaded him onto a gurney and rushed him to
Brackenridge Hospital.

And that was all Laney had been able to get from
the cop who'd taken her statement. She rubbed her
forehead and replayed the events, wishing she'd done
more, reacted faster. She desperately wanted to get to
the hospital now and find out what was happening.

Footsteps on the asphalt. A pair of black wing tips appeared in her field of vision.

"Hi."

She didn't look up. His hand rested on her shoulder, and she felt the burn of tears.

"You all right?" he asked.

"I'm fine."

He took his hand away, and she lifted her gaze. His blue eyes were filled with concern . . . and something else she couldn't quite read.

"I need you to tell me what you know about Edward Gantz."

She sat up straight and cleared her throat. "Like what?"

"Is he a friend? Boyfriend?"

"Friend."

"You sure?"

"Yes."

He looked at her for a long moment. "Why are you here tonight?"

She tipped her head back. "Reed, please. I've been through this already with that cop over there. Didn't he tell you?"

"I want you to tell me."

She sighed. "He asked me to drop by."

"What time?"

"He texted me around seven. I was leaving work. I told him I'd come about nine, but I got here early."

"Why?"

"I blew off my kickboxing class and decided to get carryout. Look, you have all this already. How many times do I have to go through it?"

He eased closer and rested his arm on the door, and

she could see the gun at his hip as he towered over her. It was a very intimidating stance, and she didn't like it at all, so she stood up.

"Why'd he want you to drop by?" he asked.

"I don't know."

"You don't know."

"No, okay? I'd just gotten there. We hadn't even eaten dinner yet. He was just showing me around when . . . everything happened."

"Take me through that part."

She huffed out a sigh. "He was showing me his office. Someone came to the front door, and he thought it was one of his workmen from upstairs. He told me he'd be right back. Then I heard this sound in the front room—a thud. And then this weird noise."

"The gunshot."

"Yes, but it was muffled, like with a silencer."

"A suppressor."

"Yes." Laney's throat tightened. She glanced at the building. All the windows were lit up now as CSIs combed the place for evidence. The two workmen from the third floor were on the sidewalk being interviewed separately by detectives. Reed's boss was here, too. Since pulling up in an unmarked police car, he'd been tromping around giving people orders.

"Did he say why he wanted you to drop by?" Reed asked.

"No. Did you listen to what I said?"

"Okay, what else do you know about him?"

"What do you mean?"

"Did you know he had a sheet, for instance?" His voice had an edge now. "It's not short, either. Wire fraud, online theft, identity theft."

"What's your point?"

"I need to know what you were doing here, Laney. And don't give me some bullshit about dropping by with hamburgers."

"That's what I was doing!"

He watched her for a few long seconds. Laney's palms felt clammy, but she resisted the urge to rub them on her jeans.

"Did you get a look at the person who chased you?" he asked.

"No."

"But you said it was a man."

"It was a man's voice that I heard in the hallway. I assumed it was a man." She glanced at the building. "And his footsteps sounded heavy."

"You heard one voice or two?"

"One. At first I thought it was two, but looking back, I think it was just one. Like he was talking on his phone."

"But you didn't get a look at him," Reed stated.

"No."

"You didn't notice his clothes? His build? His race?"

"I told you I didn't *see* him."

He shook his head and glanced away, clearly annoyed with her answers.

"What?"

He looked at her. "Why are you acting like a hostile witness?"

"Why are you acting like a jerk?"

"Laney, I know you're lying to me." He stepped closer and lowered his voice. "I can see it in your face. And if you think I'm being a jerk, just wait until those FBI agents start taking apart your bullshit story."

She glared up at him.

"I'm trying to help you get ahead of this thing. Your *friend* has a record as long as my arm. And an FBI file. And he was shot twice while you happened to be at his apartment." He eased closer, and the intensity in his look sent a chill through her. "I need you to tell me what the hell you're doing here, because I'm ninety-nine percent sure whatever it is has to do with my murder case. The case you're *no longer working on*. The case I specifically pulled you off of for your own safety!"

She didn't say anything. She was trembling now, head to toe. She hugged her arms against her ribs and stared up at him. She'd never seen him so upset, and she was upset, too. It was on the tip of her tongue to spill everything she knew, here and now, in front of all these cops. But she held back.

She *would* tell him. She'd decided to tell him everything, but she needed to do it when they were alone.

Footsteps approached, and she turned to see a pair of men walking over. They wore full suits, with ties and everything. These would be the FBI agents who wanted to pick apart her story. The taller of the two flashed his badge as he stopped in front of her.

"Ms. Knox?"

"That's me."

"We have a few questions."

• • •

Reed juggled his phone as he stripped off his holster and dumped it on the kitchen counter alongside his keys.

"There's something screwy about this case," Jay told him. He was calling from the station, and Reed could hear the bullpen noise in the background.

"Yeah, tell me about it."

"Gantz doesn't have a cell phone."

Reed opened his fridge and remembered he hadn't been to the store in weeks. He had nothing, not even a beer.

"Everyone has a cell phone." He took out a glass and filled it with tap water. As he looked out the window, he noticed all his neighbors' trash cans and recycle bins parked along the curb. "Shit," he muttered.

"What?"

"He has a phone, trust me," Reed said. "I'll ask Laney about it."

"Want to try her tonight?"

"No."

Reed went to the garage and jabbed the button for the automatic door. As it lifted, a pair of headlights turned into his driveway.

"You sure?" Jay asked. "I bet she's up."

"I'm sure."

The lights switched off, and Reed recognized the silhouette of the car. And then the silhouette of the woman getting out of it.

"First thing tomorrow, then," Jay was saying. "We need to get hold of those phone records."

Laney walked through his garage and straight up to him. When he'd last seen her at the crime scene, she'd looked pale and shell-shocked, but she didn't look that way now. She looked like she was on a mission. She strode past him into his house.

"I'll see what I can get," Reed told Jay. To hell with

the trash cans. He closed his garage and returned to the kitchen, where Laney was leaning against the counter eavesdropping.

"And that's not the only thing," Jay said. "I just came from the hospital."

"Which one?"

"Brackenridge. Guy's still in surgery, but I caught one of the nurses. Get this—*two* GSWs, and they're saying he might pull through."

Laney reached up and opened a cabinet.

"I mean, can you believe that?" Jay asked. "Is that fucked up or what?"

Everything about this case was fucked up, as far as Reed was concerned, starting with the fact that one of the key witnesses was in his kitchen rooting through his liquor cabinet. She took out a bottle of Jack and poured two shots. She left one on the counter and went into Reed's darkened living room, where she stood beside the sliding glass door and stared outside.

"This Gantz has got to be the luckiest son of a bitch on the planet," Jay said.

"Maybe it's not luck."

"How do you mean?"

"Maybe the shooter's an amateur."

Laney glanced over her shoulder.

"With a suppressor?" Jay asked.

"It's possible."

"I'm not seeing it."

Laney slid open the door and stepped out onto the deck.

She shouldn't be here. She was neck-deep in his case. She'd lied to him and to the FBI, and he didn't know why. He didn't know what she was hiding or if she was protecting someone. What he *did* know was that she was twenty-four, and beautiful, and the dead last woman he should get involved with.

"Reed?"

"Who's there now?"

"Where?"

"At the hospital with Gantz."

"The feds hung around at first, hoping he'd wake up. But sounds like he's going to be out a while with the surgery and everything. And that's *if* he pulls through."

"So he's alone?"

"The lieutenant posted a uniform there overnight. I told her to call me if there's any news."

"Okay, keep me informed."

"Will do."

Reed ended the call and tossed his phone onto the counter beside his holster. He grabbed the drink and went to the door. It was dark out except for the moonlight. Laney, lit only by the full moon, stood against the rail of the deck and stared out at the wooded area where there had been a creek before the drought.

She looked solitary. And vulnerable. And she'd come here for something. He thought he knew what it was, but he didn't know if he could give it to her.

Reed stepped outside. She wore the same form-fitting black tank top she'd had on before. Same jeans, too, but she'd traded her bloody sneakers for sandals, and he noticed the glittery silver paint on her toenails.

"Nice deck," she said. "What is it, pine?"

"Cedar." He approached her.

"You build it yourself?"

"Yeah."

She turned to face him, leaning her hip against the railing. "Where do you keep your boat?"

"Don't have one."

She tipped her head to the side. "Then why do you have a boat trailer in your garage?"

"I've been planning to get one. Haven't pulled the trigger."

"Why not?"

"Haven't found the right one yet."

"There are plenty of boats in Austin. You must be picky."

He sipped his drink, watching her over the rim of the glass. He had a feeling they weren't talking about boats now. She gazed up at him for a moment, then turned and looked out at the woods again.

It was a still night, hot and humid, and he could already feel the sweat trickling down his back. He looked at Laney's slender shoulders and felt a pang of frustration because she'd lied to him tonight.

She turned around again and leaned back against the rail, and her eyes were dark and luminous in the moonlight.

He drained his glass and set it down. "Delaney—"

"Don't. Please?" She eased closer and rested her hand on his chest. "I don't want to answer any more questions tonight. I just want to be here."

He watched her, reading the look in her eyes. It was right there in front of him—a dare. She held his gaze, and his pulse picked up. She could read him. She knew exactly what he was thinking, what he'd been thinking since he first saw her.

He bent his head down and kissed her. She tasted sharp and sweet from his whiskey. Her hands slid up around his neck, and he felt her fingertips tangling in his hair. He shifted her, pressing her back against the railing, and she made a low moan and tipped her head back.

He kissed her jaw, her neck, breathing in the scent of her skin. He pulled her hips against him and kissed the tender spot just under her earlobe, and she made a soft, feminine sound that filled him with need. Her skin was salty, and he knew she'd been crying earlier for reasons she didn't want to tell him. She didn't trust him, not fully. But still, she'd come.

Her nails dug into his scalp, and she brought his mouth back to hers, and he kissed her hard and deep as her hand slid down to his belt. She gripped it, curling her knuckles against him.

"Reed." She pulled away. "Let's go inside."

CHAPTER 18

He stared down at her for an endless moment, and she knew he was thinking of some reason to reject her. But then he took her hand and led her back to the house, leaving their glasses outside.

Hot, jittery excitement filled her as the glass door slid shut with a *thunk*. She'd been wanting this to happen. From that first night, she'd wanted to feel his body against hers, wanted his hands on her bare skin. She was tired of waiting, and now she wanted all of it, everything she'd been thinking about. For the rest of tonight, she wanted to be the center of his attention.

He pulled her down the dark hallway. His grip on her hand was firm, but he didn't seem hurried, and a little tremor of anticipation went through her as he stopped in the doorway of his bedroom. He glanced around, maybe taking inventory or thinking about the mess. She leaned her hand against the doorway and started taking off her shoes and then her jeans as her eyes adjusted to the darkness and she looked around his room.

He pulled the jeans from her hand and tossed them away, then backed her against the wall, kissing her roughly. He slid his hand up her bare thigh and gave a low moan of approval as his fingers encountered the strap of her bikini panties. She hitched her leg up and pulled him closer, kissing him as roughly as he was kissing her.

She loved the feel of his body against hers. She loved the way he kissed. Every touch was strong, confident, and all her past experiences melted away in comparison. Everything about him was manly, nothing boyish or tentative. He pulled back to look at her, and the determined gleam in his eyes made her insides tighten.

He tipped her head back and moved down, sliding his hand under her shirt and stroking his thumb over her nipple. His mouth closed over it through the fabric, and she squirmed against him. He dragged her shirt up, then moved her bra aside, and his mouth on her bare skin was an electric shock.

He had a thing about her breasts, she'd noticed, and he seemed intent on them now as he lifted her arms and yanked her shirt over her head and tossed it away. His hands stroked over her, and then his mouth, and she tipped back her head and gave herself over to the maddeningly hot sensation of everything he was doing. The stubble of his beard scraped her sensitive skin, sending shivers through her as he played and stroked until her body throbbed. He returned to her mouth again, and she rocked her hips against him and made a low needy sound in her throat.

Suddenly, he lifted her up, and she wrapped her legs around his waist as he walked her to the bed. He lowered her onto it and leaned over her, and she realized he was still completely dressed while she was down to nearly nothing. He seemed to realize this, too, and started unbuttoning his shirt, his gaze never leaving her body. She got onto her knees and batted his hands away, wanting to do it herself. She'd been think-

ing about this, about getting him out of his starched
shirt and getting her hands on those hard muscles. She
finished his buttons and pushed his shirt off, and he
pulled his white T-shirt over his head. A rush of excitement filled her as she sat back on her knees to look.

"Wow."

"What?" He leaned forward and caught her mouth
with his.

She didn't bother explaining, just kissed him and
made quick work of his belt. He got rid of his pants,
and then the bed sank under his weight as he rested
his knee between hers. She glanced at his muscular abs
and the dark line of hair that trailed from his navel to
the top of his black briefs.

He wrapped his arm around her and scooted her
back into the center of his bed, then kissed her deeply,
and she wrapped her leg around him to pull him close.
She wanted his weight on her, hard and heavy. But
before she could settle him where she wanted, he slid
down her body and got started on her breasts again.

"I like this," he said, peeling down the straps of her
flimsy black bra. He moved the fabric away and stroked
his hands over her skin. "This, too," he said, licking and
teasing her. His hand glided behind her back and deftly
popped the clasp, and then he pulled her bra away and
kissed her some more, and his stubble sent hot little
darts through her.

She propped herself up on her elbows and watched
him, smiling because she wasn't exactly used to com-
pliments on this particular part of her anatomy.

"What?" He glanced up.

"Nothing."

She lay back down and ran her hands over his muscular arms and his broad shoulders. She loved his warm skin and the tension she could feel running through him. She tugged at the waistband of his shorts, and he got rid of them. She scooted down the bed and reached for him, but he clamped his hand around her wrist and planted it firmly beside her head. He gave her a look of warning as he kissed his way down her body again, sliding her panties down and over her legs, and she heard the whisper-soft sound of them hitting the floor.

She tipped her head back and sighed as his mouth and his hands moved over her, sliding and exploring. She let her legs fall open and let the sensations wash over her. He knew exactly how to touch her, exactly where. He noticed every sigh and shiver and homed in on precisely what she wanted, what she craved, and didn't have to be shown a thing. The heat built inside her, and she gripped the bedspread in her hands. His mouth moved over her until she was squirming and moaning, and still he didn't stop. She arched her hips.

"Reed."

He seemed to know she was losing it and kissed his way up her body, settling between her legs like she'd wanted, but it still wasn't enough.

She grabbed his head and kissed him, pressing herself against him, loving the hot pressure of his skin. He pulled back, breathless, and his gaze on her was intense.

For a moment, she blinked up at him in the dimness, shocked that they were actually here together, actually in his bed after all her fantasizing.

He reached across her and dragged open a drawer, and she took the opportunity to kiss his chest and stroke her fingers over the hair there.

"Fuck." His body went rigid.

"What?" She sat up on her elbows.

But then he relaxed. "Nothing."

She caught a glint of foil as he slapped a condom on the nightstand. Disaster averted.

And then he was back again, kissing her, but it was harder and hotter now because the teasing was over. He shifted her under him and leaned his weight on his elbow as he covered himself with a condom. She reached for him in the darkness and tried to help, but he moved her hand to his hip as he pushed her legs apart. And then his gaze locked on hers, and she braced herself as he drove into her.

It was hot and painful and *good*, and she gripped his shoulders as he pulled back and did it again, slowly this time. And again.

She wrapped her legs around him and pulled him closer because she wanted more. But he was already there, already changing the pace, going harder and deeper until she clutched her arms around him and dug her nails into his back. The rhythm built until he hit a perfect, blissful stride, and all she could do was hold on as he pushed her and pushed her until she didn't think she could stand it. He was breathing fast now, and his muscles bunched under her hands as he drove into her again and again. She was reaching her limit, but she still wanted more. She made a high, pleading noise that didn't even sound like herself as she clutched her legs around him and pulled him as close as she possibly could. And then he reared back and gave a stunning thrust, and every nerve in her body exploded as he crashed against her, pinning her beneath him at last.

She lay there, dizzy. She couldn't move or even

breathe. She opened her eyes, and her face was pressed against his neck. She felt his pulse racing against her cheek and a surge of giddiness that she'd made him work.

He pushed himself up, blinking down at her in the dimness, then rolled to his back.

She closed her eyes. With his weight gone, she filled her lungs with air again. Her body felt numb. Her heart was still pounding, and her toes actually tingled.

"You okay?"

She glanced at him, surprised by the note of concern in his voice. "Why?"

"I was kind of . . . rough."

She smiled. She rolled to him and rested her head against his side. His skin was damp and hot. He smelled like sex and sweat and man, and she took a deep breath and nestled closer.

She drifted off. Minutes or hours, she didn't know. But when she opened her eyes again, the room was darker. Quieter. She lay with her back against his front, and she felt the heavy weight of his arm on her waist.

She blinked into the darkness, and her gaze landed on the window of his room and the faint pattern of horizontal lines created by moonlight shining through the blinds. She spied her bra on the nightstand, and her brain slowly clicked into gear.

She should go. It was late, and there were things she needed to do tonight. And not do. Spending the night at Reed's house was on the "not do" list. But his body was warm against hers. And his arm on her waist felt . . . safe.

She couldn't remember the last time she'd felt totally safe going to sleep.

Maybe she'd stay, just for a few more minutes. She tucked his arm closer and let herself drift.

. . .

"I thought you went home?"

Veronica glanced up from her computer to see Jordan standing in the doorway of the evidence lab. "I did," Veronica said. "Got called back on this shooting thing. Hall put a rush on the slugs we recovered from the apartment."

"Why?"

"Damned if I know. And I'm not sure we'll get much, because they're pretty misshapen. But it's worth a try."

"Hmm. Well, I'm out," Jordan said. "Don't stay too late."

"I won't."

Veronica returned her attention to her computer and uploaded the files. Instead of sending them to DPS, which was notoriously backlogged, she was sending them to the ballistics lab at the Delphi Center. The slugs themselves had already been couriered over.

There was something up with Hall. He'd been all over this shooting case, even visiting the crime scene, which he seldom did. The lieutenant hated blood and was known for losing his lunch at homicide scenes. But he'd shown up tonight anyway and even insisted on walking the building with Reed Novak, getting the detective's take on how the shooting had gone down. It wasn't Hall's usual response to a nonfatal incident, and Veronica didn't know what was going on, although she had a sneaking suspicion it had something to do with the two recent murders.

The crimes were getting tons of press, and for once Veronica didn't think the media was going overboard. She'd watched the news reports and read the stories, and even the most lurid accounts didn't include the details she thought were truly frightening.

An image flashed into her mind of April Abrams sprawled on the floor with her head bashed in, her T-shirt pushed up around her armpits. Veronica tried to imagine the horror of waking up in the middle of the night and realizing you weren't alone.

"Still here?"

She jumped and whirled around. "Don't sneak up on people."

Jay stepped into the room and walked over. "I wasn't." He looked over her shoulder. "What's that?"

"Photos of the slugs."

"Already?"

"Hall put a rush on everything. We're sending this to Delphi." She glanced up, and he was reading the email she'd been composing. "Do you mind?"

"Sorry." He stepped back.

"Any idea why he's got a bee in his bonnet about this one?"

"No," he said, but the tone of his voice told her he did know.

"I was thinking it had to do with Reed's cyber-detective friend," she said. "I saw her at the scene being interviewed."

"Yeah, she knows the victim."

Veronica lifted an eyebrow. "You think she's involved?"

Jay didn't respond.

"Does Reed think she's involved?"

Again, nothing.

"Fine, don't tell me." She turned her attention to her computer. "I'll figure it out soon enough anyway."

Jay leaned against the counter. "So I was wondering." He cleared his throat. "You eaten yet?"

"Had a Twix a minute ago."

"I meant dinner."

She sent the email and exited the program, stalling for time so she could think. Was he asking her out? She hadn't been asked out in a while, but that's what it sounded like. Then again, maybe she was reading too much into it. Jay was a big man and probably had an appetite to match.

She glanced up at him, and he was watching her. Damn it, he had pretty eyes, too. They were brown and watchful and definitely interested in her response. He wasn't just hungry.

"You want to get dinner together or . . . ?"

"I don't go out with cops."

The corner of his mouth curled up in a smile. "Seriously?"

"Seriously. No offense."

"None taken." He was definitely smiling now as she gathered up her papers and slid them into a file.

"If you had to *guess* why Hall is so worked up over this shooting," she said, "what would you think?"

"I don't know," he said. "But it might have something to do with the FBI turning up at the crime scene."

"We didn't call them?"

"Nope."

"Hmm. Curiouser and curiouser."

"So why don't you?" he asked.

"Don't what?"

"Go out with cops?"

She tilted her head to the side. "You're a detective. See if you can figure it out."

"I don't know." Another smile. "I'm thinking of some gun jokes, but they're a little crude."

Veronica rolled her eyes and stepped past him to stack the files on her desk. She glanced around the lab to make sure everything was off for the night.

"Really, what is it?"

She looked at him. Did he truly not know?

She'd learned the hard way that cops talked. A lot, especially the detectives. They shared evidence, swapped stories. It was one reason they were good at their jobs, but from her perspective, it was a problem. She had to work with these guys day in and day out, and she didn't want to be fodder for a bunch of locker-room gossip. So even though she'd been asked out a lot over the years—by detectives and beat cops and even lab technicians—she made a habit of saying no.

But this time, she felt tempted.

"Come on." Jay stepped closer, evidently taking her silence for ambivalence. "One dinner."

"It's almost midnight already."

"I know. You must be starving."

She grabbed her purse off the back of the chair. "You're very tenacious."

"Tenacious, huh? I like that." He smiled sheepishly. "I was worried I might be coming across as desperate."

She sighed. "Listen, it's really nothing personal, but—"

"We can go to the IHOP over by campus. You can catch me up on your work, I'll catch you up on mine. It'll be like a staff meeting. But with food."

She folded her arms over her chest but didn't say anything.

"Come on. What else do you have to do tonight? Go home and watch *Bones* reruns?"

That was exactly what she'd planned to do, damn it. She couldn't help it—she smiled. "You detectives are really obnoxious. You know that, right?"

• • •

Reed glanced at the clock. After three. He rolled out of bed and grabbed a pair of jeans off the back of the chair in the corner.

He watched Laney sleeping as he zipped up. She was out cold. He walked to the front of the house and checked the lock, then peered through the window at Laney's car in the driveway. He checked the garage door and the slider, frowning down at it because he'd thought he'd left it unlocked.

He glanced back at the kitchen. A pair of glasses sat on the counter beside the sink, and Laney's purple phone was plugged into his charger.

She was sneaky. He hadn't even felt her slip out of bed. Reed flipped on the back porch lights and re-turned to the bedroom.

He paused in the doorway. She lay on her stomach now, her arms tucked under the pillow. Her back was pale and smooth, and the sight of her asleep in his bed made his chest feel tight. For a moment, he couldn't move—he just stood there in the doorway, wondering what he'd gotten himself into.

She was evasive. And infuriating. And unpredict-able. But there was something about her that pulled at him. She was a mystery he still hadn't managed to unravel. Just seeing the dark curtain of hair against her cheek stirred something inside him, something raw and emotional that he hadn't felt since that first year with Erika, before they'd even been married. He'd been twenty-five and practically a kid then, about the same age Laney was now.

This was so fucked up. He was much too old for her, and they had nothing in common, really.

But they had chemistry.

He'd been drawn to her in a deep-down, yearning kind of way since the moment she'd bumped into him in that coffee shop. He'd thought sleeping with her might snap him out of it, but it looked like he'd been wrong.

She rolled onto her side. Then she lifted her head off the pillow and glanced at the empty side of the bed.

"Hi."

She sat up and looked around. "What time is it?"

"Late."

She swung her legs out of bed and grabbed his shirt off the floor. She shrugged into it, and he thought she was headed for the bathroom, but she walked right past him into the hallway.

"You okay?"

"Hungry," she said over her shoulder.

He followed her into the kitchen, where she quickly discovered he had nothing to eat. He'd meant to order some carryout, but he'd gotten sidetracked.

He propped his shoulder against the wall and watched her frown at the contents of his fridge. His shirt went almost to her knees, but she'd left it open in front, which had the effect of waking him up.

"Pathetic." She glanced at him.

"I know."

She tried the freezer. "But . . . there's hope." She grabbed a pint of Ben & Jerry's and read the label. "Phish Food. How'd you know?"

He opened a drawer and got her a spoon as she peeled off the lid. She sauntered past him into the breakfast room, where she glanced out the window at her car in the driveway.

"You should have security lights," she said, digging into the ice cream.

"I do. They're motion-sensitive."

She sat back against the table, watching him as she slid the spoon from her mouth. His imagination was kicking into gear now. "I called the hospital," she said.

"And?"

"He got through surgery." Her voice was somber. "He's still in recovery, so they don't really know . . ."

Reed pulled out a chair and sank into it. He hadn't expected to talk about this again tonight, but no reason to put it off. "How'd you get that? Usually, they only talk to family."

"I spoke with the nurse I met when I was there earlier. She thinks I'm his sister."

Reed scrubbed his hand over his face, fully awake now. He leaned forward, watching her. "You have any idea why the FBI was there tonight?"

She looked at him warily. "You guys didn't call them?"

"Why would we call them?"

She poked at the ice cream. "I don't know."

He waited. She wanted to talk, he could tell. But he had a feeling he wasn't going to like what she had to say.

"I wouldn't be surprised if Scream's business has put him on the FBI's radar," she said.

"You're talking about Edward?"

"Yeah, that's his nickname. I'm pretty sure they've been watching him for a while."

"Why?" Reed leaned back in the chair, trying to ignore how his shirt gaped open in the front.

"He sells zeros. Software bugs that can be exploited and used to gain secret access to companies. It's a lucrative business, but not all of what he does is strictly legal, so . . ." She shrugged.

"And I'm guessing he's made his fair share of enemies along the way?"

"Probably."

Which meant plenty of people had a reason to want him dead. And his getting shot *might* not be related to Laney's visit. She could simply have been in the wrong place at the wrong time.

But Reed didn't know why she'd been there. Because she still hadn't told him.

He watched her pick at the ice cream. The purple lock of hair hung in her eyes, but he didn't need to see her face to know she was feeling all kinds of guilt right now.

"Did he say—"

"Look, I don't want to talk about this now," she said.

"When?"

"Not now."

Laney had come inches away from being dead herself. She'd dodged three bullets. *Three.* And now she was sitting here in his kitchen, holding out on him and trying to distract him with sex.

She still wouldn't give him the full story. And the

only other person who could provide it might be dead by morning.

She glanced up at him with those doe eyes. "Tomorrow maybe."

She was lying again. He could see it on her face.

"I don't want to fight with you right now." She set the ice cream aside and eased closer to him. She was still leaning back against the table covered with mail and bills. And his shirt was still floating around her, giving him glimpses of skin.

His gaze locked on hers. "What is it you want to do?"

Slowly, she stepped over his legs and lowered herself onto his lap. "I don't know." She leaned close, resting her arms on his shoulders, and her breath was warm against his ear. "Anything besides fight."

CHAPTER 19

Reed was already in a foul mood when the doorbell rang the next morning. He strapped on his holster and crossed the house to find Jay on his doorstep.

"You're early."

"The meeting's bumped up." Jay stepped inside. "I sent you a text."

Jay followed him into the kitchen. Reed saw him notice the liquor bottle on the counter, the glasses by the sink, the mail scattered on the floor around the breakfast table.

"Late night?" Jay looked at him.

Reed ignored the question and unplugged his phone from the charger to read his text messages. Jay had written him a book. The meeting with the Delphi Center DNA tracer had been bumped up an hour, and Hall had scheduled a meeting at eleven.

"Veronica sent the slugs in."

Reed glanced up. "Already?"

"She processed everything last night. Hall put a rush on it." Jay leaned back against the counter. "Hey, you got any coffee?"

"No."

Reed scrolled through the rest of his messages. One from Erika, one from his lieutenant, nothing from Laney.

Not that he'd expected anything.

He had woken up at six fifteen in an empty bed. He wasn't used to women sneaking out on him. In fact, he couldn't remember a single time it had happened, and the more he thought about it, the more it pissed him off.

Reed slid his phone into his pocket and grabbed his jacket off the chair. With any luck, he wouldn't need it today. With any luck, he wouldn't find himself knocking on some poor woman's door to tell her that her husband or her son or her daughter was never coming home.

"You ready?" Jay asked.

"Yeah."

"Oh, hey, and I called the hospital. Gantz made it through the surgery."

"Maybe we'll actually get to interview him, get some answers."

"Wouldn't count on it," Jay said. "I hear the guy's chances are slim."

• • •

The hospital wasn't nearly as busy as it had been the night before, which would make Laney's task more difficult. As she walked toward the nurse's station, she noted only two people in the waiting room—an elderly woman watching *Good Morning America* and a guy in a suit standing beside the watercooler texting away on his phone. Laney's gaze lingered on the suit a moment, trying to decide whether he was FBI. His striped shirt looked a little flashy, and anyway he was using an iPhone. So not a fed, then.

She approached the nurse's desk and tried to look confident, even though she didn't recognize anyone.

"I'm here to see Edward Gantz."

"Are you family?" a nurse asked without looking up from her computer.

"I'm his sister."

The woman stopped typing and gave Laney a once-over, pursing her lips. Despite her cheerful *SpongeBob* scrubs, she didn't look friendly.

"I spoke to Nurse Molina last night?" Laney glanced around. "Is she still on duty?"

"No." The woman looked Laney in the eye for a long moment, then tapped something into her computer. Her expression changed, and Laney felt a pang of dread. "His condition's been downgraded, I'm afraid. He's listed as critical."

"Is there any way—"

"No visitors right now. Doctor's orders."

Laney stood there, debating whether to push her luck. The nurse was watching her, stone-faced, and she decided to quit while she was ahead.

"Thank you." Laney glanced at her watch. "I'll check back later."

She returned to the elevator, pulling out her phone as she went. Reed had called again, and Laney's stomach tightened as she stared down at his number. She'd managed to avoid him this morning, but that wouldn't last long.

The elevator doors slid open, and an orderly stepped off, pushing a cart filled with covered food trays. Eggs and bacon, from the smell of it. Laney held the door for him and stepped into the empty car just as the neighboring elevator *dinged*. Several men in suits walked out, and Laney's pulse jumped. They were the FBI agents from last night. She jabbed at the close button and held her breath.

As the doors slid shut, a man lunged between them. "Not so fast," he said. "Who the hell are you?"

CHAPTER 20

Laney reached for the alarm, but he caught her wrist.

"Get the fuck off me." She yanked her hand away and lurched back, bumping against the wall.

"You're sure as hell not my sister. Who are you?"

Laney pressed herself against the wall and stared at him. It was the guy from the waiting room. Scream's brother.

"What's your name?" he demanded.

"Delaney Knox. Who are you?"

"James Gantz."

He stepped closer. He was even taller than Scream. He was thin, too, and had blue eyes, but the resemblance stopped there. With his overgelled hair and perfectly tailored suit, he looked slightly less subversive than his brother.

"How do you know Edward?" he asked.

Laney reached around him and pressed the ground-floor button before the doors could pop open again. "We're friends."

He stared down at her.

"We worked at the Delphi Center together."

He seemed to take this as proof of her legitimacy, and his posture relaxed. He ran his hand over his hair, and she saw that his eyes were bloodshot.

"How's he doing?" she asked. "They wouldn't tell me much."

The elevator stopped, and he held the door open as she stepped out. He glanced around, then ushered her out of the traffic flow to a spot beside a gift shop that sold balloons and teddy bears.

"I honestly don't know." He planted his hands on his hips. "The doctor said the surgery went okay, but then he took a turn this morning. They think it's his kidney."

Laney bit her lip.

"So . . . are you his girlfriend?"

"Friend."

He looked down at her, and she could tell he didn't buy that. "Do you have any idea who would want to shoot him?"

"No."

He sighed. "The FBI doesn't, either."

"How do you know?"

"Because I've been in town about three hours, and they've already interviewed me twice." He shook his head. "I know my brother was into some shady stuff, but . . ." He looked away.

"But what?"

"He's smart. I thought he knew not to get mixed up with anyone dangerous."

A toddler skipped past them into the gift shop, followed by a woman pushing a stroller. James paused to watch them, and Laney took a moment to study him. He looked exhausted, like maybe he'd been up all night.

"Are you the brother who lives in Houston?" she ventured.

"How'd you know that?"

"He mentioned it."

"I drove in as soon as I got the call." His phone buzzed, and he pulled it out of his pocket to check the screen, then tucked it away again.

"So, Delaney . . . you know what Ed was working on lately? The FBI seems to think this might have something to do with his company."

"I don't really know."

"I talked to him Wednesday, but he didn't say anything about it. Not that he would tell me." He gave a wan smile. "He never talked to me about his work. Computers are his thing, not mine." He paused for a moment, looking at her. "They said they interviewed a female witness last night. I assume that's you?"

"Who said?"

"The police."

She hesitated, unsure of what to tell him. "I didn't actually see it happen. I was back in the office."

He held her gaze for a moment, then glanced at the window display beside him where there was a row of teddy bears wearing T-shirts that said "Get Well Soon!" His eyes teared up, and he turned away.

"Would you mind if I got your phone number?" she asked. "In case I need to get in touch."

He cleared his throat. "Sure." He tugged a business card out of his wallet and handed it over. The card said he was a senior sales associate for a software company she'd never heard of.

Computers are his thing, not mine.

Laney glanced up. He didn't seem to catch the irony. And she realized he reminded her of Ian Phelps from ChatWare, yet another software salesman who knew nothing about computers. Unlike Ian, though, this guy didn't seem like a total prick.

"You know, he'd been throwing around money lately," James said. "I don't know what he was doing, but I should have pressed him on it. I should have asked questions."

"Maybe it's better you didn't."

His brow furrowed, and she regretted saying it. His phone buzzed again, but this time he didn't pull it out.

Laney slid the card into her pocket. "If I hear anything new, I'll give you a call."

"Same goes." He offered her his hand. "Nice to meet you, Delaney. You take care of yourself."

• • •

Mia Voss didn't look old enough to be one of the nation's foremost DNA experts. Probably the freckles, Reed thought as he followed her into a conference room. The ponytail didn't help, either.

Then again, everyone seemed young to him these days.

Reed and Jay took chairs around the table as the doctor sat down and flipped open a file.

"I completed your tests. The results were a bit complicated, and I wanted to walk you through everything." She straightened her papers in front of her, and Reed ID'd her as an extreme type A. Not a bad quality for a forensic scientist whose work could determine people's fates.

"First of all," she said, "I haven't finished analyzing the duct tape yet. However, I was able to finish the lightbulb you all sent in, and I can confirm that the material on it is, in fact, blood."

Jay looked at Reed. "She was right."

"Who was?" Mia asked.

"Our CSI."

"I can also tell you that it's a good thing you sent the evidence to us. We're dealing with a small sample of very low quality, so I had to use some advanced techniques to develop the profile."

"Such as what?" Reed asked.

"I'm sure you're familiar with STR testing." She glanced from Reed to Jay. "Short tandem repeats. Those are markers on the DNA strand. I used a technique called miniSTR analysis because I had so little material to work with, and some of it was degraded."

"Any idea why?" Jay asked. "I mean, we think the perp unscrewed the lightbulb just a day or two before Isabella Marshall's murder. Not too much time has elapsed since he touched it."

"Yes, but I'm talking about the material he *deposited* on the lightbulb. That material is much older and, as I said, degraded. It could be a lot of factors—humidity, ultraviolet light, bleach. It all depends on the circumstances. You're operating under the assumption that this material rubbed off from gloves worn by the perpetrator?"

"We think he uses a murder kit," Reed told her. "He brings certain items to the crime scenes—condoms, duct tape."

"The murder weapon," Jay added.

"So, if that's the case," she said, "you're theorizing his kit includes a pair of gloves."

"He has a favorite hammer," Jay said. "We figure, why not gloves, too? This guy's pretty particular."

"Well, however this sample got deposited—and a glove worn by the killer is a definite possibility—it's old and low-quality, but it *is* blood."

"Whose?" Reed asked, trying to keep the impatience out of his voice.

"Not Isabella Marshall's, I can tell you that." She consulted her notes. "Preliminary testing indicates that this profile is consistent with a sample submitted by the Clarke County Sheriff's Office. The sample is from a woman named Olivia Jane Hollis."

Reed looked at Jay. Veronica had been right again. Reed's pulse was thrumming. It was a major break, and suddenly, his crap morning was looking a little better.

"Her DNA was entered into the database two years ago, shortly after she went missing," Mia said.

"Then you're essentially telling us he wears the same gloves all the time," Jay summarized. "Including when he scopes out the place ahead of the murder. And with Isabella, he got a previous victim's blood on her porch light when he unscrewed it."

"I'll leave you guys to determine a plausible scenario," she said. "I'm simply relaying what the evidence says, which is that blood from Olivia Hollis is on the lightbulb in question."

"Since you haven't mentioned it," Jay said, "I guess it's too much to hope that there's any other DNA on that lightbulb? Like maybe some male DNA that could belong to the killer?"

"Unfortunately, no. I ran a standard amelogenin procedure, used to determine sex. The genetic material here came from a woman."

"Damn," Jay muttered.

"Sorry."

"No, don't be." He looked at Reed. "It's the best break we've had. It connects the two crime scenes, which puts us at three, and that makes it official."

"Official?" She looked at Reed.

"Three connected murders," he said. "We're dealing with a serial killer."

CHAPTER 21

It was just like at Urban Grounds, only this time Laney saw him coming. She was standing in the Delphi Center's lobby coffee shop, and Reed walked right up to her as she collected her extra-large no-whip latte.

"Can I talk to you?" He darted a glance at Ben, who quickly took the hint.

"See you upstairs, Lane."

She watched Ben leave and felt a twinge of panic. She stepped away from the bar into a quieter corner of the store.

Reed gazed down at her, looking perfectly calm. "You disappeared," he said.

"I had to get to work."

"So did I."

She stared up at him, at a loss for a comeback. Her heart was racing now. She hadn't thought this through. She'd known she'd run into him, but she hadn't expected it to be so soon.

His eyebrows tipped up. "That's it? We have amazing sex all night and then you sneak out at six in the morning?"

"What else did you want?"

He stared down at her for a long moment. Then he looked away and shook his head, laughing, although he didn't look like he thought anything was funny.

"What else? Okay." His gaze locked on hers again. "For starters, how about we finish the conversation we were having?"

The conversation about Scream, he meant. The one they'd been having when she crawled onto his lap. She thought of his mouth and his hands, and her cheeks flushed hot at the memory.

"We were talking about Edward," she said.

"About what you were doing at his place when he got *shot*, yeah."

Laney wanted to duck out of this again, but she was all out of tactics. And he'd see right through her anyway. He was way too perceptive and always homed right in on the slightest lie or misdirection.

"You have to promise me you won't share this with the FBI," she said.

"I can't do that, Laney."

"You have to promise to try."

He folded his arms over his chest and watched her. Finally, he nodded.

"I told you how Scream finds back doors into places. He's really good at it."

"Better than you?"

"Yes."

She glanced around the coffee shop, but the mid-morning rush had subsided, and they had the place mostly to themselves. She lowered her voice anyway.

"I asked him to help me with Mix," she said. "I told you how I redesigned their security last fall? I wanted him to see if he could penetrate it. Because someone obviously did."

Reed's jaw tensed. "What'd he find out?"

"Nothing."

He looked surprised.

"But that helps us, too," she said. "It confirms what I already thought, that Mix's security is tight. Which means whoever managed to breach it knew what they were doing because there was no back door, not after my team and I overhauled everything."

"So how did he get in, then?"

"We didn't get that far." Her stomach clenched as she remembered the muffled gunshot.

"And this is what you were talking to him about when you went over there?"

"Yes."

"I'm sure you have a theory. What is it?"

She nodded. "Well, in any system, people are always the weakest link. My idea is that the killer used social engineering. That's basically penetrating a system through human contact."

"You're saying it's an inside job?" His gaze narrowed. "We've already looked at all their employees."

"Not an inside *job*, necessarily, but I think he used an insider. He could have used a phishing scheme to get a high-level employee's password. Or he could have covertly entered the building. Or maybe he got hold of someone's computer and tampered with it to give himself a portal. If he was clever enough, he could use someone to gain access without them even knowing it happened."

"Let's assume he's clever enough. Now what?"

"Now . . . we have to check it out. Confirm. If we can find out who he used, and how, that should tell us something about who he is. We might even get an ID."

"*We* aren't doing anything. You're not on this case anymore, remember?"

She just looked at him.

"Have Ben do it. Or Mark," he said. "But I don't want you involved."

"I'm aware of that."

"You're aware, but you plan to ignore me, right? God damn it, Laney."

She didn't bother answering. She figured her silence was answer enough.

● ● ●

"Not happening. We're not involving the FBI."

Reed looked at his lieutenant across the conference table and clenched his teeth. It wasn't the answer he'd wanted, but it was what he'd expected.

"Sir." Jordan cleared her throat. "I'm not sure you're seeing the implications—"

"I see just fine," he snapped. "And I'm telling you no. Everything's circumstantial. It's not enough."

"With all due respect, sir, what more do you need?" Jordan asked. "April Abrams's and Bella Marshall's murders are obviously connected. And now we have DNA evidence linking them to Olivia Hollis. That's three victims."

"And probably more," Reed said. "The Delphi Center's profiler believes he started well before now, maybe years ago. He believes he's pursuing a *list* of women, monitoring multiple targets."

"No FBI," Hall said firmly.

"What about ViCAP?" Jay asked. "If we could at least run it through their database of violent crimes—"

"No is no," Hall said. "I don't want the feds involved. Period. So far, we have two homicides in this city"—he

looked at Reed, as if daring him to contradict him—
"which is more than enough trouble. We don't need
to go advertising the fact that there's a serial killer out
there. The last thing we need is the FBI swooping in
here and setting up some task force and creating a
media circus. And that comes straight from the chief."
He crossed his arms and stuck out his chin, looking
remarkably like Reed's five-year-old nephew when he
didn't get his way.

Reed's temper festered. This went beyond turf wars.
Hall was protecting someone. Was it Mix.com or one of its
executives? Or was this whole thing coming down from
Aguilar, and the chief was protecting someone? Much of
Austin's economy was based on the rapidly growing tech
sector, and there were some pretty cozy relationships between the business community and city hall.

"We done here?" The lieutenant shoved back his
chair and stood, looking directly at Reed. "We'll meet
same time tomorrow. And by then I want a list of via-
ble suspects."

Hall walked out, leaving his top three detectives
staring after him.

"Anyone want to explain the stick up his ass?" Jordan asked.

"Got me," Jay said.

She looked at Reed.

"No idea."

But he planned to find out.

• • •

Veronica stood back to admire her work. The virtual
crime scene was perfect, down to the damaged wooden

finial at the top of the stair railing. She glanced up and down the hallway checking for inaccuracies, but the computer-generated image had everything. Only a few minor details, such as the fine dusting of sawdust on the floor and the smell of primer that permeated the air, hadn't been captured by the computer. But structurally speaking, everything was true to life.

"We ready, Veronica?"

She made a few adjustments, refusing to be hurried. Reed had been tapping his foot since he got here.

"It doesn't have to be perfect."

She looked up. "Are you doing this, or am I?"

Reed glanced at Jay, and Veronica read the message loud and clear. Yes, she was in a snippy mood, but they could just deal. She was having a rough week, and she was fed up with overbearing detectives who wanted everything yesterday and didn't see fit to tell her what was going on.

She made a final adjustment to the brightness of her image. "Okay, come take a look," she said, pivoting the computer on the portable stool she'd set up in the hallway outside Gantz's apartment. "See the chip in the doorframe there? Based on that and where the bullet entered the victim, we've been able to calculate the bullet trajectory." She tapped a few keys, and a red line appeared on the screen. The detectives eased closer.

"You sure that's accurate?" Reed asked.

"Are the measurements you gave me accurate?"

"Yeah."

"Then it's accurate," she said. "The victim is six-one, half an inch taller than that when you count the shoes he was wearing at the time of the shooting. So the bullet was fired from here"—Veronica pointed to a spot on the screen—"and followed the path delineated here, chipping the doorframe and then grazing the victim's cheek, shattering the bone before becoming lodged in the wall."

Reed and Jay looked back at the spot where the shooter would have been standing.

"So he was sheltered behind this corner," Jay said.

She nodded. "That's my take."

"He probably knocked on the door, moved back, and waited for Gantz to step out, then fired the shot," Reed said.

"Based on the blood spatter, it looks like Gantz stumbled backward, probably clutching his face as he fell," she said.

"That's when he closed in for the second shot to finish him off," Jay said.

"And that's where it gets interesting." She opened a new screen showing a different view of the hallway, this one much closer to the victim's door. "For the second shot, he stood about ten feet back and pointed the gun downward. That's consistent with the entry and exit wound you gave me." She glanced at Reed to confirm. "And you're sure those measurements are correct?"

"Talked to the surgeon myself." Reed walked over to the place where the shooter would have been standing for shot number two. He glanced at Veronica. "Your software program puts him here."

"That's right."

Reed's back was flush against the wall of the hallway. He unholstered his service weapon and pointed at the now empty spot in Edward Gantz's apartment. Veronica walked over with her laser pointer and used it to create a line from the muzzle of Reed's gun to the gouge on the floor where she'd recovered the slug after it passed through the victim's body.

"Lower." She adjusted his arm. "See? Which tells us he's shorter than you are. What's your height, six-two?"

Reed didn't answer, evidently lost in thought.

"Something's funny," Jay said.

Veronica nodded. "I agree."

"You'd expect him to walk right in there, stand over the guy, and finish the job," Jay said. "Instead, he stays out in the hallway."

"Also, he missed his first shot," Reed said. "He's hiding behind a corner waiting, his target steps into the hallway only fifteen feet away, and he basically hits him with a flesh wound."

"So we know it wasn't a very good shot," Veronica said.

"It was crap." Reed walked back to the spot in the hallway where the first bullet had originated. "Go back to the first view again."

Veronica pulled it up on the screen.

"See that?" Reed pointed. "Let's say he's standing here aiming at the target in the doorway. He's using the wall for cover." Reed held out his gun one-handed to demonstrate. "Either he aimed for the center body mass and the gun jerked up when he fired it, so he hit the guy's face. Or he was trying for a head shot, but his aim was off and he only grazed him. Then, instead of finishing him off up close, he stands out in the hallway."

"Even though he used a suppressor, this is no professional hit," Jay said. "This guy's an amateur. Everything about this shows hesitation."

"Exactly."

"So that puts a crimp in the feds' theory."

"What's the feds' theory?" Veronica asked.

Reed darted a warning look at Jay, but Jay answered anyway. "Feds think this was some kind of corporate-espionage thing, that Gantz probably pissed off someone powerful. But in that case, you'd expect a professional job."

"Well, what else would it be about?" She looked from Jay to Reed. "No drugs or cash stashed anywhere, and believe me, we turned the place inside out. And the victim isn't even moved in yet, so there wasn't much furniture to search. Our canine team was in and out of here in no time." She waited for him to offer another explanation. "If this isn't about drugs or money, what's it about?"

"Who knows?" Reed said with a shrug, and Veronica felt her annoyance returning. He was keeping his theories to himself.

Maybe this whole thing had to do with Reed's girlfriend, who happened to have been on the scene when everything went down. She was part of it, Veronica would bet her right arm.

Jay pulled out his phone. "I told you last night this thing was screwy," he said.

But Reed didn't answer. He walked over to the doorframe again, and the crease in his brow deepened. "And you're sure about these measurements?" He glanced at Veronica.

"*Yes*, Reed. Jesus."

He paced back to the top of the stairwell and examined the wall the shooter had presumably used for cover. Reed had that look that he got when something didn't add up. But in this case, it *did*. She'd just done the math for him. She'd walked him through a beautiful demonstration. His problem was that he didn't like the implications.

Nothing she could do about that. The facts were the facts, and they didn't lie. Unlike people. It was why Veronica preferred crime-scene reconstruction to eyewitness testimony any day of the week.

"And like I said, the shooter is shorter than you, based on these trajectories," she said. "That should help you a little, at least."

Reed didn't respond. She shook her head and started packing up her computer.

"Shit," Jay muttered. He glanced at Reed. "You read your email lately?"

That got his attention. "No. Why? We get a hit on the duct tape?"

"No, but we got that phone dump you wanted."

"Laney's phone?"

"Yeah, Laney's," Jay said. "And you're not going to like it."

CHAPTER 22

Baggins gave Laney the evil eye as she tapped in her alarm code and dropped an armload of mail on the counter.

"No sulking tonight, Baggins. For either of us."

She went straight into her bathroom, where she stripped off her T-shirt and splashed water on her face. She patted her cheeks dry with a towel and studied her reflection in the mirror.

A purple bruise had formed along her hairline from when she'd crashed into the wall in Scream's house. She leaned forward to examine it, touching it gently with her fingertips. Then she stood back to look at herself.

She felt drained and sore, like being hungover. And she couldn't remember every detail of last night, but certain ones stood out.

The sickening thud of Scream's body hitting the floor. The terrifying sound of footsteps pounding behind her in the dark stairwell.

And Reed.

She remembered the taste of his mouth and the warm slide of his hands. She remembered his breath against her neck when they were done, and she'd wanted to cling to him then, but instead she'd let her arms fall lax against the bed.

Those moments together in the dark had been bone-meltingly hot. But somehow everything seemed unreal to her now, as though it had all been a dream.

She sighed and tossed the towel into the sink, then went into the living room to pull out her laptop computer. She checked her email to see if there was any word on the decryption program she and Dmitry had been working on all day.

"Come on, come on," she muttered, skimming through messages.

Dmitry was their top encryption expert, but it would take him a while. Scream didn't just encrypt things, he *encrypted* them. And the thumb drive he'd given her last night before the shooting was no exception. She hadn't told Reed about the drive. Or the FBI. She didn't want anyone to know about it until she figured out what was on it.

Baggins hopped onto the table and rubbed his chin against the corner of her computer. Laney got up and filled his bowl, then took a quick look inside her fridge. Still empty. She returned to the futon, where she rummaged through her bag but didn't manage to find even a pack of Twizzlers.

She sat back and stared glumly at her screen. Physically, she was exhausted. She needed sleep, or she was headed for a systems crash. But she felt restless. Distracted. She'd felt that way all day.

She was totally off her game, and she blamed Reed. Not the night they'd spent together but his coffee-shop ambush. She'd known when she slipped out of his house that he'd get ticked off over it. She'd even figured he might be nursing a bruised ego. But at the coffee shop, she realized she'd actually managed to hurt him. Just a little but enough to put a pinch in her heart. He was a good man. And the way he'd touched her . . .

Well. No point in thinking about it now. She'd sabotaged any future they might have had by blowing him off this morning. And deep down, she knew she'd done it on purpose. She wasn't comfortable in relationships, especially with men, and she always managed to push them to the fringes of her life.

Laney put her computer to sleep and returned to the kitchen, this time for a look at her pantry.

Her phone chimed. Butterflies flitted in her stomach as she retrieved it from her bag and stared down at Reed's number. Should she answer it or not? She couldn't decide.

And then she decided she was being an idiot. She answered the phone.

"Hi," she said.

"Hi."

She could tell from the background noise that he was in his car or maybe outside.

"Are you alone?" he asked.

"Why?"

"I wanted to see if you'd like to have dinner."

The butterflies were back. "What, you mean now?"

"Yeah, tonight."

She picked up a bottle cap from the counter and spun it around. He was asking her out. Right now. It sounded like a date, but it wasn't. There was a tightness in his voice that told her something was wrong.

So not a date, then. She spun the bottle cap some more and considered it.

It was almost certainly a bad idea. They'd left things

how they'd left them, and that was good. She had what
she wanted, a clean break.

Not that there had been anything to break, really.
They'd spent a night together, which wasn't exactly a
relationship, but—

"You there?"

"I'm thinking," she said.

"You're making this too hard, Laney. Have you had
dinner or not?"

"Not."

"Then have it with me."

He sounded so confident. Not at all like a man nursing a wounded ego, and Laney's pulse picked up, because she liked that. Damn it, she was going to cave.

"Where did you want to go?" she asked.

"I was thinking Bangkok Palace."

It was her favorite restaurant. How on earth had he
known that? Of course, he hadn't. It was a lucky guess,
probably because it happened to be in her neighborhood.

"I prefer Jimmy's," she said. "It's a little sports bar
located—"

"I know it. Okay, Jimmy's it is. I'll pick you up in
fifteen minutes."

"Twenty," she said. "And I'll meet you there."

• • •

Laney's words from this morning ran through Reed's
mind again.

What else did you want?

It was a good question. What *did* he want? He wasn't
looking for a relationship. He hadn't been. They'd spent

the night together, and she'd let him off the hook, and he should be good with that. Relieved. But he wasn't good or relieved, he was pissed.

He wanted to see her alone again. He wanted to make her talk to him and spill her guts and tell him everything behind those dark, solemn looks.

He walked into Jimmy's and spotted her right away. She was perched on a stool at the far end of the bar and already had a beer in front of her, even though he was right on time. She wore a strappy black top—this one was cut lower than the others—and black jeans with biker boots. Reed stopped to watch her as she leaned forward to say something to the bartender.

He watched her moves, her body. How had he ever thought she looked girlish? She was all woman. And he knew now that those slender arms were strong, and those legs were powerful enough to make him lose his mind. He'd told himself he wasn't going to do this, but he wanted her again. Now. Tonight. He needed to rein in his thoughts before—

Too late. Her gaze zeroed in on him as he crossed the bar. He reached her stool, and she watched him as she tipped back her beer.

"You want to get a table?" he asked.

"Sure."

She motioned to the bartender to let him know they were moving, and Reed steered her to a booth. She ignored the menus tucked behind a green banker's lamp.

"What's good here?" he asked.

"Wings. But only if you like hot."

The waitress stopped by, and they both ordered wings. When she was gone, Laney leaned back against the seat and watched him, her expression unreadable.

She wore heavy black eyeliner, and she'd used makeup to conceal the bruise on her forehead.

She seemed content to let him kick off the conversation, so he started with what had to be on her mind.

"How's Edward doing?" he asked.

"Same."

Same wasn't good. Last Reed had checked, the man was in critical condition.

"I talked to his brother a couple hours ago." She turned her beer on the table. "He may need another surgery."

"His face?"

"His kidney. It's not responding like they wanted, so they might have to remove it, which is bad because he had kidney disease when he was a kid, so he's down to one already. They may need to do a transplant."

Reed watched her talk, unsettled by the pain he heard in her voice. She obviously cared about this guy.

"A transplant—that's serious but survivable."

"I know."

The waitress brought over Reed's beer.

"You know, if he makes it, the feds are going to want to interview him," Reed said.

"They're wasting their time. He won't talk to them, not unless he's doped up on painkillers or something. He hates cops."

"What about cops trying to solve his case?"

"He probably won't cooperate with them, either. He despises law enforcement."

"Why?"

"It's part of his antiauthoritarian philosophy. He hates all the federal antihacking laws, believes they're a form of thought control because they dictate what sort of code people can and can't write." She turned her beer on the table. "Computer code is really just language, so limiting it or banning it is like banning free speech. Scream thinks cops, especially federal ones, are essentially the thought police."

"What about you?"

She shrugged. "It's a fair point. Any program I write is essentially numbers and letters. It's a form of expression. Some people would even say it's an art form, like poetry."

"No, what do you think about cops?" He very much wanted to know.

"Depends," she said. "Some are good, some aren't."

The waitress appeared with two baskets of wings and dipping sauce. Reed watched Laney dig in.

"Don't say I didn't warn you." She nodded at his plate.

The wings were fire-hot, and he chased the first one down with a swig of Shiner.

"How's your investigation going?" she asked.

He tipped his eyebrows up.

"The murder investigation," she clarified.

"We're making progress."

"I saw a news story that Isabella's ex-husband was brought in for questioning?"

"He was," Reed said, keeping his tone neutral. It was a purely routine interview, and Reed knew he had Erika to thank for the carefully leaked news tidbit. It was a decent strategy, but she wouldn't be able to keep the attention on the victim's family for long, not with another homicide still so fresh in everyone's mind. And the minute the press got wind of the Olivia Hollis connection, forget it.

Laney wiped her hands on a napkin. "What is that, spin?"

"What?"

"It's standard procedure to interview the husband," she said. "So this focus-on-the-family thing, I'm guessing that's something your ex-wife cooked up?"

Reed stared at her. "You don't miss much, do you?"

"I've been around investigations." She picked up a wing and dipped it in sauce. "It won't work, you know. At best, it buys you a couple days' time."

He turned his attention to his food, not sure why he felt annoyed to hear her state the obvious. "We're developing other suspects."

"When?"

"Right now. As we speak." As he sat here having a beer with the woman who'd rocked his world last night. The woman he couldn't stop picturing naked. The woman whose soft, pleading sounds had been playing in his head all day.

Meanwhile, Jay and Jordan were still at the station toiling away on the case.

Laney was watching him now, her look intent. Could she read his thoughts? Just what he needed. Time to get to the point.

"This thing with Edward Gantz, the FBI believes it has to do with his business," Reed said. "They believe a corporation he hacked, or possibly one of his rivals, is out to kill him. Me? I believe they're wrong." He paused to watch her reaction. "Gantz's phone records tell a different story."

She didn't say anything or even move, but he could see her wheels turning.

"Any ideas on that?" he asked.

"Edward's phone records," she stated, her brow arched in disbelief.

"That's right."

She leaned back against the booth. "Edward has a no-contract phone. And I happen to know it's virtually untraceable."

"Virtually?"

"No, you're right. It *is* untraceable." She folded her arms over her chest. "Whose phone records are we talking about here?"

Reed watched her. He'd succeeded in getting her back up, which was his first objective. His second objective was to pin her down. She'd lied to him multiple times. Some of it was by omission, but still he couldn't let it go. Why wouldn't she tell him the full truth?

"Yesterday Gantz texted you," he said. "He said he had something for you."

"I can't believe this." She shook her head and looked away. "You didn't *guess* my favorite restaurant, you've been snooping through my goddamn phone, my emails. Violating my privacy. Have you pulled my credit card, too?"

He didn't answer.

"You're unbelievable, you know that?"

"You think?" He held her gaze. "Because from where I'm sitting, it seems totally believable. When you consider how we met."

Her eyes simmered, but she didn't argue. She didn't give a flip about privacy unless it was hers.

"Gantz gave you his address and told you to come at nine," he said. "You were early."

Fear crept into her eyes. "What are you saying?"

"I believe Gantz's attacker knows about you. I believe he knocked on Gantz's door intending for him to think it was you. I believe that person planned to kill Gantz *before* you showed up to hear about whatever Gantz knew. And then, when the shooter entered his apartment looking for any evidence of it, he was surprised to find you already there."

Her face was pale, her eyes big with dread. But she didn't look surprised.

She'd known this or at least suspected it. All he was doing was confirming her fear that someone was spying on *her* communications. And that she was a key reason her friend was near death right now. He saw the pain on her face, but there was no getting around it, and it was better this way, like tearing off a Band-Aid.

Or a strip of duct tape.

"I asked you to back off this case, Laney. But you didn't. I told you it was dangerous, and you ignored me. Now I'm not asking you, I'm telling you." He leaned forward. "Stay. The fuck. Away from this."

Something changed in her eyes. He watched it happen. The fear he'd been using to help drive home his point morphed into something else.

Defiance.

"You need me on this case, Reed, and don't act like you don't. If it weren't for me, you wouldn't even know about Mix."

"This thing goes way beyond that."

She scowled. "How?"

"Think about it, Laney." He stared her down, determined to get through to her. "What is the *one* thing that all these crimes have in common, including what happened to you and to Gantz? And it's not a dating site."

She just looked at him.

"This person is a hacker. Your boss said it himself—he inhabits the darknet." Reed waited a beat. "*So do you.* Look at your job. Look at how you got that job in the first place. Don't you see it?"

"See what?"

"You and this UNSUB operate in the same world. You crossed paths with him somewhere. You were one of his early targets, and you were lucky to survive that time, but now you've caught his attention again."

She was trying hard not to react, but he could tell his words were having an effect. He was scaring her, and he meant to. She was so damn headstrong, and he needed her to hear him.

"What do you expect me to do, Reed? Just walk away?" She sounded angry now. "This investigation needs me, and we both know it. Who are you going to get to do what I'm doing? Jay? Paul?" She shook her head. "You don't have the resources to find this guy. You don't even know where to look."

"Wrong," he said. "As of this morning, we've confirmed we're dealing with a serial offender. We can get FBI resources. We can use Quantico."

She sneered. "Right. Your chief—the same guy who's been trying to downplay this—is now suddenly willing to call in the cavalry?"

"It might take some convincing, but yes, he will be." Reed planned to make sure of it. "So we don't need your help anymore, Laney. You or the Delphi Center."

The look in her eyes chilled. Her mouth compressed into a thin line.

This date was going south fast. But it had never really been a date. From the moment he'd walked in here, he'd been working her into a corner, trying to force her to listen to him.

She picked up her purse.

"So that's the end of the conversation?"

She glared at him. "Nothing I say is going to change your mind, so why bother?"

"Laney, you know I'm right."

She pulled her wallet, and his temper heated.

"That's it? Things get uncomfortable, so you're leaving again?"

The *again* part pissed her off. He could see it.

She slapped some bills on the table and stood up. "You do your job, Reed. And I'll do mine."

CHAPTER 23

After Laney left him high and dry at the bar, he returned to the station house, hoping to work out his frustration on a mountain of reports. No dice. Around midnight, he drove home to his empty house, where his bottle of Jack was still out on the counter and Laney's ice cream spoon sat beside the sink. He ignored everything and went to bed, but her scent was all over his sheets. Finally, he gave up on sleep and parked himself on the couch, where he watched ESPN and was luckily spared a recap of his investigation on the local news. He figured his luck wouldn't last long, though, probably not past the morning staff meeting.

When he arrived at work and saw Erika in the lobby, he knew he'd been right. She strode over and greeted him with a perky smile.

"Good morning, detective."

"Hi."

"That's it? 'Hi'?" She batted her lashes at him. "How about a little thanks for the present I gave you yesterday?"

"Thanks."

She followed him toward the elevators, and he halted. This wasn't a conversation he wanted to have around other people.

"Why are you here, Erika?"

"I've got a meeting with the chief." She tipped her head to the side and smiled. "How's your little girlfriend?"

Little. Erika was six feet in heels, which made her a head taller than Laney. But she was referring to age.

"Who would that be?" He checked his watch.

"The pretty young techie I met back at the crime scene?"

Reed just looked at her. Had she actually *met* Laney? Reed hadn't seen it. But then, he hadn't been around Laney every second. He made a conscious effort to give her space when other people were around, something he seemed incapable of doing when they were alone.

"Did you need something?" He checked his watch again. "I've got a meeting in five."

"So do I. I just wanted to mention, that nice media diversion I kindly provided for you? That's not going to last."

"I'm aware."

"You might want to think about getting some actual suspects together. You know, before the case goes cold? We've got classes resuming at the university in two weeks."

"It's on my calendar, honey. I'll be sure to have things all wrapped up by then with a nice red bow."

"Stop being a smartass. I'm simply reminding you of the time frame. The mayor wants an arrest before school starts."

"Yeah? Well I've got three dead women to think about, so I've got a different time frame. I want an arrest before he does it again."

She watched him steadily. Shit. He'd just confirmed her suspicions. And she knew him too well for him to gloss over it.

"That's off the record," he said.

"You're telling *me* that? Like I'm some reporter?" She shook her head. "You're really amazing, you know that? I'm trying to help you. You guys are in some serious shit, Reed. You don't have anything, do you? Not even a suspect."

"Erika." He sighed. "Our team's busting ass on this thing, working around the clock."

"I'm sure you are." She gazed at him with fake sympathy. "Really, I can see it. You look tired, Reed. I'm sure it's tough keeping up with those young members of your *team*, isn't it?" She smiled sweetly. "But hey, good news for you—they have a pill for that."

Fuck the elevator. Reed took the stairs. He reached the bullpen and nearly bumped into Veronica charging out of the break room.

"Whoa. Where's the fire?"

"Have you seen Hall?" she asked.

"No. What's wrong?"

She cast a furtive look over Reed's shoulder. "I just got the ballistics report back on that shooting," she said in a low voice.

"And?"

"It isn't good."

• • •

Reed ushered her into an interview room and closed the door.

"You've got two minutes," he said. "Spill."

Veronica's pulse was racing. Her stomach was in knots. She hated being the bearer of bad news.

She took a deep breath. "I recovered two slugs from

Gantz's apartment building, one from the wall and one from the floor. Based on the witness's statement, the weapon used had a suppressor."

"And?"

"One slug yielded zip." She sliced the air with her hand. "Totally deformed. The other one was usable. I photographed it myself using microphotography, and the rifling marks looked good. Then I sent it to the Delphi lab. And the shooter picked up his brass in the hallway, but we recovered cartridge cases in the stair-well from the shots fired at Delaney Knox. I sent those to Delphi, too."

His eyebrows arched impatiently.

"We got a hit." She swallowed. "This gun's in the sys-tem." She opened the file and read the words. "A Sig P226 nine-millimeter. It was used in a drug shooting back in 2012."

Hope sparked in Reed's eyes. "That's a good lead."

"No, wait. There's more." She glanced down at the report again. "The weapon, along with an Osprey for-ty-five suppressor, was recovered from the apartment of a previously convicted dealer, Carlos Garza, just last fall. He's been charged with murder two, plus posses-sion with intent to sell. He's in lockup now awaiting trial." She glanced up, and Reed was frowning.

"*Awaiting* trial."

"That's right."

"So the gun—"

"Should still be in evidence right now, yes."

But clearly it wasn't.

Unless there was some mix-up and the gun had been misidentified.

Reed stared down at her. "You're sure—"

"I'm not sure of anything! I'm just telling you what the report says." She held it up. "But if this isn't some mix-up, then we've got a serious problem. A weapon from our evidence room somehow managed to end up back on the street. Hall is going to go apeshit, and I have to tell him about this."

"Forget Hall. Aguilar is going to go apeshit."

"You're saying I shouldn't tell the lieutenant?" She instantly felt guilty for even suggesting it. She was desperate to avoid an unpleasant conversation.

"Don't tell Hall," Reed said.

"You want me to go over his head?"

"Yeah, I do."

She stared at him.

"I don't trust Hall," he said bluntly. "He's been acting strange."

The knot in her stomach tightened again. Whatever this was, it was going to be bad, and she was right in the middle of it.

"You're worried," Reed said.

"Uh, *yeah*."

"I'll do it." He nodded at the report. "I'll take it to the chief."

"No, I'll do it," she said. "I submitted it, right? It's my job."

• • •

Reed watched his lieutenant's body language as he took a seat at the end of the table.

"So where are we on suspects? Novak?"

"You mean the Abrams homicide?"

"Let's start with the law student, Isabella Marshall."

"We had her ex-husband, Michael Spencer, in for an interview yesterday. So far, his alibi checks out."

"What about his financials?" Hall asked.

"She didn't get much in the divorce," Jordan said, "but there was nothing much to get. The marriage only lasted two years. He told us they didn't really keep in touch, and the family corroborates that."

Hall didn't look happy. "Anyone else?"

"An ex-boyfriend," Jay said. "Her sister told us he was bothering her six months ago, so we checked him out."

"And?"

"Guy says he was in Reno on a business trip. We confirmed it with the airline."

"Okay, what about the Abrams woman? Any suspects?"

Reed consulted his notes. "So far . . . we have Ian Phelps. Again, the alibi seems to hold. He was captured on surveillance video leaving his office building at one fifteen A.M. the night of the murder, so the timing is tight but not impossible. Another person of interest is Dmitry Burkov."

"Who?" Hall asked.

"A local computer expert who has a rap sheet. He and April have some mutual friends, and he has the skills to hack into a website like Mix. Problem is, I checked him out, and his supervisor tells me he was at work on the night of the murder."

"We should look at Phelps again," Jay said. "Did Paul copy you on his email?"

"No. What?"

"Just a sec." Jay got up and left the room, and Reed checked his phone. No email from Paul.

A second later, Jay was back with the man in tow.

"Tell them about the secret account," Jay said.

Paul glanced around the room. "I, um . . . you remember the notebook computer recovered from April Abrams's car? I've been going through the browser history, and I found a second email account. On Gmail. She had some exchanges with Ian Phelps."

"When?" Reed asked.

"Starting last summer until a month ago, I think it was. So about eleven months. Then she started getting delivery notices, so it looks like he closed his account down."

"Is this guy married?" Hall asked.

"He's got a fiancée," Reed told him. "But he denied having any kind of romantic relationship with April, so I'll need to check this out."

"I don't get it," Jordan said. "What's Phelps's connection to Isabella Marshall? And Olivia Hollis?"

"Maybe none if the crimes are unrelated," Hall said hopefully. He looked at Paul. "What's on the emails?"

"Mostly setting up dates and times to meet. Nothing explicitly sexual, but they point to a relationship." He paused. "I can print them out if you like."

"Do it," he said, and Paul scuttled out of the room.

"It doesn't really add up." Jordan looked at Reed. "Can we talk to Delaney Knox? Find out if Ian Phelps has anything to do with this dating site?"

"I'll ask her."

"The connection to Mix is flimsy," Hall said. "There are probably thousands of local people on that site. Seems to me it's more likely a jealous-mistress scenario. Maybe April Abrams threatened to go to Phelps's fiancée and he wanted to get rid of her."

"Wait, back up," Veronica said. "Why are we ignoring the physical evidence?" She opened the file in front of her and tapped her finger on a report. "We have DNA telling us these crimes were committed by the same perpetrator. It's a serial offender."

"We don't know that," Hall said. "It's circumstantial. We don't have proof."

"I'm sorry, but . . . what more proof do you want, sir?" She pulled out a pair of crime-scene photos and slid them across the table. The pictures showed two young women on the floor with their skulls smashed in. "We have the same MO, the same murder weapon, and DNA linking the crime scenes together. Isn't it time to get some help from the FBI?"

"She's right," Reed said. "Instead of running away from this thing, the chief should view it as an opportunity."

"An opportunity for what?" Hall demanded. "To announce that there's a serial killer running around targeting young women through social media? We'll start a panic. And what do you suggest we do while we look for him, shut down the Internet? That's not a plan."

"But we've got DNA evidence of something that spans multiple jurisdictions," Reed said. "We need to bring in outside resources."

"We have. We've got that cyber unit, those people at the Delphi Center."

"Yeah, they gave us a profile," Jay said. "It says we're looking for a middle-aged white guy with a history of depression. I could have told you that. As a kid he was probably a bed wetter who liked to torture animals. Where does that get us?"

"The profiler thinks he's been doing this for a while," Reed said, "so we really need ViCAP. We might be able to dig up something where there's a similar MO. Maybe even a case where DNA or prints were recovered."

"No FBI," Hall said. "I repeat: *no feds*. That's from the chief. So quit bitching about it, and roll up your sleeves and do some old-fashioned detective work. Go through the interviews, the alibis. We're bound to have missed something. Work our list of suspects." Hall stood up, effectively ending the meeting. "This Phelps guy lied to us, which means he's hiding something, so find out what it is. As of now, he's our prime suspect."

CHAPTER 24

"You don't really think this is some guy bumping off his mistress, do you?"

Reed looked at Jay in the passenger seat. "No. Why?"

"Then why are we wasting our time with him?"

Reed didn't have a good answer. Laney had insisted from the beginning that Ian Phelps wasn't their man. And he was inclined to agree with her.

"He lied to me," Reed said. "So it's worth a conversation."

Was it a personal hang-up? Maybe. He'd had a thing about people lying to him ever since he'd caught Erika screwing around on him. He could probably get past it if he was willing to sit in a therapist's office for a few hundred bucks an hour and rehash all his emotional bullshit, but Reed would rather hold a gun to his head.

"Well, Laney knows him, right? I saw them talking at the funeral," Jay said. "If he stonewalls us, we can get her to feel him out, see if he knows anything useful."

"I told her to stay out of it."

"You told her."

"Yeah, this has gotten dangerous. I told her to leave it alone."

Jay shook his head. "Man, bad idea. You used to be married, too. You should know better."

"What?"

"Girl's a hacker. Finding ways into restricted areas is what she does. Telling her to stay out of it, you just issued her a challenge."

Reed didn't say anything.

"So what was that with Veronica before the meeting?" Jay asked.

Reed glanced at him. Jay definitely had a thing for the woman.

"She got the ballistics back on the Gantz shooting. Could be something useful there, but I have to do some more checking."

Reed didn't volunteer anything more. He planned to follow up, but he had other problems to tackle at the moment. He turned onto the street for ChatWare Solutions and glanced up and down the sidewalk. It was busy with pedestrians, lots of Austinites out enjoying the sunny Friday afternoon.

There were no free parking meters so he pulled their unmarked police unit into a loading/unloading space behind a minuscule Smart car. They climbed out, and Jay shook his head.

"I couldn't get my big toe in one of those things." He looked at Reed as they walked down the sidewalk. "You think Phelps is at his office? These sales guys travel."

Reed focused on the café on the corner. "He's in town. Looks like he's having a late lunch."

They walked to Francesca's, where the chalkboard menu listed the day's specials. Reed cut around the sign and approached Ian's table. He was on the phone again, and his expression darkened when he noticed Reed.

Reed took a chair to Phelps's right. Jay took the one on the left. The man's gaze shifted from Reed to Jay and back to Reed again.

"Um, so listen. I've got to go. I'll call you back later." Phelps put his phone down and squared his shoulders. "Detective Novak." He glanced at Jay. "And you are . . . ?"

"Detective Wallace." Jay flashed his badge, and Phelps darted a nervous look around the umbrella tables.

"I'd love to talk to you guys, but—"

"This won't take long," Jay said, settling back in his chair and taking a comfortable look around. "Nice place for a coffee break. We need one of these at the station."

Phelps pushed away the half-finished cappuccino in front of him and sat back in his chair, pretending to be relaxed. "What can I do for you?" His gaze settled on Reed.

"I asked you about your relationship with April. You told me you were friends. We'd like to revisit that topic."

"There's nothing between me and April. I told you—"

Reed held up his hand. "We have the emails, Ian, so don't waste our time. I want to know when it started."

Phelps clenched his teeth and stared at him.

Jay reached over and grabbed a scone from the plate beside the coffee. "Mind? I love these."

Phelps glanced at him, then at Reed. "Last summer. It was on again, off again, totally casual."

Reed lifted an eyebrow. "Yeah?"

"Yeah."

"So when's the wedding?" Jay asked around a mouthful of food. "I hear you're getting married."

Phelps shot Reed a glare. He looked down as he composed his story, then glanced up. "I broke it off with April weeks ago, way back in June."

"Yeah?"

"Yes. And that has nothing to do with . . . what happened to her."

Reed looked at Jay.

"Hey, I've got another question for you." Jay finished off the scone and dusted his hands over the table. "What do you know about computers?"

"What?" Phelps looked startled.

"Computers." Jay paused. "You know, those machines—"

"What does this have to do with anything?" He looked across the table, and Reed gave a shrug. He looked back at Jay. "I work at a software company."

"And what do you do there?" Jay asked. "You write code, answer phones, what?"

"I sell software. I meet with clients and manage relationships." He looked at Reed.

"Would it be fair to say you're more the 'Chat' side than the 'Ware'?" Reed asked.

"Both. What does this have to do with April?"

"We're just curious."

He sighed and looked at his watch. "I have a meeting—"

"One last question," Reed said. "You ever heard of a website called Mix?"

"Mix?"

"It's a dating site."

"I know what it is. But I don't use dating sites. I mean, come on." He smiled. "Women come to me."

"Is that what happened with April?" Reed asked. "She came to you? Or was it more like you were dogging her, getting some on the side, and she got sick of hearing about your upcoming wedding?"

"I broke up with *her*."

"Really?" Jay asked. "And she did what then, threatened to rat you out to your fiancée? And then you two had a fight? Maybe you had to get a little rough with her, show her who was in charge?"

"April and I had a consensual relationship. I broke it off. Read the emails if you don't believe me. You think I chased *her*? Right." He looked at Reed, and there was a hint of desperation in his eyes now. "*I* broke things off. I let go. Period. I'm not the guy who did this. I'm not some stalker. Go find someone else to harass." He tossed his napkin onto the table and stood up. "I've got a meeting."

"Wait." Reed put his hand on his arm.

He sat down, fuming.

"Why'd you say 'stalker'?"

Phelps looked confused. "What?"

"You said you're not the guy. You're not some stalker."

"I don't know." Phelps looked from Reed to Jay. "She was being stalked by this guy, right?"

"Where'd you get that?" Jay asked.

"I don't know. In the paper, probably."

Reed shook his head. "Nope."

"Online? I must have read it somewhere."

"Try again." Reed watched for a moment. He leaned forward on his elbows. "Did April ever tell you someone was stalking her?"

"Not really." He glanced at Jay. "Not in so many words."

"What words?" Reed asked.

"She just mentioned, I don't know, some creep at her gym. Some guy who'd watch her from his car in the parking lot."

"His car?" Jay leaned closer. "What kind of car?"

"How the hell would I know?"

"What else did she say about him?"

"That was it. We didn't talk about it."

"Sounds like you did," Reed said.

"That was all she said. It was just that one time she mentioned it."

"When was this?"

"You want a date? I have no idea."

"A few weeks ago, months ago, when?" Reed persisted.

"Sometime before we broke up."

"When?"

He sighed, exasperated. "Probably five, six weeks ago. One of the last times before I broke it off with her."

"Where were you?" Reed asked.

"At my place."

"Where was your fiancée?" Jay asked.

"This was during lunch. She met me over there from work. Afterward she was getting dressed, and she mentioned wanting to switch gyms because this guy kept watching her from the parking lot. It had happened the night before, I think."

Reed looked at Jay. They might be able to pin down the date through the emails. And then they might be able to drum up a surveillance tape from the gym. And then they might get a glimpse of the UNSUB or, better yet, his car.

It was a lot of mights, but it was a lead.

"See, here's the problem, Ian." Reed leaned forward on his elbows. "You lied to me about one thing. How do I know you're not lying about this?"

"I'm not."

"She say anything else?" Jay asked.

"No."

"You're sure?"

"Yes. I told you. She barely mentioned it." He stood up and grabbed his phone off the table.

Reed and Jay stood, too.

"Don't be late for that meeting," Jay said.

Phelps glared at them, and Reed handed him another business card.

"Call me if you think of anything else," he said. "We'll be in touch."

• • •

Mix occupied a converted loft downtown, only a few blocks away from the converted loft where Laney had once worked. She looked up and down the street, noting all the expensive cars. Hard to believe this was her old stomping grounds. Amid the office buildings were construction zones crammed with bulldozers and dump trucks. Cranes towered above everything, harbingers of the coming sprawl.

When she'd been a student at UT, Austin had been artsy and eclectic, with tucked-away street markets and hole-in-the-wall music venues. But with every new Starbucks and parking garage and Pilates studio, she felt a shift in the city's personality. It was growing, thanks in part to the tech sector, and Laney didn't mind the modernization. But there was something lacking in all of it. More cars, more high-rises, and yet there was a sense of alienation beneath it, an underlying loneliness. Plenty of people on the street but all glued to their phones. Everyone was perpetually connected, but to what?

She passed the Mix building and hung a left. She circled the block looking for a space, but every spot was full, and she cursed the Friday traffic as her phone chimed with a call from the Delphi Center.

"Hey," Ben said. "Dmitry tells me you need a hand with something. Where are you, anyway?"

"I'm at Mix again. I need you to see if it's possible to get in remotely. I've tried. Scream tried. But neither of us had any success."

"Then I'm guessing I'll have the same result."

"This man had to get in somehow."

"Maybe you're making this overly complicated," Ben said. "Could be something as simple as one of their portable devices being compromised, like a laptop or a tablet. He could have gained access that way."

"The company did away with employee laptops," Laney said. "Don't you remember? It was one of the first things we recommended to beef up their security."

"Yeah, but you know how those executive types are. Always think the rules don't apply to them. Even if they got rid of laptops for the rank and file, I guarantee you the executives still have them, and something could have been stolen."

She circled the block, scanning the streets for an open space. No free meters, but she saw Ian Phelps walking down the sidewalk. He didn't notice her—he looked to be in a hurry. Laney pulled up to the light and checked her rearview mirror.

She spotted Reed. He was standing on the sidewalk in front of Francesca's putting on sunglasses. Jay stepped up beside him, and they started walking toward an unmarked police car. Damn it, they'd been wasting time with Ian again.

"Fine, don't listen to me," she muttered.

"What's that?"

"Nothing."

"So what are you planning to do there?"

"There's a Java Stop half a block down," she said. "Thought I'd set up there, see if I can hop on their Wi-Fi and maybe find an open port."

"Sounds like a long shot."

"Well, I have to try something. He's killed three people in the greater Austin area." And that wasn't counting Laney's attack. "Plus, Mix.com is headquartered here. There's no way all that's a coincidence."

"Laney?"

"What?"

"Maybe you should take a break from this thing. You sound stressed."

"I am stressed! I think he's *here*, Ben. I think he has been for years, watching this company from the ground up, figuring out how to exploit its vulnerabilities. This whole thing's a sick game to him."

"One way or another, we'll pin him down, Lane. You know we will. They always leave a trace."

"Yeah, we just have to find it."

CHAPTER 25

Laney would have made a terrible PI.

She didn't like surveillance. Or waiting. And her bladder wasn't suited for spending long stretches of time in her car. But she'd been sitting in it for hours now, running tests. She'd found no open ports that could be exploited, no sign of any rogue wireless devices. She sat behind the wheel with her laptop open, keeping her eye on the Mix building as she exhausted her array of assessment tools.

She hadn't found anything, but there had to be a back door. And if she couldn't locate a digital one, she'd have to find a real one.

She surveyed the building through her windshield. From her parking space near Java Stop, she had a clear view of not only Mix's front entrance but a side door where employees had been popping in and out all evening. It was eight forty on Friday, nearing peak traffic time for Mix, and it looked like employees were dashing out for a last-minute coffee break before settling in for the night shift.

The phone chimed in the cup holder, and her pulse jumped at the sight of Reed's number. She hesitated a moment before picking up.

"Hey, it's me," he said in that easygoing voice. He sounded totally relaxed, as though their last conversation hadn't ended with her walking out on him. "Can you talk? I've got a couple of random questions for you."

"Yes, I can talk, and no, Ian Phelps was never on Mix."

For a few seconds, nothing. "How the hell did you know I was going to ask that?"

"Lucky guess," she said, although she doubted he'd believe her. He probably thought she was still spying on his phone.

"Okay, next question. This one's about you." He paused, and she could sense she wasn't going to like what he had to say. "Three years ago, around the time when you were attacked at home, were you a member of a gym?"

"No," she said. "I am now, but back then I wasn't."

"Is your gym, by any chance, Power Fitness over on Fifth Street?"

"It's Manny's Martial Arts over on Lamar. I take kickboxing. Why?"

"Just wondering."

Laney's mind was racing with possibilities. "April was a member at Power Fitness. Did you get a new lead?"

He didn't respond, and she felt a twinge of annoyance. Of course he didn't respond. He couldn't tell her about the case anymore, not now that she was officially banned from working on it.

"Anything else you want to ask me?"

"Yeah," he said. "How's your day going?"

She felt a warm tingle at the sound of the words and settled deeper in her seat. Until a minute ago, she'd been hot and frustrated, but now his voice was a welcome distraction. She actually loved his voice. It was low and masculine and sexy. Maybe she should tell him. *Hey, Reed, you have a knack for pissing me off, but when I hear your voice, I get all melty inside.*

Right. She couldn't imagine words like that ever leaving her mouth.

"It's fine," she said. "I'm still working, though."

"Yeah, same here. I wanted to see if you'd like to have dinner later."

The invitation surprised her. She stared through the windshield at everyone trickling in and out of Mix's side door. It was almost nine, and she wasn't nearly finished yet.

"You there?" Reed asked.

"Our last dinner didn't exactly go well."

"Okay, let's get drinks, then. Or frozen yogurt. Hell, I don't know. I just want to see you."

Laney bit her lip. When he'd told her to stay the fuck away, he'd meant the case, not him. But just thinking about their last conversation brought a lump of resentment to her throat.

"You're doing it again," he said.

"What?"

"That silence thing you do. You know, it's hell on my ego."

"Ha. Your ego is fine."

"So can I see you?"

He wanted to see her tonight. Badly. And she wanted to see him, too.

"I'm finishing something for a client," she said. "I should be home by ten thirty or so. You could come over."

In other words, she wanted to see him, but she didn't

want to go out. She hoped that being a clever detective and all, he'd get her meaning.

"I'll bring dinner," he said, definitely getting it. "Call me when you're on your way home."

They hung up, and Laney stared down at her phone, wondering if she'd made a mistake. Her heart was thudding. Her cheeks felt warm. And just the thought of seeing him soon made her insides tighten.

Her walking out in a huff the other night hadn't scared him away. Not even close. He was still pushing to see her, to spend time with her.

What the hell was she doing with this man? She had no idea. She'd been content with her routine. Not just content, she'd liked it. She spent her time immersed in work. And when she wasn't working, she went home and slid into her own private computer world, walling herself off from people and relationships and all the complications that went with them.

But now she felt restless. She wanted to talk to someone. Specifically, Reed. And not just talk to him, she wanted to be with him. She wanted to see his blue eyes go smoky with desire for her. *Her.* That was the most amazing part, the part that made her all warm and fizzy inside. He wanted *her*, and she felt giddy just thinking about it.

She glanced through her windshield again as a steady stream of Mix employees returned to work with their last-minute caffeine fix. Laney checked her watch. Now or never.

She shut down her laptop and hid it under a hoodie in the backseat. Then she settled a baseball cap on her head and grabbed her cup from Java Stop. She'd finished the coffee, but that didn't matter, since it was only a prop.

She slipped out of her car, locked it, and pretended to be focused on her phone as she joined the trickle of people returning to Mix.

A pair of women about Laney's age reached the building and veered into the side street. They were followed by a lone guy, also midtwenties, who had his phone out and was furiously texting. The woman in the lead pulled out her badge and swiped her way into the building. Her friend followed her, then held the door open for the guy behind her, who in turn held it for Laney.

"Thanks," she mumbled, not looking up as she followed him into the building, acutely aware of the security camera mounted above the door.

Laney's pulse was racing as the door whisked shut behind her. She was in an interior stairwell now, and all the traffic was going up. Laney went with the flow and ended up on the second floor in a carpeted hallway, where she spotted a ladies' room and peeled off from the group.

She ducked into a stall and stood there, breathing hard. Her heart was pounding. Her back felt sweaty. But she was in. It had been easier than she'd expected. Stupidly easy. She looked the part of a software geek, and the UNSUB probably had, too.

Laney took a deep, steadying breath. She was inside—now what?

From the hallway, she'd glimpsed a large room filled with cubicles. It was a bullpen, but for which department? Since the late-shifters had all gone in that direction, she guessed it was tech support. The maze of cubes was a social environment, which meant she had to stay away or risk getting caught. In any case, the office she wanted would be in a different area. Her people were introverts.

Someone entered the bathroom. Laney waited to hear the neighboring stall open and close and then made a quick production of washing her hands before slipping out. Back in the hallway, she turned away from the room with the cubicles and headed in the opposite direction, where she spotted a door conveniently labeled AUTHORIZED PERSONNEL ONLY. She opened it and found herself in a carpeted hallway lined with doors.

The hallway was dim and quiet. This was more like it. She walked briskly, reading the placards as she went. Most of the rooms were simply numbered, but a few were named: BUILDING MAINTENANCE, STORAGE, ELECTRICAL. It was the sort of space that code grinders liked to inhabit, and she sensed she was nearing her objective. She reached a closed door marked SYSTEM ADMINISTRATOR. Even without the label, she would have guessed it by the *Dilbert* and *xkcd* cartoons taped to the door.

Laney glanced up and down the hallway. She listened for footsteps or voices but heard nothing aside from the faint hum of a vacuum in a distant hallway. She tried the door. Open.

She slipped inside, heart galloping now. The door being unlocked was both good and bad. Good because her luck seemed to be holding but bad because no system admin worth his salt would leave his office unlocked overnight. The Styrofoam cup and half-eaten sandwich on the desk confirmed her theory that whoever worked here had stepped away only momentarily.

She glanced around the office, quickly taking inventory of numerous piles of paperwork, the shelves crammed with software manuals, the jewel-encrusted picture frames lined up on top, collecting dust. It was a woman's office, and she had about the same penchant for neatness as Laney.

In the center of the desk was a large PC with a kaleidoscope screen saver. Laney stepped behind the desk and tapped the wireless mouse, bringing up a login screen.

Damn.

She had no leads on the admin's password. She tried a few keyboard walks, to no avail. The thumb drive in her pocket contained a password cracker, but that would take time. Laney reached over and touched the Styrofoam cup. Still cold. She glanced at the door.

This was it. She could feel it. This was the soft, vulnerable underbelly of Mix's security system, a vulnerability she felt sure their UNSUB had exploited. He'd been here, right where she stood. Laney knew it in her bones, just as she knew that even the most sophisticated firewalls and passwords in the world were powerless to combat human stupidity.

Laney's gaze fell on the wireless keyboard. She stared at it a moment and got a ticklish feeling on the back of her neck.

"Son of a bitch," she muttered.

She glanced under the desk for anything unusual plugged into the wall or the power bar. Nothing. She stood up and looked around. On the far wall was a file cabinet with a stack of binders sitting on top. She crept over, then paused to glance at the door. No footsteps in the hallway, no voices. She pressed her shoulder against the cabinet and moved it away from the wall.

Binders thudded to the floor. Laney froze. She shot a look at the door but didn't hear anyone.

She glanced behind the cabinet and spotted another outlet, and this one should have been empty, but there was a small black device plugged into it.

Laney's breath caught. She crouched down, pulse racing. *He's been here. Right in this very spot.*

The keylogger could sniff keystrokes out of thin air and either record them internally or transmit them. And here it was hidden away in the office of Mix's chief system administrator, whose passwords, even if they were changed frequently, would provide universal access to the entire system.

The sudden howl of a vacuum made her jump. She looked at the door and then glanced at the keylogger again. She itched to pluck it from the wall and examine it more closely, but something made her hesitate.

The vacuum noise grew louder. Damn it, she couldn't spend any more time here. She took her phone from her pocket and snapped a picture.

She stood up and moved the file cabinet back. She hurriedly replaced the fallen binders, then paused beside the door and took a deep breath to compose herself. The janitor was between her and the door she'd originally come through, so she'd have to either walk right past him or go in the other direction.

As calmly as she could, she stepped from the office and walked away from the janitor, only catching a brief glimpse of a black-haired man pushing a vacuum. Laney busied herself with her phone as she waited for him to call out to her, but he didn't. She pushed through another door marked AUTHORIZED PERSONNEL ONLY and found herself in yet another carpeted hallway leading to a room filled with cubicles. The space was dark, and the desks were empty. The advertising department, maybe? She skimmed the room and tried to decide on an exit route.

A loud squawk had her turning around just as a man rounded the corner. A security guard holding a walkie-talkie.

Laney froze, phone in hand. Then she turned on her heel and walked in the opposite direction, struggling to keep her gait casual as she exited the door she'd just entered.

Be calm. Be calm.

"Hey!" he called.

The door whisked closed behind her. Laney kept going, making a brisk path straight past the janitor.

Stay calm. No sudden movements.

The vacuum stopped, and she heard the door being opened behind her.

"Hey! You there, this is a restricted area."

Laney plowed through the door, ignoring the rent-a-cop.

"Hey!"

She raced past the bathroom she'd used and ducked into the stairwell. She flew down the steps and ran straight for the door.

Locked.

Her heart lurched as she read the sign posted at eye level: THIS DOOR LOCKED AFTER 9 P.M.

She darted a look upstairs as the door burst open. She glanced around, then dashed down a dim brick hallway. She reached another stairwell and tried the door. Locked.

More squawking noises, followed by low talking as the security guard said something into his radio.

Laney ran down the hallway, following the exit signs in search of another way out. She rounded a corner. Another exit. Relief flooded her. She reached the door and noticed the sign: FIRE EXIT ONLY.

Footsteps in the hallway.

Laney shoved through the door, setting off an ear-piercing shriek. She was in an alley behind the building. She glanced around frantically and realized it wasn't an alley but a narrow parking lot surrounded by a tall metal fence.

She took off for the gate. The parking lot was empty except for a pair of rusty Dumpsters. Adrenaline flooded her system as the fire alarm screamed in her ears. She sprinted for the gate, spying the heavy chain securing it as she got closer.

"Crap!"

She hazarded a glance over her shoulder as the door opened and the guard burst out. His face was flushed as he barked into his radio, then took off after her.

Laney yanked on the wire mesh, creating a gap between the gate and the fence but not wide enough to squeeze through. She glanced at the top of the fence. No razor wire, at least.

"Hey! Freeze!"

Yeah, right. What was he going to do, throw his walkie-talkie at her? She kicked off her flip-flops, then grabbed hold of the wire mesh and clawed her way up the fence as the guard's footsteps slapped on the pavement behind her.

She reached the top and threw her leg over, manag-

ing to snag her T-shirt. Her heart was pounding. Her
cap fell off. But she was almost there. Just a few more
seconds, and she'd be running for her car. She wouldn't
look at the guard as she jerked her shirt free and threw
her other leg over.

Almost there, almost there, almost there.

A loud *whoop*. A screech of tires.

Laney dropped to the pavement right in front of a
police car.

• • •

Reed bumped into Jordan on his way out.

"Hey, we were just looking for you," she said. "Come
see what we got."

Reed followed her into the computer lab where Veronica was seated in front of a screen. He leaned over
her shoulder and studied the grainy video image.

"This is surveillance footage from Power Fitness,"
Jordan said. "Based on the emails between April
Abrams and Ian Phelps, we were able to identify the
day of their last lunchtime rendezvous before Phelps
supposedly broke things off."

"He indicated it was back in June," Reed said.

"That's right."

He glanced at his watch. Two hours, and still he
hadn't heard anything from Laney.

"Hey, we holding you up?" Veronica asked.

"No."

"Working backward from that date," Jordan continued, "we went back a week and checked the footage from all three nights when the victim visited her
gym. This would be right before she allegedly told

Phelps someone was stalking her or watching her at her gym."

Reed leaned closer. It was a view of a parking lot, and he recognized April's powder-blue BMW parked at the end of the row. Veronica pointed to a woman with a ponytail walking toward the car while talking on her phone.

"Here she is Monday night, leaving the gym." She pointed to a dark green car. "And see this Volkswagen Beetle back here? This car pulled in right after she did, but no one got out. It's been sitting there more than an hour. Now watch what it does."

Reed watched as April got into her car, talked on the phone for a few more moments, then backed out of her space and drove away.

The VW's lights went on. It slowly backed out of its space and left the parking lot in the same direction as the Beemer.

"What about the other nights?" Reed looked at Jordan.

"Same thing happens again two nights later, only this time she pauses before she reaches her car, like maybe she noticed the guy."

"Zoom in on that car," Reed said, getting excited now. A vehicle was a critical lead because it could be traced to a person.

"We already did," Veronica said. "What you're seeing is as close as it gets without losing resolution. And we don't have an angle on the license plate or even a glimpse of the driver."

"About all we can get from this shadow in the driver's seat is his height," Jordan said, "which looks to me to be about average."

Veronica replayed the footage. Reed straightened up and crossed his arms over his chest as he stared down at the screen.

"That looks like an old-model Beetle," he said. "Maybe a seventy-eight?"

"Good eye." Veronica nodded. "It's a seventy-nine Volkswagen Beetle, forest green."

"So assuming it *is* the killer who's following her here," Jordan said, "that means we at least have his car now."

"And you really think it's him, not just some guy who noticed her at the gym?" Veronica looked at Reed.

"The timing fits," Reed said. "This is just a few weeks before the murder. And we know he likes to watch them. He got into her computer and installed spyware. I wouldn't be surprised if he was monitoring her text messages and emails, basically tracking her every move. He's probably jerking off in his car while he watches her."

Veronica cringed. "What a sicko."

"I'm no profiler," Jordan said, "but the car seems to fit the pattern, too."

Reed looked at her. "How's that?"

"Well, it's a seventy-nine VW Bug."

He nodded. "Ted Bundy drove a Beetle."

"Whoa, really?" She made a face. "I didn't know that. That's not what I meant. I'm saying it's an old car, practically a classic. And we know the murder weapon is a body hammer, so . . . you see what I'm getting at?"

"You think he's a car buff," Reed said.

"Maybe." She shrugged. "Could be he fixes cars and whatever else. We know that he's technically inclined, right? Maybe that includes cars."

"Yeah, maybe he's one of those tinkerer guys," Veronica said. "He was probably in the computer club when he was a kid. And the Lego club."

"Hey, now. I was in the Lego club."

They turned around to see Jay leaning against the doorway. He looked at Reed just as Reed's phone buzzed. He was hoping for Laney, but it was Erika's number.

Reed stepped out of the room and answered it.

"It wasn't me," she said.

"What wasn't you?"

"You haven't seen the news?"

Reed checked his watch. "What channel?"

"All of them."

He walked into a conference room and switched on a television. It was already tuned to a local news station. A blond anchorwoman sat at a desk giving a stern-faced report. The graphic over her shoulder proclaimed, DATE NIGHT KILLER STRIKES AGAIN.

"God damn it."

"They're quoting a source close to the investigation," Erika said, "and I'll tell you right now, I had nothing to do with it."

"What's this 'Date Night' shit?"

"I don't know. Apparently, the victims were all on some dating website." She paused. "Is that true?"

Reed didn't answer, and he could feel Erika's irritation as if she were standing right there.

"Reed?"

He ignored her. The anchorwoman cut away from the reporter standing outside the police station to another eager young reporter standing at a different backdrop. Reed recognized the steps of the Clarke

County Sheriff's Office, the very place he'd spent most of last Saturday sifting through evidence.

They'd made the Olivia Hollis connection, damn it.

"They're reporting as many as four victims," he said, reading the headlines crawling along the bottom of the screen. "Where'd they get that?"

"No idea. It must have come from you guys."

"It didn't."

"Don't be so sure. Could have been a beat cop or a lab technician. Who's this fourth victim you haven't told me about?"

"I don't know."

"They don't mention a name," Erika said.

"Maybe it's a stab in the dark. They figure it's a serial killer, so there's a good chance there are more. Makes them look like they're out in front on the story."

"Or maybe they know something you don't?"

"Listen, I can't talk right now, Erika. I've got to go deal with this."

"Keep me posted."

"Right."

"I mean it. This leak wasn't me, I swear. But I need to be kept in the loop. The mayor's under a lot of pressure here."

"Yeah? And what's that like?"

"Skip the sarcasm, Reed. You're not the only one sweating over this. The mayor is, too. He's extremely concerned. It's a matter of public safety."

"I think you mean voter safety."

"I need to be kept informed, Reed. Are you listening to me? I can't do my job if I'm hearing everything for the first time on the evening news. Don't keep me in the dark."

Reed hung up with her right as another call came in. Hall. Jay walked over to Reed as he answered it.

"Novak."

"You want to tell me what the hell's going on?" Hall demanded. "I just got off the phone with the chief, and *he* just got off the phone with Greg Sloan over at Mix. com. I thought I told you to leave that company alone, Novak."

Reed didn't answer. He wasn't calling about the news report? He must not have seen it yet.

"We don't have one shred of confirmed evidence that that company's part of this thing. And then you guys go behind my back and go over there. Did you not listen to a word I said?"

Jay stepped closer. "Hall?" he asked in a low voice.

Reed muted the call. "He's ranting about Mix. What's he talking about? Did you go over there?"

"You didn't hear about Laney?" Jay asked.

Reed's stomach filled with dread. "What about her?"

CHAPTER 26

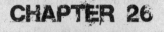

"Knox. Delaney."

Laney jerked her head up. She was on the concrete floor of a room that smelled like vomit, her knees pulled tight against her chest. A heavyset woman on the other side of the bars was staring at her.

"You Delaney Knox?"

She nodded.

"Come with me."

Laney got to her feet and picked her way through the crowd, trying not to step on any limbs. The door slid open with a *clink*, and she felt dozens of sullen gazes on her as she walked out of the cell.

The guard didn't say anything, just led her down a long corridor. Laney's jail-issued plastic shoes made squishing sounds against the concrete as she weighed the possibilities. She'd been printed and photographed, so now what? Would she go before a judge? Or maybe in the time-honored tradition of TV cop shows, she was about to get her one phone call.

A loud buzz made Laney's nerves jump. Another door slid open, and she was led into a narrow room beside a windowed chamber that looked like a tollbooth.

"Remove your shoes," the guard droned. "Stand behind the line."

Laney did as instructed, and the guard disappeared

back through the door, leaving her alone and barefoot behind a blue strip of masking tape. She glanced through the plexiglass window of the booth.

"Delaney Knox?"

She nodded, and the woman shuffled away. She returned with some papers, which she placed in a metal tray and shoved through the window.

"Sign by the X."

The papers said "DISCHARGE" at the top. Laney scribbled her name.

"I'm being released?" she asked.

The woman looked her up and down with a bored, vaguely disappointed expression that reminded Laney of her sixth-grade PE teacher. She pulled the tray back through and emptied a brown envelope into it.

Laney's pulse lurched at the sight of everything they'd confiscated during her arrest: cell phone, car keys, a strawberry Jolly Rancher.

She snatched up the phone. No signal.

"Sign the receipt," the guard instructed, and Laney scribbled her name again. But now her fingers were trembling. She hadn't even been to a bail hearing yet, and she was really getting out?

"Do you know why I'm being released?"

"No."

"So . . . are the charges dropped or—"

"No idea."

The woman jabbed a button, and another door slid open with a loud buzz. Laney followed a large male guard to a small hallway where an elevator was waiting, doors open. He directed her inside, then tapped a button and turned his back on her as they rode down.

Laney was expelled into a hallway where restless-looking people filled every available chair and bench. Bypassing all of them, she pushed through a set of double doors into the muggy summer air.

Laney stood for a moment in shock. Ninety-five degrees and ninety percent humidity had never felt so refreshing.

She whipped out her phone and stared down at it. She couldn't call her mom. Calling Reed was out of the question.

She called Ben. When he didn't pick up, she sent him an urgent text message, then shoved her phone into her pocket and looked around.

The jail was located near Austin's bar district, and the streets were dotted with groups and couples in varying states of inebriation.

Her phone chimed in her pocket, and she yanked it out.

"You've got to be shitting me," Ben said.

"Where are you?"

"O'Toole's."

"Can you come get me?"

"Now?"

"Yes!"

"Laney, seriously? I just met someone."

"*Ben.*"

"Okay, okay. Sit tight."

Laney didn't want to sit tight. She didn't want to sit anywhere near the damn police building or even stand beside it. She walked down some steps to the sidewalk, careful not to step on any glass with her bare feet. Her favorite flip-flops were back in the parking lot at Mix.

A man pushing a shopping cart filled with black trash bags eyed her from across the street. Laney stepped closer to a lamppost and looked up and down the block, trying not to appear nervous. She felt numb. Dazed.

This night was surreal. She'd been frisked and cuffed and folded into a police car. She'd been photographed and fingerprinted and *strip-searched* and then relieved of all contraband in her pockets. Her stomach growled, and she dug out the Jolly Rancher, but sucking on it did nothing to calm her. Fear and anger roiled inside her.

The fear was from being deposited in a reeking jail cell with streetwise women twice her size. The anger was from being arrested in the first place on the orders of a damn rent-a-cop.

But she was angry at herself, too. In her rush for answers, she'd been reckless. She prided herself on not leaving a trace, digital or otherwise, when she conducted intrusions. She'd never been arrested before or even discovered, with the exception of the exploit against the kiddie-porn site back when she was in college, and she'd basically gotten away with that. In fact, it had jump-started her career.

But tonight she'd damaged her reputation. And something else, too, although she couldn't say precisely what. Laney paced back and forth in front of the streetlamp, trying to ignore the looks she was getting from people in the shadows.

Finally a black Nissan Xterra turned the corner, flashed its headlights, and rolled to a stop. She climbed in.

"Shit, Laney."

"Hi."

She glanced around, feeling a ridiculous wave of relief at being in Ben's messy front seat. She adjusted the air vents.

"What the hell happened?"

She looked at him. "I got arrested."

"No shit. How?"

"Can we go, please?"

He shook his head and pulled into traffic, then shot her a look. She glanced at the side mirror and watched the police building recede.

She'd been *arrested.* The churning in her stomach started up again. Would her security clearance at Delphi be affected? She needed to talk to Mark.

And Reed.

Just the thought of him made her feel a sharp pang of panic.

"Where to?" Ben asked.

"Java Stop over by the Mix building. I need to pick up my car."

He pulled into a turn lane and stopped at the light. She felt him looking at her.

"What happened to your shoes?" he asked.

"I lost them."

"I've got some Tevas in back, if you want."

She reached around and rummaged through the junk in his backseat—wadded T-shirts, fast-food wrappers, Frisbees. She found his sandals and slipped them on her feet, adjusting the nylon straps. They were enormous on her, but at least they'd work for the drive home.

Ben looked at her again. "You want to tell me what happened?"

"No."

"What's with your arm?"

She glanced at it. A shallow cut along her forearm was caked with dried blood from where she'd scraped it on the wire fence. She'd scraped her palms, too, when she'd landed on the sidewalk.

Ben reached in back and grabbed a bottle of water from the floor. He handed it to her, then fished a stack of Taco Bell napkins from the console.

She cleaned herself up, feeling guilty for not talking to him right now. But she wasn't sure she could keep her voice steady, and the only thing more humiliating than calling him to pick her up from jail would be crying in front of him.

He wended his way through traffic until they reached Java Stop, which was shut down for the night.

"It's gone," she said inanely. She looked up and down the street, and her gaze landed on the sign posted on the side of the building: NO OVERNIGHT PARKING. VIOLATORS WILL BE TOWED.

She muttered a curse.

Ben sighed. "Where to now? Impound lot?"

That was above and beyond, even for someone she'd rescued from bars on more than one occasion.

"I'll deal with it tomorrow. Just take me home." She glanced at him. "Please."

They drove in silence, and Laney gazed out the window, struggling with her emotions. Everything was caving in on her—her job, the case.

Reed.

"Does your boyfriend know?"

She looked at him. "He isn't my boyfriend."

"Right."

She stared out the window again, feeling another kind of tension in the car now. This was the problem with not having any close girlfriends. Maybe she should have called her mom instead of Ben. But she really, really hadn't wanted to see the look on her mother's face as she picked her daughter up at a police station. Her mom was tough, but she was still a mom, and she'd go into a tailspin of worry and tell Laney her life was out of control.

Maybe it was. Laney watched the restaurants and storefronts whisk past. If she were normal, she'd spend her weekends bar-hopping and having pointless conversations and hooking up. But she wasn't normal, and all she ever did was work. It was all she cared about. And she loved the Delphi Center. She was a loner by nature, but her work was often collaborative, and Delphi forced her to get outside the walls of her comfort zone, forced her to interact. She couldn't imagine having her security clearance pulled or being fired because of such a stupid mistake. How had she been so careless?

The streets of Austin flew by. Tears stung in her eyes, and she didn't know why. She wasn't a crier. She couldn't remember the last time she'd felt so undone.

Yes, she could.

After her attack, she'd felt this way. She'd been shaken and anxious and plagued with self-doubt all the time. Nothing had felt right to her, not even writing code. It had taken her months to come out of the funk. She thought she'd left it behind her, but this case was bringing it all back—the emotion, the uncertainty, the restless nights.

The fear.

Maybe Reed was right and she should stay away. But she didn't want him to be right. She wanted to prove to him and herself that she wasn't in over her head, that she could contribute something valuable. Something necessary. Something no one else could.

At last, they reached Laney's street. The sight of the familiar porches and cars calmed her nerves a little, and she took a deep breath as Ben slowed in front of her sidewalk.

"Thank you for getting me," she said.

"No problem."

"Sorry for ruining your night." She looked at him. "I owe you one."

He lifted an eyebrow. "Yeah?"

She rolled her eyes and shoved open the door just as a pair of headlights came up behind them.

Ben checked the rearview mirror as a pickup pulled over behind his SUV. "That him?"

She sighed. "Yes."

"Good luck." He flashed her a grin. "See you Monday."

She got out and closed the door, and Ben lowered the window. "And don't forget my shoes."

Reed got out of his truck and slammed the door, watching as Ben sped away. He walked over and glared down at her, hands on hips. His sleeves were rolled up, and his thick hair was mussed, as though he'd been combing his hand through it all night.

Laney looked him up and down. "What, no dinner?" She turned and walked up her sidewalk. He followed.

Inside she silenced her alarm and made a beeline for her kitchen. She poured some food for Baggins and crouched down to pet him as he hungrily attacked his bowl.

She stood up, and Reed was leaning back against the sink, watching her. His face was taut, and she could feel the anger emanating from him. She took down a glass from the cabinet and reached around him to fill it with water.

"Drink?" she asked.

"No."

She guzzled the water, which helped soothe the lump in her throat.

Reed closed his eyes and tipped his head back, like he was counting to ten silently.

Then he looked at her. "What part of 'stay the fuck away from this' did you not understand?"

"It's not a big deal."

"No?" He looked incredulous.

"Criminal trespass is a misdemeanor."

"That's not the point, and you fucking know it. Do you know how many favors I called in to get you released tonight? I had to argue with the goddamn chief of police. I had to *defend* you, as if you had some legitimate purpose over there."

"I never asked you to do that."

"Yeah? Well, when that arrest magically disappears from your record, you have me to thank."

She set the glass on the counter. "Don't you even want to know what I found out?"

"No."

She eased closer and watched his jaw twitch. He gazed down at her, and she could feel the frustration coming off him in waves.

"Fine." She turned away, but he caught her arm, and she felt his long, strong fingers burning into her skin.

"What'd you find?"

She took a deep breath. "A keylogger."

"A keylogger."

"Yes, a hardware-based keylogger." She arched her eyebrows. "Do you know what that means?"

He released her arm and eased back, rubbing his hand over his face. "Damn it, Laney."

"It's a way to snatch passwords. Black-bag cryptography, you could call it. It's practically undetectable. Software-based antimalware programs can't defeat a system like this." She searched his face for a reaction. "That is good for us, Reed. It's an important clue."

He shook his head, obviously annoyed by the *us* in her statement.

"He was *there*, Reed. Right there in the office of their system administrator. Which means he got into the building, and we might be able to find him on their security tapes."

Reed shook his head.

"You don't believe me?"

"Yes, I believe you. What I can't believe is that you don't see what you just did."

She drew back, defensive. "I handed you another important lead."

"Yes. And it adds to the pattern of what we know about this UNSUB. He spies on women. He gets into their phones, their emails, their lives. He hijacks webcams and watches them in their homes. What else do you think he can see when he does that, Laney?"

She thought she understood what he was getting at. "April's and Isabella's webcams were dormant when I examined them. He wasn't watching—"

"What about tonight, Laney? What if he was watching that system admin's computer? What if he saw you?"

She stepped back and felt her blood go cold. She hadn't thought of that. In her frantic race to get out of there, she'd completely missed the possibility.

Reed was staring at her now, his blue eyes intense. And he was right. She'd slipped up. She'd overlooked something, something that could come back to bite her. If the UNSUB hadn't already known she was directly involved in this investigation, he might now.

Reed watched her, waiting for her reaction, and she didn't want to admit that she'd made a mistake.

"What's done is done," she said. "There's nothing I can do about it now."

"Bullshit. You can *listen* to me for once. You can stay the hell away from this thing and let the police handle it."

"Oh, like you've been doing so far?"

His eyes darkened.

"My work has been helping you," she said. "Admit it to yourself, even if you won't admit it to me."

He shook his head and looked away. "You're so damn frustrating, you know that?"

"Why, because I don't let you boss me around?"

"Among other things, yeah."

She studied his face, rigid with tension. He was angry. He liked control. In his job, in bed. He liked to control everything, but he couldn't control her, and it pissed him off.

His gaze darted down, and heat sparked in his eyes.

No matter how frustrated he was with her, no matter how pissed off, he was here now. He couldn't stay away.

She eased closer and felt the tension kick up, proving what she already knew.

This time was different. Last time, she'd invaded *his* personal space and basically thrown herself at him. Not very many men would have refused her under the circumstances, so she'd been careful not to attach too much meaning to it.

But tonight was different. The expression on his face was different. He'd come here, to *her*. And the simmering look she saw in his eyes now, the pent-up emotion, wasn't all about the case.

Excitement rippled through her. She went up on tiptoes to kiss him, but he caught her arm.

"I need to know something," he said. "Why did you call that guy to pick you up?"

She eased back. "Ben?"

"Yes, Ben. Why'd you call him instead of me?"

"Because I needed a ride, not an interrogation."

He held her gaze.

"You sound jealous."

"I am."

She couldn't believe he'd said that. For a long moment, she just looked at him, and the air between them felt charged.

He wanted her. He didn't *want* to want her. He thought she was too young, too volatile, too hard to predict. But he wanted her anyway, and the knowledge gave her a rush of excitement.

He reached out and took her hand, turning it over so he could see the cut on the pale underside of her forearm.

"What's this?" He looked at her.

"I cut it on the fence."

"You all right?"

She nodded.

His thumb stroked across the pad of her palm that was scraped raw. He lifted her hand up and kissed it so softly it took her breath away. And she stood frozen with amazement as his gaze locked on hers with more tenderness than she ever could have imagined.

Her stomach dropped a little. And then he slowly pulled her against him and lowered his mouth to hers, and it dropped a *lot*, like she was in an elevator, falling and falling, with no idea when she'd slow down.

Tenderness.

Of all things . . . she hadn't expected it, and she didn't know how to respond. She slid her arms up around his neck and combed her fingers into his hair and pressed against him as his tongue coaxed her mouth open. His lips were firm but gentle, and the warmth of him surrounded her as she pulled him closer.

"Laney," he whispered, and she cut him off. She wasn't sure why. She tangled her tongue with his, and what started out as a gentle kiss quickly became heated and demanding. She stroked her fingertips over his cheeks, loving the stubble there, and she remembered how late it was and that it had been a long day and he was tired and frustrated, and yet he'd come here for *her*.

Her blood thrummed in her veins. She pressed herself against him, rocking her hips against his, and he made a low groan deep in his chest. Laney's knees went weak, but just then, he gripped her around the waist with both hands and lifted her up onto the counter. He pushed her knees apart and moved between them.

"Ummm," she murmured, scooting closer to the edge and shifting her feet to slip off the oversized sandals. They fell to the floor with a *thunk-thunk*, and she used her bare heels to pull him in close. She liked this elevated vantage point, with his mouth against her neck and his hands tipping her body back to trail kisses over her collarbone. He tugged her shirt up, and suddenly, his mouth closed over her nipple, sucking and pulling on her through her bra, and she gave a whimper and squirmed closer. He reached around her for the clasp, and then his mouth was hot against her bare skin, driving her crazy with need as she wrestled her T-shirt and bra off and tossed them away. Cool air wafted over her. She shivered with nerves and anticipation as his gaze dropped. His big, warm palm cupped her breast, and his gaze met hers.

"You are so sexy," he said, stroking his thumb over her nipple, teasing her, and she squeezed her thighs tighter against his sides. She rested her hands against the counter and leaned her head back to enjoy everything he was doing. She loved his body, especially his broad shoulders. She stroked her hand over his arm, feeling his starched shirt beneath her fingers, and she decided she wanted it off right away. She went to work on his buttons, getting them open and pushing his shirt off his shoulders as quickly as she could, then pulling up his T-shirt. He helped her, yanking it over his head and throwing it aside, and then she skimmed her hands over all those smooth, hard muscles she loved as he bent over her breasts again.

She couldn't believe he'd come here. She'd thought he'd be mad at her tonight, maybe even avoid her altogether. But instead, they were in her kitchen shedding clothes.

In front of her window.

What if he's watching?

A cold shudder moved through her, and she pulled back.

"What?" Reed looked up.

"Bedroom."

He dragged her off the counter, cupping her butt in his hands as she wrapped her legs around him with a startled yelp. He grunted and shifted her weight and carried her down the hallway and into her room. He stepped over some discarded shoes and stumbled to a stop beside the unmade bed.

"It's a mess," she said, but he didn't seem to care as he lowered her onto the sheets and stretched out beside her.

His hand stroked down her body, only grazing her breast this time on its way to the waistband of her jeans. She pulled his head down for a kiss. She heard the soft pop of the snap and felt a surge of heat as he dipped his fingers into her panties. She shifted eagerly beneath him as she remembered how he'd made her mindless last time. She loved the way he touched her.

"Good," he murmured, kissing her, and she realized she'd said it out loud. And then she couldn't say anything at all, because he slid his fingers inside her and she went absolutely dizzy. She arched her hips, desperately wanting more and more but at the same time wanting to hold back.

He rolled off her and stood beside the bed, then slid his hands over her hips, pulling off her jeans and panties in one smooth motion. She propped herself up on her elbows, blinking up at him in the dimness as he gazed down at her and unbuckled his belt. She felt the excitement pulse through her as his gaze roamed over her body and he got rid of the rest of his clothes. And then he was back on her, settling his weight between her legs and kissing her again with even more heat than before. She kissed him with all the stored-up passion she'd been feeling, everything that had been burning inside her since she'd first met him. He was in her bed now. She had him. Right where she wanted him and for the whole night.

At least she hoped.

He sat back, catching his breath, and his gaze narrowed as he stared down at her.

"What's wrong?" he asked.

"Nothing."

He traced his hand over her arm, careful not to touch her cut. "Are you sure you're—"

"Yes," she said, rearing up. She shoved him flat onto his back beside her. She straddled him and sat back, and his look of surprise turned to desire.

She leaned over him, clamping her hands around his biceps as she kissed him—his mouth, his jaw—then trailed her tongue down over his chest, lingering on the line of hair that started above his navel, then working her way back up again. He shook off her grip, freeing his hands to stroke down her back and over her hips. He pulled her firmly against him and sat up, cupping the side of her face as he kissed her.

She pulled back and reached for her nightstand, but he already had a condom out, and she was too far gone to care where it had come from as she snatched the packet from him and tore it open with her teeth. He took it from her, quickly covered himself, and then shifted her hips as she lowered herself onto him.

"Reed."

She braced her hand on his shoulder as he pushed into her, and it was deep and *good*, and she shifted her weight on him as he did it again. She gripped his shoulder, tipping her head back as he rocked against her, over and over again, and she loved having him under her and feeling his immense power as they moved together. It was good. So good. So, so good she never wanted it to end, and she dug her nails into his arm and squeaked his name.

He heaved himself up and tossed her onto her back, pinning her with his hips. For a second, she was shocked. And then there was nothing in the universe except *him* and the perfect friction they made together. She clutched him tighter, pulling him as close as she could as she gazed up at him in the dimness. The muscles of his neck were taut as he propped his weight on his arms and drove himself into her again and again, and she thought she'd lose her mind.

And then it was too much, and she could feel the edge coming closer. She scraped her nails down his back and whispered in his ear, and he gave a powerful thrust that snapped her control, and he was with her as she came.

She went limp as he collapsed on top of her, finally settling his full weight on her body. She relished the feeling of him there but soon discovered she couldn't breathe.

He pushed up on his palms and gazed down at her, and she saw something in his face, a fleeting look, before he rolled onto his back. He stared up at her ceiling, then squeezed his eyes shut. She wondered what the look meant, if he was feeling regret.

Her heart pounded. She looked at the ceiling and tried to get her breathing back to normal and tried not to think about anything.

He got up and disappeared into her bathroom for a moment. When he came back, she was having a mini anxiety attack.

What now?

Would he spend the night? The idea made her nervous, and she tried to piece together why as he stretched out beside her in her bed. Her head was still swimming from everything that had happened. She'd spent most of the night in *jail*. And now she was ravenously hungry. And in need of a shower.

He rolled onto his side and pulled her back against him, and she closed her eyes, trying to forget everything except the solid heat of his body against her back. That part was easy. His breath was warm against the top of her head, and he slid his fingers up her arm. And slowly back down. And up again. And the soft, soothing repetition of it lulled her into a state of not caring. His hand stroked over her back. When it lingered on her shoulder blade, she tensed.

"What's this?" he asked, grazing his thumb over her scar.

She cleared her throat. "That night. When he was in my house."

His thumb went still.

"I cut myself."

He sat up on an elbow and eased her onto her back. His gaze was dark and serious. She knew what was coming, and she braced herself.

"Will you tell me about it?"

"Why?"

He reached up and stroked his thumb over her chin. "Because. I want to know you."

She stared up at him silently. Her heart was drumming now as she studied his eyes. His mouth. She couldn't think of what to say. The moment stretched out, and she could feel his disappointment like a weight, but she couldn't get the words to come.

"I don't like to talk about it."

He feathered her hair away from her eyes and tucked it behind her ear. "Someday?"

She nodded.

He leaned down and kissed her, and the unbearable sweetness of it made her chest tighten. She felt guilty for all the ways she'd lied to him. And was still lying. By omission, mostly, but it was lying all the same.

She had a feeling he knew. He was a good detective. Observant. And his cynical streak ran deep. For some crazy reason, she liked that about him, liked that he'd seen things and probably done things. She liked that he wasn't naive about the world.

She gazed up at him in the near-darkness. Would he stay or go now?

It was up to him, she decided. She wasn't going to ask.

She turned away, and he pulled her back against him, and she took a deep breath and tried to focus on the warm closeness of him. He started that stroking thing on her arm again, and she let her eyes drift shut. His hands felt so strong and masculine against her skin. This kind of intimacy was new to her, and it scared her how much she liked it. She loved his body, his scent, his voice. She wanted to soak it all up, even though she knew it would only disappear. Everything about the way he touched her felt so impossibly good.

He shifted, and she felt him checking his watch. He started to sit up.

"Stay." She put her hand on his arm. "Please?"

CHAPTER 27

Reed awoke to the sound of a phone vibrating on the nightstand. Laney's, not his.

She answered it and mumbled something hostile before slipping out of bed and going into the hall.

Reed cast a groggy look around the room. It was bright, maybe nine o'clock. He sat up and swung his legs out of bed, dislodging the cat.

He rubbed the back of his neck. He got up and pulled on his pants, and the fat tabby squinted at him from the doorway as he zipped up. He glanced around Laney's bedroom in the full light of day.

Bras and jeans were strewn across the chairs, and the closet door stood open to reveal a pile of laundry. No photos or decorative touches anywhere except a framed print hanging over the dresser where most women would have put a mirror. He recognized the picture—it was a black-and-white M. C. Escher drawing of a never-ending staircase.

Reed's gaze went to her alarm clock: 9:05. She was still on the phone, so he ducked into the bathroom to grab a shower. He kept it quick, skipping her coconut-smelling shampoo and opting for soap. When he got out, he rubbed a towel over the mirror and turned to examine a set of parallel scratch marks on his back. He glanced at the door. He wished she'd walk in right now so he could pull her into the shower with him and even lather up with the coconut stuff if she wanted. But she was still on the phone, so instead he got dressed, thinking back through everything and trying to remember exactly when she'd scratched him.

They'd been up most of the night. Reed hadn't been able to let her sleep. He couldn't stop touching her, and she wouldn't stop letting him. He'd been obsessed.

He walked into the living room and found the object of his obsession sitting on her futon with a laptop open in front of her. She wore a T-shirt, no bra, and she was deep into a computer problem, judging by the line of concentration between her brows.

Reed went into the kitchen and started opening cabinets. He found a bag of coffee and dumped about eight scoops' worth into the machine, then filled the carafe with water while he listened to her conversation. It was mostly jargon, but the tone of her voice put him on alert. As he flipped on the coffeemaker, she ended her call.

"Who was it?" Reed asked, grabbing the shirt he'd discarded on her counter the night before.

"A friend who's been working on something for me at the lab." She glanced up. "Tell me something. Why'd you ask me yesterday about my gym?"

Reed sighed, resigned to the fact that she wasn't going to leave this thing alone, no matter what he did or didn't tell her. He pulled on his T-shirt and shrugged into his button-down.

"Turns out April had noticed someone watching her at her gym a few weeks before her murder. We looked through the security tapes, and he may have been driving a seventy-nine VW Beetle."

"A *seventy-nine*?"

"Yeah, we've got a theory he may be a classic-car buff. The murder weapon is a body hammer."

Laney stared at him for a long moment. "Any chance the VW had out-of-state plates?"

"We didn't get a plate. Why?"

She carried the laptop over to the bar. Reed nodded at the computer as he buttoned his shirt. "That thing's a dinosaur. What is that, five years old?"

"It's my backup system," she said. "Here, come take a look at this."

He walked around to look over her shoulder. It was a crime-scene photo of a woman sprawled facedown on a floor, her head in a pool of blood. Reed's hands stilled on his buttons.

"It's an unsolved case," Laney said. "She was bludgeoned in her home with a hammer. The killer used duct tape on her mouth and removed the lightbulb from her back porch."

"Where'd this come from?"

"Michigan."

"No, where'd you get it?"

"ViCAP."

He stared at her. "How?"

She lifted a shoulder.

"You can't just hack into the FBI's computers, Laney."

"Actually, you can. I told you, nothing's unhackable."

He felt the blood rushing to his head. "Christ, you could go to jail. You were just *in* jail, as a matter of fact. Are you out of your mind?"

She glared at him. "*I* didn't do it. Not personally. I just happened to come by the information."

"You're going to get yourself arrested! By the *FBI*,

and it's going to take a hell of a lot more than a few phone calls from me to get you out."

"Do you want this or not?"

He stared down at the crime-scene photo that looked so much like April Abrams he couldn't look away.

"When was this?" he asked.

"The first one happened eight years ago in Ann Arbor."

"There's more than one?"

"I've got two so far. The first victim was an engineering student at the University of Michigan. The more recent case was six years ago, also in Ann Arbor." She tapped a few keys, and the crime-scene photo was replaced by what looked like a police report. Reed's phone buzzed in his pocket, but he ignored it as he read the words.

"Both victims bludgeoned, injuries to the skull," she said. "In the first case, the killer gained entry by popping open a sliding glass door. In the second case, he picked the lock. Which doesn't surprise me."

"What doesn't?"

"The lockpicking. It's a hobby in some computer circles. You see lock-breaking competitions at conventions and stuff. Defeating a mechanical barrier, that's a natural extension of what we do."

Reed skimmed the page, his gut clenching as he registered all the similarities.

"Ann Arbor," Laney muttered. "That's an interesting parallel."

"How?"

"Well, it's a college town, like Austin. And the university there has a world-renowned comp-sci department." She scrolled through a few more screens. "I still haven't gone through everything yet to see if there might be more." She glanced up, and there was something evasive in her look. "This, um, this is just a partial download of what I might be able to get."

He tried to decipher that. Did this have something to do with Gantz? Had he hacked into the FBI for her? All along, Reed had suspected that she was protecting the guy.

"Don't give me that look," she said, clearly picking up on his suspicion. "What do you care where the info came from, as long as it's solid?"

"How do I know it's solid?"

"Because you trust me."

He watched her for a long moment.

"Do you have access to ViCAP?" she asked.

"Maybe."

"Well, you want to write these names down?" She slid a pad of sticky notes in front of him and folded her arms over her chest. "You know, you could pretend to be grateful. This didn't exactly fall into my lap."

He jotted down the name and case number at the top of the report. She clicked into the second file, and he did the same.

So much for spending the day with Laney. He looked at her and felt a now-familiar combination of frustration and lust.

"I have to go in," he said. "I have to follow up." He couldn't use all this until he had it confirmed through legit channels.

"Keep your phone on," she said. "I'll call you if I get anything else."

He stuffed the note into his pocket. "I'm still pissed at you, Laney."

"You'll get over it."

• • •

Reed returned Jay's call the second he got into his truck. Eight years ago. They definitely should have had this. The similarities were uncanny.

Reed's call kicked to voice mail. Something must have gone down last night. Or this morning. Jay didn't call him on a Saturday unless it was important.

He turned out of Laney's neighborhood and headed for the station, going over the implications as he drove. Two more potentially related murders, both in Michigan. It was a major break in the case, courtesy of his hacker girlfriend.

Was Laney his girlfriend? She probably wouldn't like the label, probably didn't want to be labeled anyone's anything.

Reed had meant it when he told her he wanted to know her better. But she didn't like to talk about herself, so he was going to have to do it through observation.

Her home told him a lot. She had a bare minimum of furniture, most of it cheap. Evidently, she spent all her money on the place itself, not what was inside. Years before, she'd rented a house in a crime-ridden neighborhood. Now she lived in one of the city's safest zip codes and had a state-of-the-art alarm system. And then there was the kickboxing.

Her attack had left scars, both physical and emotional. It had made her distrustful. Paranoid. It had added another hard layer to her protective outer shell.

The thing was, she wasn't hard, not on the inside. She was soft. Compassionate. Vulnerable. And he knew instinctively that if he hurt her, there would be no second chances. He wasn't even sure he had a first chance.

So that was it, decision made. Whatever impulsive and probably illegal thing Laney had done to score this intel, Reed was going to cover for her and put his job on the line doing it. He couldn't do anything else, because she was right. This case needed her. *He* needed her. And the information she'd just handed him was potentially explosive.

He dialed Jay again.

"I was just about to call you," Jay said. "What's your twenty?"

"I'm on my way to the station. Something's come up."

"Yeah, I know. I'm at Ian Phelps's place. Reed, we need you over here."

• • •

Veronica surveyed the scene, getting together her game plan. Bedrooms were a good starting point, but this time she'd begin in the kitchen. She set her evidence kit on the counter and selected a fingerprint powder.

"You get this cell phone already?" she asked the crime-scene photographer. He was new. Tall and skinny, the kid had watery blue eyes and a blond soul patch under his lip. He snapped a picture of the breakfast room and turned around.

"What's that?" he asked.

"This cell phone," she repeated. "Did you get it yet? Everything we take with us needs to be photographed first."

He turned and snapped some pictures. When he was finished, Veronica took out an evidence envelope and carefully sealed the phone inside. Phones were a treasure trove of digital and biological evidence. Veronica wanted the biological. She'd collect prints and DNA this morning and then hand it off to the computer lab.

The phone taken care of, she turned her attention to the rest of the kitchen. Ian Phelps's notebook computer sat open on the table beside a bowl of Froot Loops, now soggy.

"The computer, too?" the photographer asked.

"Definitely. Get a couple." She stepped into the laundry room, where Jordan was poking through a heap of clothes on the floor. "Anything interesting?"

"Jeans, socks." Jordan picked up a T-shirt with a gloved hand and gave it a sniff, then made a face. "Workout clothes, I'd say."

Veronica opened the washing machine. "Well, well."

"What is it?"

"Sheets."

Behind her, the photographer sounded like he was hacking up a lung. Veronica turned around. "Hey, catch your cough."

"Sheets are good, I'd think," Jordan said.

"Always. Even if they've been washed, we might still be able to get DNA."

"Detergent doesn't destroy it?"

"Not completely. There are tests we can do."

Another coughing fit behind her, and Veronica

whirled around. "Yo, you mind not spewing phlegm all over my evidence?"

"I've got allergies." He wiped his nose on his shirt-tail.

"Then take a freaking antihistamine. Or better yet"—she stalked over to her evidence kit and grabbed a paper face mask—"put this on."

Jordan was watching her from the laundry room. "You all right?" she asked quietly.

"Fine. Why?"

"You seem a little . . . stressed today."

She meant *bitchy*, but she was too polite to say it. And she was right. Veronica had been snapping at people all morning.

She took a deep breath. "I'm fine, just tired."

Jordan lifted an eyebrow. "Long night?"

"Jay came over."

She grinned. "Oh, yeah? I thought you had a rule against dating cops."

"I do."

"So how'd he get you to bend it?"

She'd bent it because he'd asked again. And because he had kind eyes. It seemed silly now, and Veronica shook her head.

"Uh-oh." Jordan's grin disappeared. "That bad, huh?"

"Not bad, just . . ." Tense. Awkward. No chemistry whatsoever. Damn it, if only she'd kissed him first before inviting him home, they could have avoided the whole embarrassing fiasco.

Jordan was still watching her, waiting for an answer.

"Disappointing," she finally said.

"Ahem."

Jordan's gaze darted over her shoulder, and Veronica froze.

"Hey, Jay. What's up?" Jordan chirped.

Crap, crap, crap. Veronica cringed but didn't turn around.

"Novak just got here. He wants to talk to you."

"Thanks." Jordan gave her a quick glance and walked out, leaving her alone with Jay. She turned around.

"You, too, Ronnie."

His face looked blank, so maybe he hadn't overheard. Maybe.

She followed him across the condo and stepped through the front door into the blazing sunlight. The crime-scene van was parked on the street behind Phelps's black Saab.

She hazarded a look at Jay. His expression was hard now, and he wouldn't make eye contact. *Crap.*

She cleared her throat. "Back there with Jordan, what I meant was—"

"Forget it." He strode over to the crime-scene van, where Reed and Jordan were standing beside the open cargo doors.

"What time was that?" Reed was asking the detective.

"About eight o'clock," she said. "Dispatch took the call around seven fifteen. A neighbor out walking his dog happened to glance inside the car. Said he'd heard about the Abrams murder on the news and knew Phelps worked at the same company as the victim, so he decided to call it in. A patrol officer came over and did a pass-by on foot, then called the squad room. I showed up a few minutes later, and the Saab was parked here on the street."

Reed nodded at the car. "And everything was just sitting there in plain view?"

"Right in the backseat," Jordan said. "A bloodstained T-shirt and a bloody hammer."

"Where's the fiancée right now?" Reed asked.

"I hear she's out of town for the weekend," Jay said. "Left yesterday evening."

"Okay, so Jordan responded to the scene around eight A.M." Reed looked at Veronica. "And when did you get here?"

"About twenty minutes after that. I actually live not too far from here." She glanced at Jay, who was looking impressively blank again.

"What about Hall?" Reed asked Jay.

"He showed up when I did. He wanted to get Phelps down to the station to see if he'd talk to us while we lit a fire under some judge to sign off on the search warrant."

"And Phelps went in voluntarily?"

"No arguments," Jay said. "We didn't put him under arrest or anything."

"We weren't drawing attention to his car at that point," Jordan added. "He was totally cooperative."

Veronica watched Reed's reaction. He looked perplexed, and she didn't blame him. It was an unusual turn of events, to say the least.

"So where's everything now?" Reed looked at her.

"Here." She stepped over to the crime-scene van. "The shirt is sealed in an envelope already, but the hammer is in a box." She grabbed a mask and gloves from a supply kit and handed them to him. "Wear this if you want to look. The last thing we want to do is contaminate anything."

Veronica secured a mask over her mouth and nose. She carefully removed the lid to the box, and Reed eased closer to look inside.

It was a silver hammer, long and slender. The instrument was shiny and elegant-looking—except for the circular face, which was coated with dried blood. Veronica pulled the box closer, and sunlight glinted off a strand of blond hair.

Reed's eyes flashed to hers. "You have a ruler?"

She pulled a measuring tape from her pocket and handed it over. He let out several inches of tape and held it up to the face of the hammer.

"What'd you get?" Jay asked. "Does it fit the description?"

"One-point-five inches." Reed looked at him. "It fits."

• • •

By the time Reed got back to the station, Phelps had been cooling his heels in an interview room for more than three hours. Reed swung by the lab and found Veronica at a computer looking at fingerprints. She glanced up.

"You finish with his laptop yet?" he asked.

"I got what I needed and delivered it to Paul."

"What about the cell phone?"

"Same."

Reed's phone buzzed as he headed upstairs, and he recognized the number of the Ann Arbor detective he'd left a message for earlier. He took the call to his desk.

"I got your message," the detective said, and Reed pegged him for a veteran cop based on the sound of his voice. "You guys turn up something on our cold case?"

"Possibly. It looks like your case has some similarities with one down here in Austin. You remember much about the investigation? I realize it's eight years ago."

"It's not something you forget," he said. "The victim was nineteen. She'd been raped and had her skull bashed in. It was bad. And I had teenage girls at the time."

No wonder he'd returned Reed's call so quickly. The detective had probably lost a lot of sleep over the case through the years.

"According to the records, they think a hammer was used?" Reed asked.

"They never did figure out what kind. That was one of the mysteries. It wasn't your standard size, according to the pathologist who looked at the skull injuries."

"I'd like to read the file. You mind shooting it over?"

"Sure. You'll want to check the sketch, too, see if it reminds you of anyone you're looking at."

"There's a sketch?"

"Yeah, we had a witness at one point. Victim's neighbor. He claimed he saw a man around her apartment the day before the murder, maybe tampering with her lights. We had him sit down with a police artist to come up with a drawing."

"I'd definitely like to see it." Reed rattled off his email address and asked the detective to call him if he thought of anything else that might help. Almost as soon as he ended the conversation, another call came in. UNAVAILABLE, which was probably Laney's new phone. She'd given him her number this morning, admitting the possibility that someone might be spying on her digitally.

"I was about to call you," Reed said.

"I bet." She sounded sarcastic. "You tell your lieutenant about the cold cases?"

"Not yet. Where are you?"

"Just picked up my car from the impound lot. Listen, I've got some news. I talked to Scream's brother a few minutes ago."

"Gantz's brother?"

"Yeah, he tells me Edward bounced back after the last round of meds. He's doing much better now, and they decided to go ahead and release him today. I'm going to stop by and see him later."

Reed didn't say anything. He didn't like the idea of her going to visit the guy, not until they sorted all this out. And probably not even then. Gantz had a long rap sheet, and the last time she'd been to see him, she'd nearly been killed.

"He's awake and alert now," she said, "just in case you want to interview him or anything."

"You said he hates cops."

"He does, but you're not FBI, so you might have a better chance. You should at least try to talk to him."

"I will. But I've got my hands full right now with some new developments. We executed a search warrant at Ian Phelps's place."

"You—wait, what?"

"Ian Phelps."

"Are you serious? How many times do I have to tell you Ian didn't do this? Come on. He's a sales guy, not much going on upstairs. There's no way he pulled off an exploit of this magnitude."

"I know all that, Laney, but we found evidence in his car. A potential murder weapon."

"*What?*"

"A body hammer. With blood on it. And some bloodstained clothes."

"Are you making this up?"

"No. Why?"

She laughed. "Because it's utterly absurd, Reed. Who leaves evidence like that in a car?"

"Maybe someone who doesn't have much going on upstairs. Or someone who wants to get caught."

"You don't really believe that, do you?"

"I'm not sure what to believe at this point. But I definitely have some questions to ask him."

"Get me his computer," she said. "I will absolutely prove to you Ian had nothing to do with this."

"I'll see what I can do."

"Ha. You think I believe you? You're trying to fucking placate me, Reed. You don't want me involved."

"You're right, I don't."

"Well, I *am* involved. Give me an hour with that computer, and I'll disprove this stupid case theory."

"How can you be so sure he didn't do it?" Reed asked, just to hear her make her argument.

"Because I *know* the guy, Reed. Ian's a lot of things—a womanizer and a narcissist and even a halfway decent software salesman. But a hacker he is not. Ian Phelps couldn't defeat a Rubik's Cube. There's no way he could pull off an exploit like this."

Reed scrubbed a hand over his face. He was tired and discouraged and sick of arguing.

"Where's his computer now?" she asked.

"In our lab."

"Let me come in and take a look."

"Laney—"

"At least let me talk to Paul, tell him what to look for."

The door swung open, and Jordan walked out. "Damn it, there you are. Hall's looking for you. He wants to get started with Phelps."

"Laney, I have to go. Call you later, okay?"

But she'd already clicked off.

• • • •

Reed found the lieutenant in the observation room. The screen mounted on the wall showed black-and-white video footage of Ian Phelps sitting by himself in an interview room.

"We need to get cracking," Hall said. "So far, he's cocky and overconfident. He waived his Miranda rights, but we need to get things moving before he changes his mind."

Reed glanced at the screen again. Phelps look thoroughly bored. Not the reaction Reed would have expected for a man who'd been picked up by investigators before managing to stash a bloody murder weapon someplace safe.

"This is his sheet?" Reed took the paperwork from the table.

"Yeah."

He'd seen the information before. The guy had almost nothing on his record—just a half-dozen speeding tickets over the past decade.

This didn't feel right to him. None of it, including Laney going to visit Gantz today. Reed was goddamn sick of her pushing him away and ignoring his advice.

"You need to finesse this thing," Hall instructed.

The lieutenant was all hyped up, no doubt relieved to have a suspect he could parade in front of a camera just as the media was getting wind of the serial-killer angle.

"Finesse what, exactly?" Reed asked. Hall made it sound like he wanted him to pull a confession out of thin air.

"You've talked to him before, so see if you can get him comfortable, get him talking. We want him to re-tell his story about the night of the Abrams murder, catch him in some inconsistencies. Pin him down, get him to lie, but don't let him know you're doing it."

Reed shot Hall a look, then took the file and made a stop by the break room. He bought a couple of Cokes from the vending machine and grabbed some paper from the recycle bin to beef up the file. Then he walked into the interview room.

"Ian. How's it going, bro?" He tossed the file down and slid a Coke across the table.

"This is harassment," Phelps said. "I've got half a mind to call my attorney."

"You're welcome to." Reed offered him his phone, and Phelps eyed it suspiciously. "Or I can get you a private room if you want. Maybe you'd rather use a landline?"

He glanced at his watch. "Let's just get this over with. I've got a tee time at two."

"Shouldn't be a problem." Reed popped open his Coke. He opened the file and took a long look at it as he sipped. Phelps took the other Coke and watched Reed defiantly as he popped the top and guzzled it down.

"Says here you're twenty-nine." Reed flipped a page. "Where'd you go to school?"

"UT."

Reed looked at him. "University of Texas?"

"Yes." He sighed. "Come on. Is this what you waited three hours to ask me?"

Reed smiled. "We're getting to it. April Abrams, she went to Vanderbilt University, is that right?"

"Right."

"That's up in Tennessee. Nashville, I believe."

Another sigh.

"You graduated what, seven years ago? Eight?"

"Seven."

"That's undergraduate?"

"Yes."

Reed thumbed through the file, as if it contained anything relevant. "And your major was . . . let's see . . ."

"Communications." Phelps leaned forward, setting his elbows on the table. "What does this have to do with anything?"

"Just something I was wondering." He closed the file and pushed it aside. "You maybe get a master's degree along the way?"

"No."

"You ever do any summer school or maybe an internship anywhere?"

"Summer school, yes. Here in Austin."

"What about University of Michigan?"

"What about it?" He glanced at his watch again.

"You ever take any classes up there? Or live there for any length of time?"

His brow furrowed. "No."

"Ever visit any friends or family in Michigan? Maybe take a vacation?"

"No." He was scowling now. "I never set foot in Michigan."

"You never set foot there."

"Maybe I've been through an airport. So what?"

The door opened behind Reed.

"Detective?" Jordan gave him a pointed look. "Sorry to interrupt, but you've got a phone call."

Reed excused himself. Out in the hall, Jordan shot him a look. "He's pissed."

Reed walked into the surveillance room, and Hall was red as a beet.

"What the fuck, Novak?"

"I've got some information—"

"You're supposed to be talking about his timeline. What's this about Michigan?"

"There are two unsolved homicides up there, and the evidence shows multiple similarities, right down to the type of hammer used."

"Two cases in *Michigan*? Where did you get this?" His face flushed even redder. "You went to the feds behind my back, didn't you? I've had it with your shit, Novak."

Reed gritted his teeth.

"You probably went to the media, too." Hall jabbed a finger at him. "You're the source behind that leak last night."

"Wrong."

"That's it, you're done. I'm yanking this case away, and if you get near it again, I'm yanking your badge, too." Hall turned to Jordan. "You're up, Lowe. Get your ass in there, and get this guy talking."

CHAPTER 28

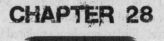

"I don't recognize him, do you?"

Reed took his eyes off the road and glanced at the composite sketch Jay held up.

"No."

"And I've got a memory for faces," Jay added.

The Ann Arbor PD had sent the file, and Reed had grabbed it off the printer on his way out the door. He and Jay were on the way to interview Edward Gantz, who might be able to either refute or corroborate the Ian Phelps theory.

"Even if all these murders are connected, this sketch could be unrelated," Jay said. "This could just be some guy who happened to be seen loitering around this girl's place the day before she got killed. You know, wrong place and wrong time, and now everyone's searching for someone who looks nothing like the killer."

"It happens."

Which was why Reed always took eyewitness accounts with a grain of salt. People didn't always remember things accurately, and even if they did, what they remembered might have nothing to do with the crime.

Reed swung into a gas station and pulled his truck up to a pump. Jay got out, sliding the composite sketch inside the file folder and tossing it onto the seat.

"I need something to eat," Jay said. "Want anything?"

"Black coffee."

"You got it."

Reed shoved the nozzle into the gas tank. He watched the numbers on the pump scroll and tried to swallow down his bitterness. He'd wanted to have it out with Hall, and he would have if he didn't have so much goddamn work to do. But Reed couldn't do anything if he got canned, and he could tell Hall was right on the brink.

Reed clenched his teeth and counted to ten. It was a technique he used to get his temper under control, and typically it worked, but not today. Everything about this day had sucked from the moment Laney had slipped out of bed.

Reed went over his strategy with Gantz. If the kid had, in fact, been the one to help Laney break into the FBI's database, then he was going to be touchy about it, especially when talking to a cop. So Reed needed to be careful. But he also needed the guy's statement, because Reed was convinced the timing of the shooting was no coincidence. Gantz had reached out to Laney to tell her he'd discovered something important, and just hours later he'd been gunned down, probably by someone who wanted to prevent him from sharing whatever he'd found.

So the big question was, had Gantz seen the shooter?

Reed finished fueling up and got back behind the wheel as a call came in from the Delphi Center.

"It's Mia Voss. Sorry to interrupt your weekend, but I finished the rest of your evidence."

"The duct tape?" Reed's pulse picked up.

"That's right. We have a hit."

Reed sat back and let that sink in.

"I always like working on duct tape, and this is why," she said. "Even the most meticulous assailants will inadvertently deposit skin cells or hair. Some people use their teeth to tear it, which leaves behind saliva."

"He tore it with his teeth?" Reed couldn't hide his disbelief. This UNSUB had been so careful, which was why Reed was having trouble believing he'd left bloody evidence sitting in his car on a public street.

"Actually, I don't think so. I didn't recover any DNA except the victim's on the tape's torn edges," she said. "But the *sides* of the tape are a different story. Picture a new roll of duct tape. It tends to be sticky on the sides, especially if it's kept stored in a warm environment, such as a garage, and people tend to deposit skin cells when they're handling it casually. Therefore, even if they wear gloves while actually committing the crime, there may be skin cells present from other instances in which they picked up the tape roll."

"So he's in the database," Reed said, clutching the phone.

"Not exactly. His DNA—and I can confirm it's a man—is in the database. The forensic index, to be precise. That means it was recovered from another crime scene, not collected from an arrestee. So we don't yet have an ID on it, we simply know that this comparison sample comes from a homicide scene."

"Let me guess. Michigan?" Reed glanced at the convenience store. Where the hell was Jay? They needed to get on this.

"How did you know?" Mia asked.

"We turned up a connection."

"Well, you're right. This happened in Ann Arbor. The victim was nineteen years old. Holly Petrusky."

"That's her."

"They found his DNA under her fingernails, so possibly she scratched him during the struggle."

"And this evidence is definitive?"

"As definitive as it gets. I had a colleague verify the results independently, which is why it took so long."

"This is a big help. If you wouldn't mind—"

"I'm sending this as we speak," she said. "Take a look at your email."

Reed got off the phone and reached for the file, casting an impatient look at the store. They needed to move on this. They could get a DNA sample from Phelps. If he wouldn't give one voluntarily, Reed could use the Coke can he'd set aside earlier. Depending on what the tests showed, they could either eliminate Phelps as a suspect or move forward full speed.

Jay opened the door and hopped into the truck as Reed flipped through the file again.

"What's up?" Jay asked, tearing open a pack of beef jerky.

"We've got the perp's DNA from the duct tape used with April Abrams. It matches un-ID'd DNA recovered from the Holly Petrusky case up in Michigan."

"You're serious?"

"I'm serious."

Reed found the sketch and pulled it out again. "That sketch looks nothing like Ian Phelps," Jay pointed out.

"I know."

Reed flipped to the interview with the witness who'd later sat down with a police sketch artist. He read through the Q and A, searching for any further details about this supposed suspect. Had the witness noticed anything else unusual that day, besides this man loitering around the victim's house? Had he noticed a vehicle, maybe a forest-green Volkswagen? Reed skimmed through the notes, but there was no mention of a car. He glanced at the top of the report, where it listed the witness's info.

The name hit him like a sledgehammer.

He read the words. He read them again.

"What's wrong?" Jay asked him.

"Holy shit."

• • • •

Reed's words echoed through Laney's head. She couldn't stop thinking about them as she made her way through town with her windows rolled down and the wind blowing through her hair.

I want to know you.

Not the most poetic phrase anyone ever uttered. But definitely the most romantic thing a guy had ever said to *her*. And he'd seemed sincere, too.

He wanted to know her.

Part of her wanted to let him. Another part of her wanted to shrug him off and remain aloof.

Reed wasn't like other men she knew. He wasn't running away.

The men in Laney's life always seemed to be looking for an exit. But Reed didn't seem daunted by her weirdness or her demanding job or her antisocial tendencies. Even the idea of a relationship didn't seem to faze him. In fact, he seemed open to one.

I want to know you.

What else could that mean? Unless she was reading too much into it, which was possible, given her somewhat limited experience with men, most of whom spent all their time either working on or playing on computers.

And just like that, she realized it. She realized what the men in her life lacked, despite all their impressive brain power.

Maturity.

Reed wasn't afraid or insecure or hesitant. He identified what he wanted, and he went after it.

Laney's heart thudded as she thought about him, about the easy confidence that had pulled her in from the moment they met.

I want to know you. No one else had ever made her feel so desired, so feminine. Emotion surged through her, and the giddiness was back. She wanted to know him, too. She wanted to be close to him.

The wind whipped around her hair as she pulled up to an intersection and glanced around, then consulted her phone again for directions. She made a left at the next corner and followed a two-lane highway past a series of warehouses. She checked her phone one more time and then hooked a right onto a road leading east out of town. To her left was a neighborhood under construction, with houses in various states of completion. By contrast, the land to her right was undeveloped. The fields were dotted with oak trees, and the late-afternoon sun cast long gray shadows across the yellowed grass.

She drove for a few more minutes and spied a sign marking the next turnoff. She slowed to read it. This was it, but she got that same niggle of doubt she'd felt when she'd pulled up to Scream's newly purchased property the other night. It didn't look like she'd expected. But if there was anything she'd learned from her investigations, it was that looks could be deceiving.

Laney turned down the narrow road, rolling up her windows and switching off the radio so she could give the surroundings her full attention. She was on the east edge of town. The houses were far apart on lots that looked like subdivided farmland, someone's back forty that had been sold and sold and sold again. Barbed-wire fences separated lots peppered with little houses and septic tanks and double-wide trailers.

Definitely not what she'd pictured. She'd thought he'd live in more of an urban setting, maybe in some kind of bachelor pad. But why had she thought that? She'd been making assumptions about him. For all she knew, he might not be single at all. He could be married with 2.5 kids, a three-bedroom house, and Labradoodle.

A mailbox came into view, and Laney read the number. This was it. She pulled into the gravel driveway and bumped along for a few minutes before rolling to a stop behind an old black pickup. The house was bigger than the others out here, with a pair of dormer windows on top and a wraparound front porch. Definitely room for a family, but Laney saw no sign of anyone as she climbed from her car.

She tucked her phone into the pocket of her hoodie and glanced around. No rope swing dangling from the giant oak in back. No trikes in the yard. No dogs, either, only a pair of pink plastic flamingos flanking the wooden stairs. The warped boards creaked as she mounted the steps and looked for a doorbell. She didn't find one, so she pulled the screen door open and knocked.

No answer.

She glanced around and waited. She stepped over to a window and cupped her hand to peer through the grimy windowpane, but the curtains were drawn, and she couldn't see anything inside.

Curtains. Another detail she wouldn't have expected. She looked again at the pink flamingos. Was it possible he lived with his mother? She knocked once more, louder this time, then let the screen door slam shut. She descended the steps and checked her watch.

"Hello? Anyone home?" she called.

A low droning noise had her turning around. It was a power tool, maybe a drill, and it was coming from the outbuilding. Laney tromped across the driveway, glancing at the pickup. It had mud-caked tires and a trailer hitch in back. Laney followed a dirt path to the building, which was made of weathered wooden slats and listed slightly to the right. It had probably been here for decades, yet it looked like it might blow over in the next big storm.

The door was ajar, and she stepped inside. The air smelled of dust and motor oil. She stood in the doorway for a moment to let her eyes adjust.

It was a large space, bigger than a garage but smaller than a barn. To her left was an old red Mustang up on blocks, no tires. To her right was a tarp-covered car and a wooden workbench littered with tools.

The back of Laney's neck prickled. She surveyed the array of wrenches and screwdrivers, the scattering of nuts and bolts. Her stomach started to sink. A faint humming noise filled her ears, blocking out all other sensory information, all other sound.

Laney's chest constricted. She couldn't breathe. She stepped back, bumping against the doorframe. She reached for her phone as something hard pressed between her shoulder blades.

"Hello, Delaney."

CHAPTER 29

Reed sped toward the police station.

"We need to take him down ASAP," he told Jay.

"You think he knows we're on to him?"

"Hell, yes. He just planted the bloody murder weapon and handed us our prime suspect on a silver platter."

"You're right," Jay said. "I bet he's the 'dog walker' who phoned in that tip."

"Just like he's the helpful neighbor up in Michigan. Who are you calling?"

"Jordan. She should still be there. . . . Hey, it's Jay. Listen, is Paul in the lab?" Jay looked at him across the truck. "Yeah, go check."

Reed tapped the brakes as he raced through another intersection.

"He's gone."

"Shit." Reed pounded the steering wheel.

"Said he planned to work from home the rest of the day," Jay added.

"We need to get a team over there. He's definitely a flight risk. Explain it to Jordan, get her to tell Hall."

Jay was frowning now, clearly unhappy about something she was telling him. "They're in the middle of a press conference," Jay said. "A SWAT team's not happening, at least not anytime soon."

"You and me, then," Reed said. "We'll scrounge up some patrol guys for backup. We can take him down and figure out the rest later. At minimum, we need to get eyes on his house. I'm telling you, when he finds out we've ID'd him, he's going to go off the grid."

Jay was shaking his head again and put the phone on speaker. "Jordan, I'm with Reed. You're on speaker."

"He's in the middle of a press conference," she said.

"Who, Hall?" Reed asked.

"Hall, the chief, a couple of PR flacks. They're announcing we have a suspect in custody."

"He arrested Phelps?" Jay asked.

"Just a minute ago, yeah."

"On what charges?"

"Making false statements. And also—"

"Jordan, listen," Reed cut in. "I need you to look up an address for me."

"What am I, your secretary?"

"It's important. I need the home address for Paul Doher."

She paused a beat. "*Our* Paul?"

"Yes, and I need it fast."

"Yeah, what's up with that? Why's everyone asking for Paul's address today?"

"What do you mean?" Reed looked at Jay. "Who else is asking for it?"

"Laney Knox called here half an hour ago," Jordan said. "She wanted the same thing."

• • •

Her chest felt hollow. Fear zinged around inside it like a trapped sparrow trying to get out.

"We're going to do this slowly," he said, and the muzzle of the gun pressed against her spine. "You're going to lift your arms, both of them."

Her hand was frozen around her phone. Would she be able to slide her thumb over the emergency call button without looking at it?

"Now. Do it."

Her heart thudded. She lifted her arms up. She heard him take a step back, then another.

"Now, turn around. Slowly."

Her tongue felt thick. She swallowed. Slowly, she turned around.

Paul's face was tight, his blue eyes squinty. The side of his lip curled up in a sneer.

"Your shock betrays you, Delaney. You don't remember me."

Her gaze locked on the gun pointed straight at her chest. He held it steadily, and the suppressor on it made it look even more menacing.

He squinted at her. "You don't remember me at all, do you?"

Remember him . . . remember him? She remembered meeting him last week, but she sensed he wasn't talking about that. And he was bigger than she'd realized. Stockier. In the computer lab, he'd looked paunchy, but now she saw that he was solidly built. He wore jeans and work boots and a canvas jacket, despite the heat. What other weapons did he have on him?

"Your phone." He nodded at it. "Toss it on the workbench."

She hesitated.

"*Now*."

She walked over and tossed it onto the table with all

the tools, and suddenly she knew what he was doing. He took another step back from her.

"Now, pick a hammer." He smiled faintly, and her blood chilled. "Any one you like. You get to choose."

Her chest squeezed. She glanced around frantically. "*Move*."

She stepped forward. On the table was a metal toolbox containing an array of slender hammers that all looked the same. She took one from the case, wrapping her trembling fingers around the handle. There was something dark stuck on the end of it.

"Good choice. That was April's."

Her gaze jumped to his. Her throat went dry.

"Smash the phone."

She stared at him.

"*Now!*"

She gave the phone a whack, shattering the screen.

"Again."

Her stomach clenched as she gave it another solid hit.

"Good girl. Now, put it down and take three steps back."

Her brain whirled. She had just destroyed her only lifeline. But she had a weapon in her hand now.

"Oooh, you're thinking, aren't you?" His smile disappeared. "Be smart, Delaney. What's faster than a speeding bullet? Not a flying hammer, I promise you. Put it down."

She did.

Then she backed away, scrounging for a plan. If she could get close enough to kick him or wrestle the gun away—

"Turn around. Hands against the wall."

She turned and leaned her hands against the rough wooden boards. Through the gaps in the slats, she could see the golden grass of the neighbor's property. How far away was that? She tried to remember the layout—

"Feet apart."

He stepped closer. He smelled of sweat and motor oil, and bile rose in the back of her throat. The muzzle of the gun caressed her neck, and she inhaled sharply.

"Spread 'em." His breath was warm against her ear. "Your detective ever tell you to do that?"

She moved her feet apart, and her stomach churned as she stared at her hands against the wood. Where was Reed right now? She should have told him where she was going, but she hadn't. She'd thought about it, but she hadn't wanted to check in with him or anybody.

His hand was in her pocket now, groping her through her jeans. Then it was inside her hoodie, fishing the car keys out.

Think.

He was smart, but she was smarter. She hoped. She just had to get the gun somehow. Or disable him and make a run for it. The neighbors weren't that far, not if she got a head start.

"I'll give you a hint," he said mockingly. The gun slid down her spine, and she sucked in a breath. "CS three-forty-six. Undergraduate cryptography with Dr. Woodward."

Laney's mind raced.

"No? Still don't remember me?" The gun pressed into her tailbone. "I read your paper on encryption security and gave you an A you didn't deserve."

Her mind came up blank. He was Woodward's TA?

It had been a huge weed-out class at eight in the morning. She remembered sitting in a sea of people and struggling to keep her eyes open. But she had absolutely no memory of Paul Doher.

The gun scraped up her back, and her heart gave another lurch.

"You bitches are all the same, lost in your petty little worlds." He stepped away from her. "Turn around, let's go."

She slowly turned around, looking for anything she could grab as a weapon. He was too far away for her to try anything, and she had a sinking feeling he knew about her kickboxing.

Of course he did. He knew everything. He'd been watching.

"Now." He jerked his head toward the door. "Let's go."

She moved slowly toward the door. He was several steps behind, but she felt the gun aimed at her back like a laser burning through her clothes. As she stepped into the sunlight, she darted a desperate look around. The neighbors were distant, maybe fifty yards. The road was even farther, and there was no traffic. She glanced at the shadows and knew the sun would be setting soon.

"To the house," he ordered.

She trudged past his truck, still grasping for a plan. Any chance he'd left the keys inside? She cast a longing look at her car as they moved toward the weathered wooden stairs she'd climbed willingly only minutes ago.

A lifetime ago.

She saw the stairs now, the warped wooden boards,

and the screen door with the chipping paint. The house loomed closer and closer.

If she went inside that house, she was never coming out.

Acid churned inside her stomach. Sweat slid down her back, and she could feel his beady blue eyes on her. She climbed a step. Then another. She lifted her foot for the final step and thrust it back, smashing her heel into something hard.

Thwack.

The post beside her splintered as a bullet landed. She ducked and whirled around, barreling past him sprawled on his back, but he quickly rolled to his knees.

Screaming, she sprinted for the nearest fence, but the closest trailer seemed miles away. She could feel him at her heels, getting closer and closer as she ran. And then her yell became a shrill wail as he caught her hoodie and yanked her back.

She fell to the ground, landing hard on her butt. A sharp blow to the back of the head. For a second, she saw stars. Then she was scrambling forward, clawing at the grass, the dirt, screaming and kicking and trying to get away. He was on her, flipping her onto her back, and she thrust her knee up, then smashed the heel of her hand into his chin, sending him rolling sideways. He gasped and sputtered and clutched his groin as she tripped to her feet and rocketed for the fence.

She darted through the trees, the scrub brush, panting and looking frantically for help. The neighboring trailer's windows were dark. No cars. The next-closest building was a double-wide with a pickup parked beside it.

She stumbled over rocks and tree roots as she

plunged through the low brush. She cast a look over her shoulder, but he wasn't behind her now, only trees and bushes. Was he hiding, or had she nailed him hard enough to keep him down?

She tripped to her knees but bounced right back up and kept running for the fence. It was a wire game fence, five or six feet tall. She'd have to scale it, which would give him a clear shot. She changed course and dashed for a section concealed by a cedar tree, stripping her jacket off as she went so it wouldn't snag. She ducked behind the foliage and cast a last look over her shoulder. He still wasn't there, at least not where she could see. She reached for the wire mesh with both hands.

Fire tore up her arms.

CHAPTER 30

Jay scowled at the map on his phone. "It's in the middle of fucking nowhere."

"Did you know he lived way out here?" Reed asked as he raced down the road.

"I didn't know a damn thing about him. The guy's like office furniture. I never gave him a second thought."

"Nobody did. Maybe that's his problem." Reed gripped the wheel, and he thought about Laney. A sour ball of dread formed in his gut. "Call the dispatcher again."

Jay did. "Hey, it's Wallace." He listened a moment, then looked at Reed. "Still nothing on Laney's cell phone."

"Ping it again."

"Try it again and call me back," Jay instructed. He hung up with the dispatcher and looked at Reed. "Emergency services has pinged her phone twice now. No GPS signal, which means it's disabled. Either the battery's been removed or it's been destroyed."

Reed clenched his teeth. Laney was there. He knew it. She'd been intent on talking to Paul about that damn computer, and she'd gone out there to see about it. He floored the pedal.

"Almost there," Jay said, checking his map again. "I'd say five minutes."

• • •

Laney lay on the ground, dazed. Her teeth hurt. Her arms felt numb. She tried to sit up and fell back, thunking her head on something hard.

Tears burned her eyes.

Get the hell up, Laney.

Her chest tightened. She couldn't breathe.

He's coming.

She forced herself to roll to her side and managed to push to her knees. She blinked down at the yellowed grass with its thin coating of dust.

Electric fence, her brain registered. She shook her head, hoping to shake off the dizziness. She stared down at her hands in the dirt. Her fingers burned as though she'd grabbed hold of a lightning bolt.

She pushed herself to her feet and belatedly realized that was a bad idea. She ducked low and lurched for the nearest tree. Her legs felt wobbly, and she fell to her knees again as soon as she was behind the relative safety of the branches. She pressed her palm against the rough bark as she gasped for breath.

Her pulse was racing, from fear and exertion and God only knew how many volts of electricity. She listened for any sign of him, but all she could hear was a high-pitched humming noise in her ears.

She gulped down a breath and looked around. Road. She needed the road. But he knew that was what she needed. It was her only way out, and he'd be waiting.

She crouched low and dashed for the next bush. Then the next. Then the next. The sun was sinking, and the long, dark shadows were playing tricks with her mind. Still she didn't hear him, but she knew he was out there lying in wait.

Something warm trickled down her cheek. She put her hand to it, and it came away red. She'd caught a splinter when the bullet had hit the post just inches from her head.

A cold shudder moved through her, and she dropped to her knees again. She had to stay down. Stay hidden. She looked out over the grass and saw the break in the fence that marked the driveway. And just beyond it the road. Probably sixty yards away, but that was her goal.

She crawled on her hands and knees, staying low and watchful as she inched her way forward and forced herself to think.

Paul Doher. He'd been in her house three years ago. He'd been in her bedroom. He'd had his weight on her and his arm against her throat, and his ski-masked face had invaded her sleep for years now. A wave of nausea gripped her, and she clutched her stomach, afraid she'd throw up.

A faint rustling. She froze.

Cautiously, she looked out over the brush. She saw no one, only a sliver of the black pickup truck through the trees. He was out there, armed and waiting for her.

She flattened closer to the ground and moved forward on her elbows, ignoring the rocks and the sticker burs and the sweat seeping into her eyes.

She wished for a gun. Reed's Glock. Or the smaller one Jordan had recommended. She should have armed herself when she'd had the chance.

She wished for her phone.

She moved steadily, painfully, toward the gap in the fence. She strained to hear, to keep the tears in her eyes from spilling over. She couldn't fall apart. The road was getting closer. She could make it.

The brush grew thick, and she got into a crouch behind the cover of a leafy juniper bush. She could see the road now, the thin band of asphalt through the gap in the fence. But she hadn't seen or heard a single car since she'd been out here.

Snick.

She dropped low and turned around. It was distant. But she'd definitely heard something. Was he in pistol range? She had no clue.

She darted a look at the road again, and suddenly all she could see was that hammer. April's hammer. And the bit of flesh stuck to the end.

Panic spurred her into action. She glanced over her shoulder and made a run for it, sprinting for the road as fast as her legs could move, straining to hear anyone behind her and bracing for the bite of a bullet. She ran and ran until her lungs burned and her muscles screamed. Closer, closer.

In the distance, an engine. A car coming? But no, the noise was coming from the house. She darted a look over her shoulder as the noise grew louder.

Her feet reached the gravel driveway, and she pushed harder, faster, racing for the road. The engine roared behind her, and she let out a hysterical sob. She looked over her shoulder as the black truck swung around the curve. The giant grille zoomed toward her, and she dived out of the way. She tripped to the ground and rolled, then scampered behind a bush, but it was small and flimsy and no match for a truck if he tried to mow her down. She dashed for the road again, but the truck roared closer. She dived behind another tree as a gray pickup suddenly skidded around a curve and sped straight for the black truck.

Brakes squealed. A deafening crash and crunch of metal. Shouts and curses and slamming doors.

"On the ground, motherfucker! Now, now, now! Hands behind your head!"

Reed's voice. And Jay's.

"Don't fucking move!"

Laney ducked behind a tree. She clutched her hand around the slender trunk, digging her nails into the bark. She closed her eyes.

"Laney!"

She sucked in air, but her lungs wouldn't fill. She couldn't make her voice work.

"Laney!"

I'm here.

"Her car's here," Reed said. "She's here somewhere."

"I'll check inside."

"I'm here," she said aloud, dragging herself to her feet. "Reed, I'm here!"

Paul was facedown in the middle of the road, hands cuffed behind his back. Reed and Jay were on either side of him with their guns pointed at him.

Reed's gaze locked with hers, and the combination of pain and relief in his eyes made Laney's chest hurt.

"You're bleeding," he said tightly, keeping his gun pointed.

"I'm okay." She wanted to throw her arms around him, but the look in his eyes stopped her.

"Stay back!" he barked, then grabbed Paul by the

arm and hauled him up. He spun him around and slammed him against the truck. "You're under arrest."

• • •

The sirens were faint at first but soon became deafening. Two police cars showed up, and within minutes she was sitting in the back of one of them with a first-aid kit in her lap.

Reed stood beside his pickup talking on the phone. The front bumper of his truck was smashed in. The front of Paul's truck looked like an accordion.

Laney dabbed her fingers with an antiseptic wipe. She had new cuts and scrapes to add to the ones from last night, and her knee was starting to swell.

She glanced across the driveway at the other police car. The evening sun shone through it, and Paul's head was a dark silhouette in the backseat. Laney shuddered and turned away, focusing on the house. Jay and a uniformed officer had disappeared inside to secure the premises.

Reed strode over, his expression grim.

"How's the cheek?" He crouched in front of her and gently tipped her chin up.

"I'd forgotten about it. It's probably just a splinter." She rested her hands on her knees because she didn't want him to see that they were trembling. "What happens now?"

"CSI van should be here in a minute. Then we get the show on the road, start taking this place apart."

She nodded at the other police car, where Paul sat with a pair of uniforms standing guard. "What's the holdup?"

Reed's jaw tightened. "There's some question about where to put him."

"What do you mean? Put him in jail."

"We've got to decide where. Hall wants him at one of the substations because the media's still all over us downtown."

"Media?"

He stared at her a moment. "I forgot you hadn't heard. We arrested Phelps. They just had a press conference to announce it."

Laney blinked up at him. They'd arrested *Ian*? She wanted to say something, but her brain couldn't find the words. She felt the fear inside her quickly becoming fury as her gaze settled on the other car again.

Reed stood up and shifted, blocking her view. Maybe he thought just the sight of Paul was too much for her to handle. "Laney."

She looked down. She curled her fingers around her knees and gripped them.

"Laney, honey."

She forced herself to look at him, and he squeezed her shoulder.

"He's going away. I promise you."

"Yo, Reed."

They glanced over to see Jay standing on the porch.

"Need you in here, man. You won't believe this computer setup."

Laney started to stand, but Reed put his hand on her shoulder.

"You should stay out here."

"Like hell."

He planted his hands on his hips and looked at her,

and she knew he hated everything about her being here right now, but he would just have to deal. He turned toward the house, and she followed him. They mounted the creaky stairs and stepped through the door.

The inside smelled oddly of Lysol. Laney glanced around. The only seating in the living room was a brown recliner opposite a flat-screen TV mounted on the wall. In front of the chair was a glass coffee table with three magazines lined up in a neat stair-step pattern in the upper right corner.

Laney walked through the room, getting a glimpse into a kitchen with mustard-yellow counters. She didn't see so much as a speck of dust on any of the surfaces as Jay led them down a narrow hallway. She expected Jay to turn into a room on the right, but he kept going and stopped where the hallway dead-ended into a built-in bookcase.

He glanced over his shoulder at Reed. "Check this out." With a gloved hand, he pressed the top of the cabinet. It rotated inward.

Jay ducked through a low doorway, and Reed followed, then Laney. She found herself in a stuffy little room, maybe eight by eight. Her attention went to the three desks lining the walls and the black swivel chair surrounded by six big computer screens. The room was dark and sour-smelling and hot as a sauna with all the machinery.

All six screens displayed the same screen saver, cascading computer code.

"Like mine," she murmured.

"What's that?" Reed turned around.

"His screen saver. It's from *The Matrix*." She surveyed the setup, then looked at Jay. "You have any more of those gloves?"

He glanced at Reed for approval before digging a pair from his pocket and handing them over.

She nudged the men aside and pulled the gloves on. Then she dragged the chair back. No way in hell was she sitting in the filthy thing. "Roll that into the hall, will you?"

The three desks were arranged in a *U* shape. The center one had a keyboard alongside a wireless mouse. She glanced under the desk. Several high-capacity servers sat beneath it, and she recognized the brand, a favorite with porn collectors.

Laney's hand hovered over the mouse for a moment. She had no password cracker here and no idea what sort of letter-number combination Paul might use. She tapped the mouse, and the screen came to life.

It was a basic desktop with a solid black background.

"You sure you should be touching that?" Jay asked.

She didn't reply as she slid the mouse to the right and the neighboring screen came to life. She slid it farther and got an image on the third screen.

"No password?" Jay looked at her.

"Maybe he thinks he's safe here in his secret little media room."

Reed leaned forward. "What is that?"

"Surveillance footage," she said.

Both monitors showed images of interior rooms. Laney noted the colors and fabrics and the clothing strewn about.

"Women's bedrooms," she said. "These are his targets."

"No fucking way," Jay muttered.

"Way." Laney leaned in for a closer look, then glanced back at Reed.

The cold, steely look in his eyes sent a chill through her.

She turned and slid the mouse left, activating the three remaining screens. All showed webcam footage of interior spaces. Dread tightened her stomach. So many victims they'd never even known about.

"He's a psycho," Jay said.

"This is how he watches them," she said. "He probably spends hours in here fantasizing until he gets up the courage to make a move."

"Holy shit, is that . . . ?"

She glanced over her shoulder at Jay, who was staring at the screen. "What?" she asked.

"That looks like . . ." His voice trailed off as he raked his hand through his hair. "I can't be sure, but I could swear that room . . ."

"Detective?" A uniformed cop stuck his head in. "You guys need to move the pickup. The CSI van's trying to get in. Garcia moved the other vehicle, but there's still not enough room, so—"

"You're supposed to be guarding the prisoner," Reed said.

"He's in the car. Don't worry, he's cuffed."

"You can't leave him alone, for Christ's sake! He's an expert lockpick."

"I didn't. Garcia's with him."

But Reed was already out the door as footsteps pounded down the hallway.

"Detective Novak? Shit, I'm sorry, I don't know what happened. He disappeared."

CHAPTER 31

Veronica's head was pounding by the time she got home. She pulled into her garage with a sense of impending doom because she knew what was coming. It always started behind her eyes, and by the time it reached the back of her skull, she'd be weak with nausea. Her only hope of avoiding it was to get one of her migraine pills into her system before the queasiness kicked in.

She gathered her groceries off the front seat and got out of her car, casting a tired look at the lawn mower on the other side of her garage. She'd planned to do her yard this weekend. And her laundry. And pay bills, too, but the day had slipped away from her.

She dumped her bags on the kitchen counter and immediately filled a glass with ice. She poured ginger ale over it and went into the bathroom for her medicine. She forced the tablet down and then stared at herself in the mirror.

Her hair was a mass of frizz, her skin looked wan, and she still had bags under her eyes from being up so late with Jay.

The thought of him put a knot in her stomach. She'd turned him down over and over again because she didn't want to be gossiped about, and then she'd done the same thing to him. She thought of his face this morning and turned away from her reflection, too ashamed even to look at herself.

She went back into the kitchen and put away the groceries. She plugged her phone into the charger and silenced the ringer, then kicked off her shoes and sank down on her sofa, slowly leaning her head back. It would take a while to kick in, if it even worked. The pills were no guarantee. She closed her eyes and waited.

Lawn and laundry and bills, all tomorrow. She had to water her plants and call her sister, too. And she probably wouldn't do any of it because she'd be curled up in bed with the blinds shut tight as she prayed for the pain to stop.

She opened her eyes and looked around her living room. The pale yellow glow of the lamp was starting to hurt her eyes. She glanced at her back door and forced herself to her feet. At least she could get the plants watered before she found herself down for the count.

She stepped outside and discovered exactly what she'd expected. Her petunias were wilted, and even the hearty bougainvillea looked shriveled. She gave everything a nice long drink and then rolled up the hose. She wiped her feet on the welcome mat.

"Damn it!"

She stepped inside and pulled up her foot. Her big toe was bleeding. She'd cut it on something sharp.

She stared at the cut. An icy trickle of fear slid down her spine. Slowly, she lowered her foot and looked around the patio. In the lamplight spilling through the window, she saw glistening shards of glass.

Her chest tightened. Her breathing grew shallow. She forced her face to relax, to show no expression, nothing at all.

Purse on the counter. Phone on the counter. Keys on the table.

She walked toward the kitchen on legs that suddenly felt like noodles. She passed the table and decided to skip the keys, the phone, everything. She just needed to get out. Out, out, out, before he realized that she knew.

Her pulse was racing. Her chest constricted. She trained her gaze on the front door and crossed the living-room carpet. She was almost there. Ten more steps. Nine. Eight.

A shadow leaped from the hall.

She screamed and lunged for the door. But he had her by the hair, yanking her back and throwing her to the floor, then landing heavily on top of her. She bucked and kicked under him, clawing at his face, his eyes, the thick black ski mask that covered his cheeks.

His knees were on her arms, pinning her down, digging into her biceps, and she flailed under him, but he was like a rock. He gazed down at her with hateful blue eyes, and she bucked and screamed as he calmly pulled a roll of duct tape from the pocket of his jacket. He ripped off a long strip of it, and her heart seized with terror. A loud keening noise tore from her throat as the tape slapped over her mouth.

No, no, no!

She kicked beneath him, enraged and helpless and petrified all at once. Her heels pounded against the floor, but his weight on her chest was heavy and suffocating, and she was losing breath as the masked face loomed over her. She heard the tear of fabric as he yanked her shirt. And then he said something, and spittle landed in her eyes, but she was too shocked to hear or understand anything except exactly what was happening to her, exactly what he intended to do. And a vision of her own brutalized body and her own bludgeoned head flashed into her mind.

No, no, no! She bucked and kicked. The edges of her vision blurred as she put every ounce of strength she possessed into heaving him off of her.

A great *boom* behind her, and suddenly she was surrounded by legs and boots. Two giant arms reached down and lifted him off and hurled him against the wall.

A blinding light shone in her eyes. She rolled to her side, choking and gasping as she pulled off the tape and flung it away. And then her face burned, and she felt like she'd ripped off her own lips.

"Veronica."

She crawled toward the door, tried to get to her feet.

"Veronica." Someone was at her side, pulling her up and away from the chaos. "Are you okay?"

Jay.

She blinked at him in shock. And then she saw Reed and a swarm of uniformed cops kneeling on her floor and slapping cuffs on her attacker, and he was flapping around on the floor like he'd been Tasered.

"What—how—" She tried to form a thought, but her mind wouldn't work. She shook off Jay's hands and backed away, bumping into the wall. Her living room was filled with men holding guns and Tasers and shouting orders at one another.

"Veronica, answer me. *Are you all right?*"

She looked at him, gradually comprehending his words as she tugged at the hem of her torn shirt.

Was she all right?

Was she *all right*?

"Hell, no," she said, and burst into tears.

CHAPTER 32

Reed walked into the bullpen and spotted Jay coming out of the computer lab. It was swarming with FBI agents. Now that they'd actually apprehended the killer, everyone wanted a piece of the case.

Reed tossed his keys onto his desk and intercepted Jay on the way to the break room.

"You hear about the Chevy?" Reed asked.

The search of a sixty-eight Chevy pickup on Paul's property had turned up a cache of travel supplies, including money, two burner phones, and a phony passport. Investigators also had recovered a Sig P226 pistol, probably the one missing from the evidence room that had been used to shoot Gantz.

"Yeah, I heard. Sounds like he was planning to skip town."

Jay looked at him, and Reed knew what he was thinking. He wished he'd just fled instead of making one last compulsive stop for his next target.

"How's Veronica?" Reed asked.

"Mild concussion." Jay sighed heavily. "They discharged her from the ER half an hour ago, and she went home with her sister."

"Good."

"How's Laney?" Jay looked around. "I heard she's back here?"

"She told me she was going home."

Jay's brow furrowed. "I just talked to Jordan. They were working together down in the evidence lab."

"You sure?"

"Yeah."

Reed went downstairs and found Jordan seated in front of a computer. She glanced up.

"You just missed her," she said.

"Laney was here?"

"She wanted to make sure we had all the ViCAP info. We've been going through it the last hour." She glanced at the clock. "She walked me through everything on the two murders up in Michigan and also a home invasion up there that we think might be related. Boyfriend scared off the intruder, but everything fits the profile. She tell you about it?"

"No. I didn't even know she was here. What time did she leave?"

"About ten minutes ago. And I have to say, she looked a little shaky."

Reed muttered a curse.

"I offered to drive her home, but she wouldn't let me. She said she felt fine, just tired." Jordan lifted an eyebrow. "And if you believe that, you're a moron."

Reed turned to go.

"Hey."

He looked back at her.

"She's a good investigator. Any chance we can hire her away from the Delphi Center?"

"I wouldn't bet on it."

He headed back upstairs to close out. It was after midnight already, and he had a mountain of paperwork on his desk, but he needed to get to Laney's, so he grabbed his keys and left everything where it sat.

Hall called out to him as he passed his office. Reed stepped in and found the man seated behind his desk. The tie he'd worn for the afternoon press conference was askew and loose around his neck.

"Where's Delaney Knox?" Hall got to his feet.

"Home."

"We need to bring her in for questioning tonight." He glanced at his watch. "Tomorrow morning at the latest."

"I'm not bringing her anywhere," Reed said. "She's recovering."

"I need to hear her statement."

"She gave one already. You can read it."

Hall's gaze narrowed. He came around the desk, and Reed felt his blood starting to boil. "I heard about your little affair, Novak. You should know the FBI's looking at her for hacking charges. They might be looking at you, too. We don't need this kind of publicity now."

"Publicity?" Reed's hand clenched into a fist at his side.

Hall stepped closer, oblivious. "You led an unauthorized raid on a suspect's home. You botched the arrest. I should suspend you."

"Bring it on. You better do it quick, though."

He scowled. "What's that mean?"

Reed gritted his teeth. He glanced at the clock. Twelve-fucking-thirty. He didn't want to do this right now, he wanted to get to Laney's. "All this time I thought you were protecting the chief," Reed said. "But you weren't protecting Aguilar at all, you were protecting yourself."

"What—"

"I know about the IPO at Mix. Your brother-in-law's on the board there and stands to make a shitload of cash when the company goes public. You stymied this investigation every fucking step of the way to protect that company from any bad publicity." Reed poked a finger into Hall's chest. "You refused to look at the facts, you refused to use outside resources, and because of your negligence, two women almost died today."

Reed watched the fear come into Hall's eyes. Reed had been working on this angle of the case with a financial reporter from the *Austin Business Journal*, and he didn't have everything nailed down, but he could tell from Hall's reaction that he'd gotten it right. Reed didn't have the evidence yet, but he suspected Hall was getting a payoff for everything he'd done.

"You can't prove a damn thing," Hall said.

"I don't have to. By Monday morning, you're going to have federal investigators crawling up your ass." Reed clapped him on the shoulder. "Better not plan on taking any vacations."

Reed walked out of the station and into the hot summer night. He spotted his pickup with its mangled front bumper parked in a fire lane with a ticket tucked under the wiper blade.

Reed tossed the ticket inside, got behind the wheel, and drove to Laney's. He rolled his windows down, hoping the fury he'd had locked inside him all day would somehow seep out of him before he reached her. He made a detour by a convenience store, rolled up to her place at exactly 1:05, and was relieved to see the purple flicker of a television in her front window.

Reed parked in the driveway and stared at her

house. He wanted her with a fierceness that shocked him. He hadn't wanted anything—truly yearned for anything—in years. He'd thought it was burnout creeping into his life and causing the apathy. But that was gone now, replaced by this intense desire. He wanted Laney to need him. It was ironic, because she was about the least needy woman he'd ever known.

He approached her door, combing his hand through his hair and feeling strangely nervous.

If you believe that, you're a moron.

Reed didn't believe it. Not for a second. Laney was anything but fine, and still Reed predicted she was going to try to push him away. He stood under the glare of her porch light and waited for her to answer the door. He could almost feel her on the other side of it debating with herself.

The door swung open.

"Hi," she said.

"Thought you'd be asleep."

"Really?"

He stepped inside and closed the door as she reset her beeping alarm. She turned around. She wore a strappy white tank top and plaid boxer shorts. The television cast a purplish hue on everything, making the cut on the side of her face look black. Just seeing it put a twist in his gut.

"I brought ice cream." He held up the bag.

She took it without a word, and he followed her into the kitchen. She got out two spoons as Reed rolled up his sleeves and washed his hands. She took the ice cream into the living room, and Reed grabbed a beer from the fridge and followed her.

She sat down beside her cat on the futon, and he

joined her. He felt anxious. He waited for her to tell him he shouldn't stay long, that she planned to go to sleep soon.

She ate a few bites of ice cream, then put the carton on the table with her spoon sticking up.

"Want any?" she asked.

"I'm good with beer."

Actually, he didn't even want the beer. He rested it on the table and settled back beside her. There was so much he wanted to say to her. And ask her. But she was giving off a vibe like she needed space, so he was grateful just to be here.

Someone had tried to kill her tonight.

She'd had to fight for her life. Again. And Reed had almost been too late.

The fury was back again, making his shoulders tense and his chest tighten.

"I'm binge-watching *Game of Thrones.*" She scooted closer.

"It any good?" Reed pulled her against him and tucked her head against his chest.

"Sometimes."

Reed stroked his fingers over her in that way that seemed to relax her. He felt the tension draining out of her. Or maybe out of him.

"I watch it when I can't sleep."

He traced his fingers up her pretty arm, then down. Then up again. He pulled her closer, and his heart squeezed when she nestled her head against him.

"That happen a lot?" he asked quietly. "Not being able to sleep?"

She shrugged.

Reed closed his eyes and tried to just be in the moment with her without demanding anything. But he felt that anger again, that white-hot rage that had been coursing through his veins since he'd seen her bleeding and terrified at Doher's place.

"I'm sorry," she whispered.

He pulled away and looked down at her. "You're sorry?"

"For not figuring it out sooner."

Jesus Christ, he wanted to hit something. "I think that's my line. I'm the one who's sorry." He pulled her against him, hugging her tightly as he kissed the top of her head. "Driving over there, I don't think I've ever been so scared in my life." He squeezed her again, and she gave a little yelp.

"What?" He instantly let go.

"Nothing, just . . . my knee."

He looked at her knee. It was swollen and mottled with bruises.

"What the hell happened?"

"I fell. When I was running to the fence."

"We need to get you checked out."

"I'm fine."

"I'll take you to the ER." He sat forward, and she grabbed his arm.

"Reed, I'm fine. I iced it. There's nothing else to do."

He looked at her in the dimness, at the stubborn tilt of her chin. He could tell she'd made up her mind.

She rested her hand on his thigh. "I want to be home tonight. With you." She slid her hand up his leg, and her eyes darkened. "No more questions. No talking. Just be with me."

He watched her for a long moment. He had so much to say, so many things crowded in his mind. But she didn't want to hear any of them right now.

He picked up the remote and turned off the TV, plunging the room into darkness. He reached for her and gently pulled her against him. He found her mouth, and she was hot and sweet, and he knew she'd been waiting up for him, waiting for this. He slid his hands under her shirt to touch the smooth softness of her skin, and she arched against him. She felt so good and tasted so perfect, and he wanted to give her exactly what she wanted.

"Hold on to me," he whispered.

She slid her arms around his neck. Reed scooped her up and carried her to bed.

CHAPTER 33

Veronica had a nervous knot in her stomach as she pulled up to Jay's apartment. His black Tahoe was in the parking lot, and she took a deep breath. He was home. She was all out of excuses.

She grabbed the cookie tin off the seat beside her and strode up to his door before she could change her mind. She gave a sharp rap. The door opened after a few minutes, and he looked surprised to see her. He had on basketball shorts and a T-shirt that stretched tightly over his broad chest.

"Good, I caught you," she said. "You're probably on your way to the gym, right?"

"Good guess." He gave her a puzzled look for a moment before swinging the door back. "Come on in."

She stepped out of the heat into the chilly dimness of his hallway. His first-floor unit backed up to a greenbelt, and she caught a glimpse of thick woods through his back windows. She turned and looked at him. "Here." She thrust the cookie tin at him. "Chocolate chip."

"You made me cookies?"

"They're okay. A little overdone, actually. I'm not really a baker."

The corner of his mouth curved up. She stood there empty-handed, trying not to fidget as he opened the lid and popped a cookie into his mouth. He offered her one.

"No, thanks."

"These are great." He glanced around. "You want to come in and sit down or—"

"No, really. I just stopped by."

He walked deeper into the apartment and put the cookie tin on the counter separating the kitchen from the living room. His place was all single-guy stuff, from the oversized leather sofa to the giant television. A sliding glass door in back led to a patio where he had a black Weber grill.

He was looking at her face now, specifically the bruise at the side of her forehead. It had gone through a rainbow of colors throughout the week, and today was a sickly greenish brown.

"How are you doing?" he asked.

"Fine." She cleared her throat. "That's actually why I came. Part of the reason. I wanted to thank you."

His eyebrows tipped up. "For what?"

"For, you know, kicking my door in. Getting there in time." She tried to sound casual, but the words came out glib, and he looked down at the floor, clearly uncomfortable.

"Yeah, wish we would've been there sooner." His gaze met hers. "And how'd you know it was me who kicked your door in?"

"I measured the shoeprint. Thirteen and a half. Who else would it be?" She smiled and glanced away.

This was even more awkward than she'd imagined it would be as she'd spent her day off baking the damn cookies. She'd burned the first batch and had to go to the store for more ingredients.

She looked at him, determined to get this done. "The other thing is I owe you an apology. For the other day."

His eyebrows tipped up again.

"For what I said to Jordan about us."

He winced and looked away.

"I'm really sorry."

He shook his head. "Forget it."

She stepped closer. "No, I really am. I didn't want to go out in the first place because I didn't want anyone gossiping about me, and then I did it to you. I feel like a bitch."

"You're not." He laughed and looked over her shoulder. "Actually, I wouldn't have minded gossip, if it had been good."

"I'm sorry. Really."

He shook his head and blushed, clearly embarrassed. "Yeah, well, I'm sorry you were disappointed."

"I wasn't."

He gave her a baleful look.

"Not like that. I just meant . . . damn it, I'm making it worse, aren't I?"

"Can we just forget it?"

A scratching noise caught her attention, and she glanced around him to see a cat pawing at the door.

"Your cat wants in."

He turned and sighed. "It's supposed to stay outside."

" 'It'?"

"She. Whatever."

The cat mewed and rubbed against the glass, and Jay walked over and let her in. She made a dash for a bowl in the kitchen.

Veronica looked at Jay. "That's the stray calico April Abrams was feeding."

He sighed. "Maybe."

"Not maybe. I tested all that damn cat fur. It's the missing cat from the crime scene." She went around the counter into the kitchen and crouched down to pet her. The little thing was old and had a torn ear.

She glanced up at Jay. "What's her name?"

"Damned if I know. She doesn't have a chip or anything."

"You took her to a shelter?"

"Yeah."

"Why didn't you leave her?"

"I don't know. I was going to." He rubbed the back of his neck. "But it was like Death Row in there. They're overrun with cats. Who'd want to adopt that skinny old thing?"

The cat purred and rubbed against Veronica's hand.

"I'm thinking of taking her to my sister's," he said. "She lives in Brenham, and she could probably use a mouser around the barn."

"A mouser? This little one?" Veronica lifted the cat up and snuggled her against her chest. "She'd get picked off by the first coyote."

Jay gazed down at her and sighed. He'd already decided to keep the cat, she could see it in his face.

She put the cat down at his feet and stood up. He wasn't looking at the cat anymore but at her. And he had that look on his face again, the warm, interested look that had put a flutter in her stomach and made her want to go out with him.

"You're a good man, Jay." She went up on her toes and kissed him. As she eased away, he pulled her back in and kissed her again, harder. As he let her go, she felt a surge of attraction.

"Sorry." His hands dropped.

"No, it's good." She caught his hand and squeezed it.

And then she stepped back, because she was sending him mixed signals, and she needed to leave him alone until she got her head straight.

He gave her a puzzled smile, and she smiled back, and she felt a swell of relief because things felt right between them again. She was glad she'd come.

He cleared his throat. "I should get to the gym," he said. "Thanks for the cookies."

She followed him down the hall. "Thanks for kicking my door in," she said.

"Anytime."

• • •

"Your cop's here."

Laney glanced over her shoulder to see Tarek standing in her cubicle. He wore a black T-shirt with his favorite slogan stamped across the front in tall white letters: "RTFM." Read the fucking manual.

Laney tried to shake off the daze.

"My what?"

"Your detective guy," Tarek said. "He's down in the lobby."

Laney got up and glanced at her phone. She didn't think she'd missed a call, but then again, maybe she had. She'd been coding feverishly all afternoon, immune to all distractions, even thoughts of Reed. Now a buzz of anticipation filled her as she rode the elevator down to the lobby.

He'd been called to a crime scene at 3:20 A.M., and Laney had woken up alone with a dull ache in her chest. Reed had spent every night at her house for three weeks, and it amazed her how quickly she'd gotten used to his warmth in her bed and his truck in her driveway and his razor on the side of her bathroom sink.

When she stepped off the elevator, he was standing beside the reception desk.

"Hey, I was about to call up there." He held up a cardboard coffee cup. "Extra-large no-whip latte. I figured you skipped lunch."

She took it. "Thanks." She glanced around the lobby. "You want to go outside or—"

"Come on." He pushed through the glass doors and led her around the side of the building to a tree-shaded spot with a picnic table. But instead of heading for the table, he took her hand and pulled her close to the building.

"What—"

He cut her off with a kiss, easing her back against the concrete and tipping her head back the way he did. He took her mouth with his until she was pliant and dizzy and she didn't even care where they were, she just wanted to be with him.

He stepped back and looked down at her. "Missed you this morning."

"How was it?"

"Okay."

Which meant bad, she was learning.

She walked over and set her coffee on the picnic table. He hadn't bought any for himself, so he'd probably been mainlining it all day.

"I wanted to get back over before you left for work,"

he said. "But I had to swing by my house, get a shirt, put my trash cans out on the curb. Place is starting to look abandoned."

She leaned back against the picnic table and looked up at him, trying to read his expression. Was this his way of telling her something?

A warm breeze wafted up, stirring the limbs of the pecan tree above them.

"We could sleep at your house sometime," she said. "We don't always have to stay at my place."

"I don't mind." He swept the lock of pink hair from her eyes. "You've just been through something. I know you feel safe at your place. With your security system. And your ferocious guard cat."

He smiled, but she knew he was serious. He was trying to be supportive. He was trying to help her through the traumas, past and present, that she never liked to talk about. He'd been so patient with her, watching her with those long, steady looks and waiting for her to open up to him. And she was, gradually giving him pieces of herself. But she worried it wasn't enough. Every time they made love, the raw intimacy of it blew her away. He demanded everything, every fiber of her being, and then some. And she'd lie next to him, sated and blissed out and stunned that she could feel so close to someone.

"Hey." He slipped his hand around her waist. "You're giving me that look."

He bent his head down and kissed her again, long and deep, while the warm breeze swept over her skin. He stepped back and let her go.

"I did have a purpose in coming here, believe it or not," he said. "I wanted to ask you out to dinner tonight. Someplace good."

"Hmm. How about Bangkok Palace?"

"I was thinking Adrienne's."

She drew back. "Adrienne's is *nice*. And expensive."

He smiled and shook his head. "I'm trying to take you on a date here. Every time I ask you to dinner, you storm out on me, or one of us gets called into work, or we end up at a crime scene. You're making it damn hard to court you, Laney."

"You're courting me," she stated, and felt a tingle in her stomach.

"That's what people do at the start of a serious relationship."

The ache was in her chest again. She pressed her hand to it as she looked at him, searching his eyes. "Is this a serious relationship?"

"Don't you think?"

"I don't know," she said. "I've never been in love before."

He smiled slightly and took her hand. "Hurts, doesn't it?"

She nodded.

He pulled her against him, and her heart was racing. Then he kissed the top of her head. "I'll pick you up at eight."

She swallowed. "Eight's good."

"If anyone asks you to work late, tell them to go to hell."

He walked her back to the entrance, then gave her a quick kiss good-bye. Her gaze followed him down the sidewalk toward the parking lot.

Laney stepped inside the cool dimness of the building. She walked across the lobby feeling slightly dizzy again. She stopped beside a cluster of people waiting for an elevator and stared down at her feet.

Reed Novak was courting her. He wanted to take her to Adrienne's tonight. What the hell was she going to wear?

"Coming, Laney?"

She glanced up to see Dmitry staring at her from inside the elevator. It was filled with her coworkers, young guys in T-shirts and cargo shorts and flip-flops, all bent over their cell phones playing games and texting—all except for Dmitry, who was watching her expectantly.

"On or off?"

She stepped on and turned around to face the doors as they eased shut. *I've never been in love before.*

God, what had she done?

She shot her arm out, and the doors sprang open. She rushed across the lobby to the windows and spotted Reed at the edge of the parking lot. Her heart lurched. She hurried outside as he reached his truck and pulled open the door.

"Reed!"

He turned around. He shielded his eyes from the sun with his hand, watching her as she caught up to him. When she reached him, her cheeks were flushed and her pulse was pounding. He rested his arm on the door and gazed down at her, and she couldn't read the look in his eyes.

She took a deep breath to summon her courage. "You never responded to what I said."

He looked at her a moment. "The love thing."

"Yes." Her heart actually hurt now, like he had it gripped in his fist.

He stepped closer, his gaze intent on hers. "I didn't want to freak you out."

"You won't freak me out. Just tell me the truth."

He slid his hand around her waist and lifted the other to cup her face. "You sure?"

She nodded.

"I'm crazy, stupid, out of my mind in love with you, Laney." He tipped her chin up and kissed her, and the grip around her heart loosened. It was beating wildly, like it might beat right out of her chest, and she clung to him as his words sank into her mind, her soul.

He eased back to look at her, and the tenderness she saw in his eyes made her breath catch. He was right. It *did* hurt. But it was a good hurt, a joyful hurt, and she felt hot, joyful tears coming to her eyes.

"Think you can handle it?" he asked her.

She pulled him back and kissed him.

From the next heart-pounding Tracers novel
by Laura Griffin . . .

Coming from Pocket Books in 2017

Everything about this felt wrong, and Tessa couldn't believe she was here as they bumped along the gravel road, their headlights cutting through the tunnel of trees. When they reached the clearing James rolled to a stop and shoved the car into park.

Tessa gazed straight ahead at the moonlight shimmering off the inky lake.

"This okay?" he asked.

"Fine."

He turned off the music, and she listened to the drone of the cicadas and the guttural croak of bullfrogs outside. An electronic chirp sounded from her purse. Crickets, her sister's ringtone. Tessa silenced the phone and dropped it into the cup holder.

"Who is it?" he asked.

"No one."

The car got quiet again and James reached for her, pulling her across the seat and sliding his warm hand under her shirt.

"Wait. Maybe we should talk first."

"We don't have much time." He squeezed her breast.

"James, I mean it."

He leaned back and sighed. "Talk about what?"

"Us. This."

His face was shadowed, but still she could see the heat in his eyes as his hand glided up her thigh.

"So talk." He kissed her neck, and she inhaled the musky scent of his skin—the scent that drew her to him in the most primal way, in a way she'd never been able to resist no matter what the consequences. She responded to this man on a molecular level, with every cell in her body.

He kissed her mouth, softly at first, then harder. He pulled her close, shifting her until she was almost in his lap.

"I can't stop thinking about you." His breath was warm against her throat, and whatever she'd wanted to talk about was gone now. He slid his hand down her shirt, deftly popping open the buttons one by one. Then the fabric was off her shoulders, and cool air from the vent wafted over her skin. She reached for his belt buckle.

A sudden flash of light made her jump. She squinted over her shoulder at the blinding white as a car pulled up behind them.

James went rigid. "Damn it, a cop."

Her heart skittered as the car's door opened. She hurriedly pulled her shirt on and darted a look at James.

"Don't talk," he said sternly.

A light beamed into the driver's side, and she shrank back against the door as James buzzed down the window.

"Evening, officer."

"This your vehicle, sir?"

"Yes, it is."

The flashlight beam moved to Tessa's face, then dipped lower. She tugged the sides of her shirt together and looked away.

"Step out of the car, sir."

James gave her a warning look and pushed open his door.

She sank down in the seat. Perfect. This was just what they needed. Could they be charged with something? Trespassing? Or public lewdness, maybe? Her cheeks burned and she glanced back at the cop.

Pervert. He probably staked out this lakeside park every weekend and waited for couples to pull in. He probably got a sick thrill from embarrassing people.

Pop! Pop!

The noise rocked the car and she lurched against the window, shrieking. Terror seized her as she gaped at the open door.

He's shooting. He's shooting. He's—

The flashlight shifted. Tessa scrambled for the door handle. She shoved open the door and lunged from the car, landing hard on her hands and knees.

Pop!

The sound reverberated through her brain, her universe. She clawed at the grass and stumbled to her feet. Adrenaline spurted through her veins as she raced for the woods.

He was behind her, right behind her. She sprinted for the cover of the trees, screaming so loud her throat burned.

No one can hear you. You're all alone.

An icy wave of panic crashed over her and her cries became a shrill wail. Her heart pounded as she ran and ran, waiting for the bite of a bullet.

Hide, hide, hide!

She plunged into the woods, choking back her screams as she swiped madly at the branches. Thorns tore at her skin, her clothes, but she surged forward. It was dark. So dark. Maybe he wouldn't see her in the thicket.

He killed James. He killed him killed him killed him. The words flashed through her mind as she swatted at the branches.

She had to get out of here. She had to get help. But she was miles away from anyone, stumbling blindly through the darkness. Branches lashed her cheeks, and they were wet with blood or tears or both as she plunged through razor-sharp brush and her breath came in shallow gasps.

She tripped and crashed to her knees. Pain zinged up her legs, but she pushed to her feet and kept going, deeper and deeper into the woods. No one was out here. Her only chance was to hide.

She smacked hard into a tree. She swayed backward, then caught herself and ducked behind the trunk, forcing her feet to still, even though her pulse was racing.

No noise. Nothing.

Only the whisper of wind through the branches and the wild thudding of her own heart. She dug her nails into the bark as she strained to listen. She couldn't breathe. It felt like someone was squeezing her lungs in a big fist. She shut her eyes and tried to be utterly still as she fused herself against the tree and waited.

In the distance, a soft rustle. She turned toward the sound and felt a swell of relief. Had she lost him?

Please, God. Please, please, please . . .

A faint *snick* behind her, and Tessa's heart convulsed. She hadn't lost him at all.

He was right there.

• • •

Dani Harper steered her pickup truck down the narrow road toward the whir of lights. She reached the clearing and pulled up beside a white van, surveying the scene through the mist. A pair of uniforms stood off to the side. Beyond a line of haphazardly parked vehicles, swaths of yellow tape cordoned off a silver sedan.

She glanced at the logo on the van and her nerves fluttered. The Delphi Center. Her boss must have called them. The lieutenant didn't like using outside help, but San Marcos PD didn't have the resources to handle a scene like this.

Dani reached for the poncho she kept in back, then thought better of it. It would be hot as a trash bag, and she was already soaked from her yoga class. She pushed aside the grocery sack containing the frozen dinner she wouldn't be eating anytime soon and grabbed a baseball cap. She settled it on her head and pulled her ponytail through the back as she got out. Her cross-trainers sank into the muck.

One of the uniforms trudged over, and Dani recognized him as he passed under the light of a portable scene lamp. Jasper Miller. Six-three, two-fifty. He was a rookie out of Houston, barely six months on the job.

"Hey, Dani." He smiled, catching her off guard again with those boyish dimples that seemed at odds with his huge build.

"Tell me you didn't touch anything." She pulled a pair of gloves from the box she kept in the back of her truck.

"I didn't touch anything."

She tugged the latex over her hands and took out a mini-Maglite. She picked her way across the damp grass, careful not to step on any sort of evidence.

"When did you get here?" She ducked under the scene tape.

"Oh, about—" He checked his watch. "Fifteen minutes ago? Call came into dispatch about nine twenty. Old lady that lives off the highway thought she heard someone shooting off fireworks here in the park. First responder got here fifteen minutes later."

"And them?" She nodded at the two crime scene technicians crouched behind the sedan examining something. A tire impression, maybe? Whatever it was, they'd erected a little tent over it in case it started to rain again.

"They showed up five minutes ago," Jasper said.

The car was a late-model Honda Accord, squeaky clean right down to the hubcaps. It must have arrived before the rain. The driver's side door stood open, and Dani's stomach tightened with dread as she walked around the front, sidestepping a numbered evidence marker. She halted and stared.

The victim lay sprawled in the grass. Khaki pants, button-down shirt, short haircut. He had a bullet hole just below his neck, and flies were already buzzing around it, making themselves right at home. They hovered below his belt, too, where the front of his pants was dark with blood.

Dani felt a wave of dizziness. Then it was gone.

She stepped closer, glancing up at the blue tarp someone had thoughtfully erected over the body. She switched on her flashlight and crouched down for a closer look. On the victim's left hand was a wedding ring, and Dani's heart squeezed.

Some woman's whole world would be shattered tonight. It was shattered already—she just didn't know it yet.

She glanced up at Jasper. He looked nervous and eager for something to do.

"I've got a portable field lamp in the back of my truck," she said. "You mind?"

He trekked off, and she focused on the victim again. Given the location at this park she'd expected a teenager, but he looked more like an accountant. She studied his face carefully. His lifeless eyes were half-shut and wire-rimmed glasses sat crooked on his nose. A determined line of ants had already formed a trail into his mouth.

Dani aimed her flashlight inside the vehicle.

No wallet, no cell phone, no computer case. The wallet was likely in his pocket, but no one could touch him until the ME's van arrived. She moved her flashlight around the car's interior, paying close attention to the floorboards and cup holders.

Jasper returned with the lamp and started setting up.

"Was this other door closed when you got here?" she asked.

"I told you, I didn't touch anything."

She looked back at the CSIs pouring quick-dry plaster into an impression on the ground. Roland Delgado glanced up at her.

"Hey there, Dani Girl."

"Hey. Who else is here?"

"Another one of your uniforms." Roland nodded at the trees near the lake where flashlights continued to flicker. "He's combing the woods with Travis Cullen."

Travis Cullen. So no Scott tonight. Dani felt a twinge of relief as she stood up.

She leaned into the car and popped open the glove compartment. The insurance card was sitting right on top inside a protective plastic sleeve.

She stepped away from the Accord and turned her back on the victim as she dialed Ric Santos. He answered on the first ring.

"Where are you?" she asked.

"On my way. What do we got?"

"White male, thirty to forty, gunshot wound to the chest and groin, point-blank range."

"Groin?"

"That's right."

"Damn. What else?"

A low grumble had her turning toward the road. Her nerves skittered as a gunmetal gray Dodge pickup pulled into the clearing and glided to a stop beside the crime scene van.

"No ID yet," she told Ric. "But there's an insurance card inside the vehicle. James Matthew Ayers, 422 Clear Brook Drive."

"That's near the university."

"There's a hangtag on the mirror. A university parking permit."

Scott Black slid from his pickup and slammed the door. He reached into the truck bed to unlatch the shiny chrome toolbox. He pulled out his scene case and glanced up.

Their gazes locked.

"Dani?" Ric asked.

She turned away. "What's that?"

"The permit. Is it A or B?"

"B," she said. "Faculty parking."

"Shit."

"What's your ETA?"

"Five minutes," he said.

"You'll probably beat the ME."

She ended the call and closed her eyes briefly. Raindrops dampened her face and water trickled between her breasts. She was in yoga pants and a tank top, and she wished she'd had time to change into something better suited for detective work, because it was going to be a long night.

She took a deep breath and made a mental list. She had to interview the first responder. And she had to get a K-9 team out here. She sent her lieutenant a text coded 911 for urgent.

Roland and the female CSI were still crouched behind the car, and the woman was snapping pictures. She had to be the Delphi Center crime scene photographer, but Dani had never met her.

Scott stood beside the Accord now, his back to the victim as he skimmed his flashlight over the ground. The ballistics expert was tall and broad-shouldered, with the super-ripped body of a former Navy SEAL. Instead of his usual tactical pants and combat boots, he wore jeans and a leather jacket tonight, so maybe he'd been out when he'd gotten the call. Dani knew from experience that his jacket had nothing to do with the weather and everything to do with the Sig Sauer he carried concealed at his hip.

Something glinted in the grass, and Scott crouched down to tag it with a numbered marker. Two minutes on the scene and already he'd discovered a piece of evidence. He stood and squared his shoulders, and Dani felt a pang deep inside her as he approached.

He stopped and towered over her. "Was the passenger door closed when you got here?"

"That's right."

"Where's the girl?"

"No sign of her." She nodded at the woods. "One of our officers is searching near the lake with Travis."

Jasper joined them by the car. "How do you know there's a girl?"

Scott knelt beside the body. "He didn't come all the way out here to jerk off." He looked at Dani. "You have an ID yet?"

"Nothing confirmed."

He watched her for a moment with those cool blue eyes. His gaze shifted to the woods. "You need a K-9 team."

She bristled. "I know."

He strode over to his truck and opened the toolbox again. He took out a metal detector, which would help him locate shell casings or bullets, and maybe even the second victim if she was wearing jewelry or a belt.

Then again, the killer might have taken her somewhere else. Dani glanced back at the road and got a queasy feeling in her stomach.

"You coming?" Scott asked.

She nodded at the body. "I'll stay with him until the ME shows."

Scott walked off, and Dani let her gaze follow him until he disappeared into the woods.

She turned her attention to the lake, visible just beyond the trees. It was a scenic spot, usually—a tranquil little oasis for couples. But not tonight.

The medical examiner's van rolled up, followed closely by Ric, and Dani's nerves jangled as she thought of everything she didn't like about this case. And it wasn't even an hour old yet.

Ric walked over, his expression grim as he took in the scene. "The media has it," he said.

"That didn't take long."

"It was all over the scanner," he told her. "I give us ten minutes, tops, before they roll in here with their cameras. We need to barricade the road."

"Daniele."

She turned toward the sound of Scott's deep voice calling her from the woods. He was a tall silhouette at the edge of the trees, and from his tone Dani knew it was bad.

"What is it?" she yelled back.

"I found her."

LOVE LAURA GRIFFIN?

Then don't miss her brand-new e-book serial, Alpha Crew!

These elite operatives will go to the ends of the earth to complete their mission . . .

AT THE EDGE: Alpha Crew, Part 1

When Emma Wright's plane goes down in the jungle,
it's Ryan Owen's job to get her home safely . . .
even if she is a heady distraction.

EDGE OF SURREN

Ryan has one job: kee
scorching-hot romance
began in *At the Edge: Al*
Part 2 of this sexy,